The Widows of Eden

ALSO BY GEORGE SHAFFNER

One Part Angel

In the Land of Second Chances

The Arithmetic of Life and Death

The Widows of Eden

a novel by

George Shaffner

ALGONQUIN BOOKS OF CHAPEL HILL

2008

Published by

ALGONQUIN BOOKS OF CHAPEL HILL

Post Office Box 2225

Chapel Hill, North Carolina 27515-2225

a division of

WORKMAN PUBLISHING

225 Varick Street

New York, New York 10014

This is a work of fiction. While, as in all fiction, the literary perceptions and insights are based on experience, all names, characters, places, and incidents either are products of the author's imagination or are used fictitiously.

Library of Congress Cataloging-in-Publication Data

Shaffner, George.

   The widows of Eden : a novel / by George Shaffner. — 1st ed.

     p. cm.

   1. City and town life — Fiction. 2. Nebraska — Fiction.

   3. Widows — Fiction. 4. Life change events — Fiction. 5. Traveling sales personnel — Fiction. I. Title.

   PS3619.H345W54 2008

   813'.6 — dc22   2008000429

10 9 8 7 6 5 4 3 2 1

First Edition

To Kathy,
with apologies for the
Great Dishwashing Gambit
of 1962.

With thanks to Kathy Atchison, Dean DeBoer, Bill Dittrick, Jane Dystel, Antonia Fusco, Rodney Liesveld, Dick Resseguie, Grace, and the kids.

The Widows of Eden

Chapter 1

....

DUST BOWL DAYS

M Y NAME IS WILMA PORTER. I own the Come Again Bed
and Breakfast, which is the last of its kind in Ebb, Nebraska, and the only B & B in Hayes County that is listed in
seventeen Internet directories. I have lived in rural America all
my life, and I can tell you that it will bend a man's back and try
his spirit in the best of times, but last year's growing season was
the driest and most inhospitable in seven decades. On Thursday,
July the sixth, smack in the middle of summer, the fire station
recorded our one-hundredth consecutive day without a drop of
rain. It was hotter than Beelzebub's oven outside, even in the
shade if you could find any, the soil was harder than a cast-iron
skillet, and a thin layer of dust hung over the fields and roads
like a gritty yellow fog. All the old people were talking about
the "Dust Bowl" days over at the Corn Palace, and not like it
was past history.

Clifford Yelm, a third-generation bean farmer and hog caller,
got to worrying that Sunday because Rufus and Winnie Bowe
weren't at church, so he hopped in his pickup and drove over
to their place to see what was going on. A withered old heifer
was grazing on parched, dead grass in the front yard, which is

a peculiar way to care for a lawn even in these parts, and the windows were wide open. Nobody answered the doorbell, so Clifford invited himself inside.

The house was as empty as a politician's promise. The furniture and the rugs and the pictures were all gone, Rufus's and Winnie's clothes were missing, and the pantry and the refrigerator had been cleaned out. According to Clifford, it was eerily quiet. All he could hear were the drapes flapping in the breeze and the echoes of his footsteps on the hardwood floors. Under a gray, bone-dry dirt clod on the kitchen counter, he found a handwritten note that read:

To Whom It May Concern:
    We couldn't make a go of it any more. I am so sorry. We will miss you all. May God be with you. He wasn't with us.

                                        Winnie (and Rufus) Bowe

The bank started soliciting bids for the property from the usual out-of-state agricultural conglomerates two days later, which caused a huge commotion on Main Street. An amendment to the state constitution was supposed to prevent the sale of family farms to big corporations, but it turned out to have more loopholes than a cheap shag rug. The number of farming operations in Nebraska has dropped by twenty percent in the last two decades anyway, and every time we lose one, another rural business goes bust.

Clement Tucker, my fiancé and the richest man between Omaha and Oklahoma, could have stopped the sale of the Bowe place with a single telephone call, and it's not like I didn't ask a zillion times, but he was in no mood to discuss it—because he had just been diagnosed with skin cancer. A man of his age ought to have known better, but he refused to see Doc Wiley until I made him go. By then, the cancer had spread to his internal organs, and he was angrier than a wet cat about it, like it was somebody's fault besides his own!

For those of you who may not be familiar with the history of Ebb, a mysterious traveling salesman named Vernon L. Moore appeared out of nowhere to save our bacon twice before, although there is an ongoing controversy about what he did or didn't do. I had no idea how he could fix a drought, not to mention a deadly case of cancer, but I got down on my knees and begged the Lord to send him back for a third time anyway. Then I didn't hear so much as a peep until two weeks later, at the town Starbucks, no less.

I was gossiping in a booth with my best friend, Loretta, and her daughter, Laverne, who is all of three-and-a-half years old and my perfect little goddaughter. Out of the blue, Laverne looked up from her chocolate milk and announced, "Daddy's coming." It was a plain, factual statement, like, "Mee-maw is on the phone," or, "You left the light on in the kitchen."

Loretta kissed her on the forehead. "Of course he is, darlin'. He went to Omaha for a business meeting, but he'll be home by suppertime." Last spring, Loretta married Calvin Millet. He is the chairman and majority owner of Millet's Department Store, plus he manages the Tucker family trust for Clem now, so he travels nearly every week.

The child looked straight into her momma's eyes. "Not that daddy, my other daddy. He's coming."

Laverne's biological father, her namesake, and the love of Loretta's life until she fell for Calvin, was none other than Vernon L. Moore. Laverne hadn't seen him since the autumn before her second birthday, and for only a week at that. None of the rest of us had seen hide nor hair of him either, and we never spoke of him in her presence. In my simple, country girl's mind, that raised a few questions.

"When?" Loretta asked with a puzzled look on her face. "When is your other daddy coming?"

My cell phone rang as Laverne was about to answer. I fished it out of the bottom of my pocketbook and said, "Wilma Porter speaking."

From the other end I heard, "This is Dot Hrnicek, your friendly neighborhood sheriff. I just got a surprise call from the state police." Besides being the top lawperson in Hayes County, Dottie is a good friend and the squarest, most manly-looking woman I've ever known.

"What kind of surprise?" I asked, a bit mystified by why she had phoned. I can be a little slow on the uptake sometimes.

"Apparently, two of their cruisers are escorting a blue Ford Mustang down Interstate 80 at a high rate of speed. You'll never guess who's driving the Mustang."

"Steve McQueen?"

"That would be hilarious except he's deceased. Now, do you want to know who's driving the Mustang, or not? I'll give you a hint: his first name starts with 'V' and his last name starts with 'M.'"

"It is not!"

"I can't tell a lie, Wilma; I'm wearing the badge. He's to have a late lunch with the colonel in Lincoln, and then he'll be accompanied to the Hayes County line. I was told to expect him at four p.m."

"Today?"

Loretta could read me like a book. She looked me in the eyes and mouthed, "Is it Vern?" I nodded in the affirmative and she went rigid, like she had lapsed into a catatonic state. That worried me some, and not just because of her medical history. As far as any of us knew, Mr. Moore was unaware of Lo's matrimonial history, meaning her recent marriage to Calvin.

Dottie answered, "No, Wilma. They're playing pocket pool in Panama till Thursday. Cowboy up, girl. I assume you've got his room ready."

"Uh huh," I lied.

"Stick a six-pack in the fridge when you're done making it up. I'll be over just as soon as I finish the day's paperwork."

"You'll be . . . ?"

"I know you've got first dibs, Wilma, but we have a history, your Mr. Moore and me. I have some questions for that man."

I squeezed the cheek of my sweet little goddaughter and replied, "Don't we all, sweetie pie. Don't we all."

Chapter 2

....

GREAT EXPECTATIONS

LORETTA WAS AS STIFF as an Indian totem pole for so long that I began to contemplate my options: 9-1-1, CPR, a bucket of ice water over the head, a poke in the ribs with one of those flimsy wooden swizzle sticks you get at Starbucks. I was leaning toward the ice water when she turned to me and said, "When is Vern supposed to arrive?"

"I was told to expect him at four. Unless he's changed into somebody else, I'll get a peck on the cheek and he'll be on your doorstep by 4:02."

"Uh uh! That's a problem. I'll need to warn my husband first."

"Warn Calvin? How come? He knows all about you and Mr. Moore."

"He's a good man, Wilma, but he's just a man. He'll need to be reassured."

Truer words were never spoken. "How much reassurance time do you think you'll need?" I asked.

"Cal doesn't get home until six, if that. Can you keep a leash on Vern till eight?"

"Eight? How in the world . . . ?"

"Feed him. Tell him what's happened in the two years since

he last saw his child. Tie him to the bedpost if you have to; just keep him busy until eight o'clock."

As if we needed to be reminded, Laverne repeated, "Daddy's coming, Mommy." I wouldn't say she was giddy. Laverne is never giddy, but I could tell she was excited.

I put my hand over Lo's again. "We'll be fine. I'm sure of it."

"No you aren't, Wilma. You can't be. Vern will change things when he comes, but we have no idea what he's going to change, do we?"

"We don't for a fact, but I have my hopes. I hope he spends some quality time with his daughter and his friends, I hope he can save Clement from cancer, and I hope he can make it rain. After that, his time is his own."

Loretta smiled. "I'm glad to see that your expectations are in check, darlin'. While you're at it, why not ask for world peace? We could use some of that, too."

"Mock me at your own risk, Lo. Mr. Moore has a track record. You should know that better than anybody."

"My other daddy's coming, Mommy. Can we go now?"

Laverne was right; it was time to go. I said my good-byes and set off on foot, but I had forgotten to wear my panama hat so there was nothing between me and the searing summer sun except dry, dusty air. I measured my gait and stayed in the shade as much as I could, but I was perspiring like a pipe fitter by the time I got home.

The Come Again Bed and Breakfast is a three-story, turreted Victorian that was built by Silas Tucker the Second a few years after the Civil War. Five generations later, I bought the place from Clem Tucker, the seventh in a direct line stretching back to Silas the First, after he determined that he didn't need nine bedrooms and seven bathrooms all to himself. Between you, me, and the fencepost, I believe that Silas the Second was giving him the willies, too. Silas is an infrequent ghost, but he has been haunting the place since he died of consumption in 1887.

A few years after I turned the house into a B & B, Clem's older sister, Clara, moved out of a sanatorium in Lincoln and into the entire third floor of the Come Again, which I had renovated per her instructions. Clara is a twice-widowed, sixty-odd recluse who likes to exercise, play cards with my grandson Mark, and watch old movies and TV shows. She's not exactly talkative either. Other than the first time Mr. Moore came to town, she hasn't uttered a word except "yes" and "no" since the Bee Gees had a hit record.

As soon I let myself in, I went straight to my den to check my voicemail. That turned out to be an error. I had messages from Lulu Tiller, Hail Mary Wade, Lily Park Pickett, and half the other women in town. It was all for the same reason, of course: they had gotten word that Mr. Moore was coming to Ebb and they knew he would be staying with me at the Come Again.

I have an admission to make: my left ear is as flat as a pancake because there is hardly anything I would rather do than gossip with my friends on the telephone; but I had a higher calling that afternoon. I went upstairs to remake Mr. Moore's bed, and then I vacuumed and dusted his room, washed out his sink and tub, and made sure he had fresh towels, soap, and toilet paper. After I was satisfied that everything was in tip-top condition, I went downstairs to the parlor and sat by the window. I don't know why, but I just wanted to sit still for a minute.

The house was as silent as an empty church. It was so peaceful and calm that I started to doze off—something I never do at church, thank you very much—when the gosh-darned phone rang! I nearly had a heart attack, which is the number one killer of women in America. I grabbed the handset by the neck and practically shrieked, "What?"

Luckily, it was only Dottie. Without a word of lead-in, she said, "Is he there yet?"

"Don't you know? I figured you'd have sentries posted across the county line."

"I do, but I thought he might've snuck by us."

"It's barely three-thirty, Dot. He's probably still on his way."

"Maybe, but will you call me when he arrives; just to make sure?"

"If you'll do the same. Are you still coming over tonight?"

"Does a brown bear shit in the woods? Of course I am."

"Can you stay for dinner?"

"What're we havin'?"

"I don't have a clue, Dot. I'm making this up as I go along. Get here early, okay?"

"Early? How come? Are you expecting a disturbance? Except when he's saving my town from vicious evildoers, that Vernon Moore of yours is a bundle of trouble and strife." Dottie was referring to Mr. Moore's last visit to Ebb, when he managed to rid the county of a dangerous religious sect in his spare time.

"Loretta needs time to prepare Calvin. Your job will be to keep Mr. Moore occupied until eight o'clock. Get here as soon as you can."

"No problem, Wilma. I'm good at keeping people occupied. I carry a sidearm."

"You're a dear, Dot," I declared, and rang off.

The Come Again is as cool as a mausoleum, even in the heat of summer, but little beads of perspiration began to appear on my forehead. Another woman in my age bracket might've blamed "the change," but I knew that my body was reacting naturally to the pressure of a no-warning dinner party. Considering the quality of the company, store-bought pot pies were out of the question, and it was too late to put in a roast, so I took some meatball marinara sauce out of the freezer to thaw and threw together a four-bean salad with vinaigrette dressing. When that was done, I went into the dining room to set dinner for three on my best china and flatware. The linens I chose were a wedding gift from my dear departed Aunt Delphie, who was a suffragette in her youth and later became wealthy the old-fashioned way: via alimony. At the reception following my wedding to Al, my ex, she whispered in my ear, "Love, honor, and obey, Wilma, and keep detailed records." I should have listened, but my ears were plugged with love.

After the table was set, I zipped into the kitchen and happened to glance at the wall clock. You could've knocked me over with a feather. It was 4:05, but there had been no knock at my door, and I hadn't heard a peep from Dottie either.

Mr. Moore had slipped past Dot's patrol cars, just like she had feared, but he had knocked on a door other than my own. I blame myself. Mr. Moore believes that uncertainty is the spice of life. I should have expected nothing less.

LORETTA TOLD ME later that she knew who it was the instant her doorbell rang. Apparently, so did Laverne. She jumped up from her little red reading chair in the library and sprinted to the front door. When Loretta caught up, Mr. Moore was on one knee in the foyer, giving Laverne the kind of hug a sailor gives his child after years at sea.

He has crinkly blue eyes and dove-white hair, but his age is a matter of debate. He is not a big man either, but he is fit and straight as a rail. On that day, he was dressed in a gray, pinstriped business suit, a light-blue shirt with a starched white collar, a burgundy-colored tie, and zillion-dollar black shoes polished to a high sheen. According to Loretta, he was as cool as a cucumber, as if he was immune to the heat.

She stopped at a safe distance. "Welcome back, Vern. Somebody missed you."

Mr. Moore stood up and wiped a speck of dust from his knee, then he looked into Lo's eyes and remarked, "When we first met, I thought you were the most beautiful woman I'd ever seen, but you're even more beautiful now. Are you well? Are you healed?"

Two years ago, Loretta was beaten so badly that she lapsed into a coma and eventually died, but Mr. Moore called in a lightning bolt that brought her back to life. I know what you're thinking, but I was standing outside her hospital room when he did it. It was unmistakable.

Lo took a step backward. "I'm well, thanks to you, and married. To Calvin Millet. We sent you an invitation. Did you get it?" She held out her hand so that Mr. Moore could see the ring, which was a two-carat solitaire that had once belonged to Calvin's mother.

"I couldn't come, Lo. I wanted to, but I just couldn't make it."

"Why not? If not for me, then for Lovey and Cal. He feels like he owes you a great debt. It almost kept him from proposing. Did you know that?"

"I didn't. I'm so sorry."

Laverne, who is three and a half going on thirty-five, said, "That's okay, Daddy. Mommy isn't mad; she's just frusterated."

"And she has every right to be, sweetheart. But I'm here now and I want you to tell me everything that's happened while I've been gone."

Laverne looked up at her mother, who said, "Wilma is expecting you for dinner, Vern. Perhaps you can come back later; say eight o'clock?"

"That would be fine. Thank you."

Mr. Moore picked up his daughter and hugged her again. She whispered in his ear, "Can I ax you something?"

"You bet."

"I could tell that you were coming, but Mommy and Mee-maw couldn't. How come?"

"That's a very good question. I'll make sure you get an answer; maybe not tonight, but before the end of the week. Is that okay?"

Like most of the women in Ebb, Loretta has a finely tuned sense of hearing. "Her mother has a few questions, too. Do you suppose you can fit her into your busy schedule?"

Mr. Moore put his daughter down for the second time. "Why not tonight? If at all possible, Calvin should be with you. People are coming."

"People are coming? Here?"

"With your indulgence, yes."

"With my indulgence?"

Mr. Moore stepped forward and kissed her on the cheek. "You sound like an echo, Lo. Relax. It'll be interesting."

"Interesting?"

He put his finger on her lips ever so lightly, then he left without another word.

A BLUE FORD MUSTANG rumbled into my parking lot not three minutes later. It was a low-slung, fast-looking affair with fancy chrome wheels, but the poor thing was waist-high in dust, as if it had forded a stream of medium beige blush-on. Through the parlor window, I watched Mr. Moore retrieve a large, roller-style suitcase from the hatch and pull it across the lot to my porte-cochere. Before he could knock, I yanked the door open, grabbed him around the neck, and wailed, "Thank you for coming, Mr. Moore. Thank you, thank you, thank you. Clem is so sick. He's on death's doorstep."

I was just warming up, but my sobs were drowned out by a

police siren, and then a county sheriff's cruiser came screaming around the bend with red-white-and-blue cherry poppers
flash-dancing across its roof. Two shakes later, Dottie Hrnicek
pulled under my porte-cochere with an ear-splitting screech. She
shut the tumult off, thank God, and then she got out of the car
and walked purposely up to my doorway, where she declared,
"Vernon Moore, you are under arrest." Then she looked at me
and added, "What the hell's wrong with you, Wilma?"

I was slack-mouthed, but Mr. Moore acted like he had been
in that sort of fix before. "Who dropped the dime on me,
Sheriff?"

"How many folks in Ebb drive a three-hundred-horse Mustang with custom wheels and Ohio plates? I got half a dozen
calls." Dottie checked her watch. "What I'd like to know is how
you got past my deputies . . ."

"Your deputies?"

"I got a tip from the state police that you were coming. They
were posted at the county line."

"Oh, sorry. I took a detour through Nebraska City to see
some friends. Perhaps your deputies weren't expecting me to
come in from the east."

"Apparently not. I was just kidding about the arrest, by the
way. You all can go back to hugging and crying now. I'll see
what's cookin' on the stove."

She strode past us both with a big grin on her face and headed
toward my kitchen. Once she was out of sight, my infrequent
lodger inquired, "Is there room at the inn?"

Instead of answering like a grown-up woman, I started to cry
again. Maybe it was "the change," but I don't believe it was.

Chapter 3

PAWNEE WISDOM

B Y THE TIME I had dried my eyes and gotten back to the kitchen, Dot was nursing a bottle of cold beer at the table and reading the Lincoln paper. I was about to suggest that she make herself at home when the phone rang.

She was closer than I was, so she grabbed it and chatted for a minute, then she hung up and said, "That was Mary. Her nose is a little bent out of joint."

Hail Mary Wade is the county attorney and the Queen Bee of the Quilting Circle, which has had the effect of making her nose double-jointed.

"Does she know that Mr. Moore is in . . . ?"

Dot held her hand up like a traffic cop. "Of course she does, but don't worry yourself for a minute. She's just got a bee under her bonnet, that's all, a jealous little bee."

The phone rang again and Dottie took a message. It was Dana Yelm, Clifford's wife, who had also gotten the news of Mr. Moore's arrival. She wanted to make sure that I told him about the drought and the Bowes' disappearance, as if I needed a reminder. Two shakes later, I got a call from Billie Cater, who had the same identical concern.

When the telephone rang the fourth time, Dottie said, "For

God's sake, Wilma. Turn the damned thing off! If you don't, we'll never have a moment's peace."

The proprietor of a B & B cannot unplug the telephone. It's in the manual. While I was putting it on auto-answer, I heard a faint, electronic rendition of "There Is No Place Like Nebraska" coming from another room.

"Goldarnit!" I exclaimed.

"Is that your cell phone?"

"It sure is."

"Where is it?"

"On the settee in the den, inside my pocketbook."

"You cook; I'll shut it off."

Dot was back at the table and into her second beer when Mr. Moore came down the kitchen stairs. His outfit—a white oxford shirt with a button-down collar, creased blue jeans, and running shoes—reminded me of what the hip boys wore at Hayes High in the sixties, when I was too young to have a boyfriend but old enough to have a fresh crush every week.

My brief reverie was interrupted by a peck on the cheek. " You must be the woman of the hour," he said. "The phone's been ringing off the hook."

Dot took a swig and replied, "It's not us, hon. Everyone's calling about you, and they've all got the same question I have. They want to know whose lives you plan to rearrange while you're in Ebb."

"Excuse me?"

"I'm sorry; that was the beer talking. Who do you plan to see this trip?"

"My daughter and her mother, Wilma, old friends. Why?"

"Why? The last time you blessed us with your presence, Mr. Vernon Moore, I had to run double shifts, call in reinforcements from Gage County on two separate occasions, fib about your whereabouts to the same state police who just bought you lunch, and coordinate an arson investigation with the fire department—in one week. If you're planning to save us again, I'd like to warn my superiors."

"Does Ebb need to be saved again, Sheriff?"

I blurted out, "Clem does! He has cancer!"

Mr. Moore and my Clement have a history that dates back to his first visit four years ago. It was like they were joined at the hip from the get-go, but nobody could tell whether they were working together or against each other from one trip to the next.

"I heard, and I'm so terribly, terribly sorry," he said mournfully. "What are his chances?"

I hung my head. "The odds are not in his favor, Mr. Moore. He's resting at the River House for now while the chemotherapy does its work, but he has to return to Omaha at the end of the week for a big operation. I'm driving down to see him after dinner tonight. Could you come along?"

"I'd love to, but I'm due at Loretta's after dinner. Would you ask Clem if I can drop by in the morning, say ten o'clock?"

Maybe I shouldn't have, but I felt like a ton of bricks had been lifted off my chest. I answered, "Oh, I don't have to do that. He's been expecting you."

Dottie chimed in, "Half the town's been expecting you, but it has nothing to do with Wilma's Fiancé in Perpetuity. It's because of this godforsaken drought."

Mr. Moore frowned, and then he looked at me like I was the local news expert and asked, "Is it as bad as the papers say?"

"My Aunt Delphie once told me that Nebraska was the Pawnee word for bad weather," I reported, "and now I know why. We haven't seen a drop of rain for a hundred and seventeen days running, the corn stalks are knee high and half dead, nobody's got any beans to speak of, and there isn't enough alfalfa in the entire county to make up a hayride. A few weeks ago, Winnie and Rufus Bowe pulled up stakes and left without a word of warning. Winnie was a founder of the Quilting Circle, for heaven's sakes! They left behind their farm and all their friends . . ." My voice trailed off. I didn't want to think about it.

"Has the governor declared the state a disaster area?"

"He must've forgot," Dottie said. "He left Friday on a trade mission to China. I hear he plans to sell them some USDA prime Nebraska steak. If they like it, maybe they'll buy a heifer and a bull and we'll get cheap, rice-fed beef in five years. Won't that be tasty?"

"No doubt. What's the weather forecast?"

"Hotter 'n hell and clear as a bell for as far out as anybody can see. Water is being rationed in thirty eastern counties including ours, plus most of Iowa and northwest Missouri. Surface water irrigation has been flat-out banned; half the water was evaporating before it hit the ground. You can't barbecue on the grill or water your lawn, and don't wash that car of yours either; that's banned, too. But the Ogallala Aquifer, which has supplied this state with water since the Ice Age, is disappearing anyway, and faster than free booze at a Marine reunion."

"That fast?"

"This fast." Dottie chugged the last of her beer, and then she peered down the neck and observed, "Another dead soldier. May he rest in peace."

DOT SAW A FEW too many dead soldiers that night, so Mr. Moore bundled her into the cruiser after dinner and drove her home. She lives with Shelby Eisenhart, her partner of the past eleven years, on a little spread southwest of town. It must've taken Mr. Moore a while to walk all the way back to the Angles House, which is two blocks north of Main and across from the county courthouse, but at least it was cool by then.

Besides being ultramodern, the Angles House is the only residence in Ebb that has been built from the ground up since 1985, as opposed to being towed in on a flatbed. Calvin bought the place from Clem Tucker—big surprise there—who had it built because he got tired of commuting all the way to town from the family hunting lodge, which is every bit of eighteen minutes away during rush hour, and eighteen minutes when it's not.

When Mr. Moore knocked, Calvin himself came to the door. He is a tall, redheaded man with green eyes and a gentle but weary smile. "Welcome, Vernon," he said. "I'm sorry I missed you this afternoon, but I'm glad you could come again tonight."

Mr. Moore saved Millet's Department Store the first time he came to Ebb, plain and simple. If he hadn't, the downtown would be deader than Roy Rogers's horse. Some folks say he saved Calvin Millet, too, although others have a different view.

The two men shook hands across the entryway. Mr. Moore said, "How are you?"

"If it wasn't for the drought and the illness of a good friend, I'd be happier than any man has a right to be. Thank you for giving me a reason to live, or should I say two?"

"It wasn't easy, but you're welcome."

Mr. Moore began to step inside, but Calvin blocked the doorway. "Just to make sure," he declared, "you haven't come to take them back, have you?"

"No. I'm just here to visit."

"Are you certain, Vernon? It'll be guns or knives on the courthouse lawn at dawn if you've come for Loretta and Laverne. I'm not losing a second family, not even to you."

"You always had an admirable sense of honor, Calvin. I'm glad to see that it hasn't waned in the service of the Tucker Trust, but I'm a little worried about your inferential skills. I requested a get-together with Lo and you this evening. Would that have been the best opening move if I was planning to steal her away?"

"Probably not, but I wanted to make sure that there were no misunderstandings between us. Come on back. Loretta is in the library."

"If you turn around, you might find that she's standing about three feet behind you."

Calvin's faced turned beet red. "You're kidding."

Loretta said, "If you don't let that man in this house, my left foot will have to be surgically removed from your tight vanilla butt."

Truth be told, Lo is a few years older than her husband, maybe more than a few, but a person could never tell. There is not a line in her milk-chocolate countenance and she has the figure of a debutante. That evening, she was wearing an ankle-length purple silk robe and pretty gold sandals. I don't recall if her toenails were painted, but they usually were. Loretta owns the local beauty salon, so it's not like it costs her anything.

Calvin stood aside. Loretta said, "You're late, Vern. Where have you been?"

"Uh, the sheriff needed my assistance with a small transportation problem."

"So you're back in form, and so soon. The girls will be glad to hear it. Come in."

The Angles House may be modern on the outside, but Loretta redid the interior after she and Calvin tied the knot. The living room is filled with antique mahogany furniture, the lamps and statuary are art deco, and the walls are lined with theater bills from the vaudeville era. You'd think you were stepping into the Roaring Twenties.

"You have a lovely home. Have I met the decorator?"

"She has many talents," Lo said, referring to herself in the third person. "Would you care for a drink?"

"No, thanks. Too much spaghetti."

"Wilma fixed spaghetti? Damn! I wish she'd called. I would have invited us over."

Mr. Moore followed Loretta and Calvin to the rear of the house, where Lo had converted Clem's billiards room into her library. Tall, glass-covered bookcases lined the walls, and an oblong-shaped conversation pit filled the center of the room. Calvin and Loretta sat down on a leather sofa while Mr. Moore took an Ames chair at the end, opposite a little red chair. "Did I miss Laverne?" he asked.

"It's past her bedtime, but she's expecting to see you tomorrow. Cal had to turn off the phones so she could get to sleep. Do you know why?"

"I don't, actually."

"You're too modest, Vern. Half the women in town called—about you. They all want to know when you're going to make it rain. I told them to check with Wilma. She usually keeps your calendar, but she must've turned her phone off, too."

Mr. Moore sat forward. "Did I hear you correctly, Loretta? Did you say that the people of Ebb expect me to make it rain?"

"You set a certain level of expectation on your last trip, Vern. You can't be surprised."

Calvin interjected, "Clem has an expectation, too. Did you and Wilma have a chance to discuss his condition?"

Poor Mr. Moore must have felt whipsawed to death. Nobody had seen him in two years, but all anybody wanted to talk about was the weather and my fiancé. "We did," he replied. "I was very sorry to hear about it."

"He's in deep, deep kimchee, Vernon. That's why he sent for you."

"Clem sent for me?"

"He has a business proposition for you. He believes you can help him and he wants to make it worth your while."

Mr. Moore glanced at Lo. She replied, "Don't look at me. What could I tell the man?"

"Has he shared this proposition with you, Calvin?"

"No. I have my suspicions, but you'll have to ask him yourself. When can you see him?"

"Wilma's setting something up for the morning, assuming he's well enough."

"Don't worry about that, Vernon. He'll be well enough, and it'll do his spirits a world of good. Give me a shout if I can help."

"Thanks, but what could be easier than curing cancer, unless it's calling in a rainstorm? While I'm at it, there's a favor I'd like to ask the two of you—if you don't mind."

When Loretta is curious, her left eyebrow jumps halfway up her forehead but the right one stays put. "Why do I get the feeling that this favor is the main reason you came back tonight? Is it related to the 'people' you mentioned this afternoon?"

"A few friends of mine are on their way to Ebb. With your permission, I'd like to introduce them to you and Laverne."

"Friends? That's a surprise, Vern. Everybody thought you worked alone. What kind of friends are they? Business associates? Salespeople? Fellow miracle-workers?"

"Fellow travelers, and widows."

"Widows? How many of these widows are coming?"

"Three."

"I see. Do they have names?"

"Eloise, Marion, and Bertha."

Calvin muttered, "Well, at least they aren't Caspar, Melchior, and Balthazar."

Loretta gave her husband a look that mothers save for naughty little boys, then she said, "You were a mystery when you left Ebb the first time, Vern, but now you're a legend. People around here believe that you can raise the dead, make evil-minded preachers vanish into thin air, and beat Clem Tucker at his own game with one hand tied behind your back. Now, you're bringing friends. The citizens of Ebb will wonder why you need the help."

Mr. Moore shook his head. "The widows are the nicest, sweetest women on earth, Lo. They want to meet you and Laverne. That's all."

"Are they bearing gifts?" Calvin asked.

Loretta shot him another naughty-boy glance. "I apologize for my husband, Vern. He can forget how much he owes you. When do your friends arrive? I assume it's soon."

"They get here sometime tomorrow, but you'll probably hear before I do."

"I'll hear? Before you?"

"They have a way of making an entrance."

Loretta giggled. "Well, why the heck didn't you say so? Any woman who can make an entrance will be a fast friend of mine."

Chapter 4

MR. MOORE BRINGS A DELUGE

I GOT DOWN TO my kitchen at oh-dawn-hundred the next
morning, which was day one hundred and eighteen of the
drought, but Mr. Moore was already sitting at the table in his
usual spot, sipping a cup of tea and reading the Lincoln newspaper. Normally, lodgers were not allowed to sit in my kitchen
unaccompanied, but Mr. Moore had the run of the house. I offered him a waffle and bacon for breakfast, which he accepted,
so I went about whipping the batter while we talked. Here's a
little hint: I use club soda instead of milk in the batter. It may
sound odd, but the waffles come out extralight and crispy, and
they're super low in cholesterol.

Mr. Moore put down the paper. "Last night, Loretta said
that the townsfolk expect me to make it rain. Have you heard
anything like that?"

"I suppose I should have warned you myself. That's what all
those calls were about last night."

"Does everyone expect me to make it rain?"

"Drought is an equal opportunity disaster, Mr. Moore. Everybody's desperate, and some of the residents of Ebb have seen
you do things that a normal person can't do. You can't hardly
blame them for being optimistic."

"Optimism is good, Wilma, but within reason."

That may have made sense to Mr. Moore, but it confused the heck out of me. "I thought optimism was what you used when reason didn't work," I replied.

The batter was whipped, so I got the bacon out of the refrigerator and put seven slices into the skillet, four for Mr. Moore and three for me. It wasn't the healthiest item I could have put in the pan, but I have a country girl's weakness for good, thick bacon.

Mr. Moore inquired, "How was Clem last night?"

"Not good, I'm afraid. The doctors cut so much skin out of his back that they had to transplant a swatch from the inside of his thigh. The leg is infected now and his temperature is running at a hundred or more most all the time. Doc Wiley says the chemotherapy is affecting his body's ability to fight infection. It's also causing him to feel sick to his stomach, and he has no appetite to speak of."

"Will he be up to seeing me this morning?"

"Oh, yes, Mr. Moore. He even offered to send John for you." John Smith is Clem's chauffeur plus bodyguard and my most recent son-in-law. He and my elder daughter, Mona, a divorcée herself, got hitched last spring, just five weeks before Calvin and Loretta. Luther Salevasaosamoa, the county chief of corrections, married Louise Nelson, too, but she kept her last name. All in all, it was a backwards year in Ebb from a matrimonial point of view. Women usually come here to get unhitched, not the other way round.

I brought Mr. Moore up to date on all the latest news while we ate, starting with my eldest grandson, Matt. If it wasn't for Mr. Moore, he would be serving life in prison and then some. As it is, he's taking college correspondence courses in a medium security facility in Iowa and he could be paroled in only five years. Mark, his little brother, will be graduating from college around then. He's going to be Ebb's next tycoon.

Mr. Moore waited until breakfast was over to bring up his widow friends. I guess running a B & B gets in your blood. Of all the questions I could have asked the man, the first words from my lips were, "Will they be staying with me?"

"They won't need rooms, but I'd appreciate it if they could use the parking lot."

"The parking lot?"

"They travel in large RVs, recreational vehicles. They may need to hook up to your electrical power, but they usually prefer to sleep in their own beds."

I had had the odd RVer at the Come Again before, so I wasn't caught completely off guard. "If that's all they want, it's perfectly fine with me. Will I need to feed them?"

"Once at most, if you don't mind. They're a self-sufficient bunch, and they won't want to impose. Add whatever it costs to my bill. Add the cost of the electricity, too."

"Oh, don't be silly. I won't need to do that."

"Put it on my bill, Wilma. They'll be here for several days, and their drivers may need an occasional shower, too. It saves water in the RVs."

That was a cork-popper if I ever heard one. "Your widow friends have chauffeurs, for RVs? I've never heard of such a thing? May I ask why?"

"Certainly."

Here's another hint: if you request permission to ask a question, Mr. Moore will usually grant it, but then he'll wait for you to spit out the actual question. "Why do they have chauffeurs?" I asked.

"Because the widows don't drive."

That was his entire answer. I suppose I should have expected it.

MR. MOORE WENT for a walk after breakfast. Since the noonday temperature averaged upwards of a hundred and four during the drought, most of the downtown stores opened early so that the people with any money left could do their shopping in the morning. According to eyewitness reports I received later, Mr. Moore stopped by Millet's Department Store, the Starbucks for a mocha, and the library. Everywhere he went, people asked him to make it rain. Oddly, there was disagreement about how he responded. Some folks thought he was amenable, others reported that he was noncommittal, and a few told me that he was downright negative.

In the meantime, I finished up the breakfast dishes and meandered back to the den to check my e-mail. Naturally, I had to delete the spam first. Here's a question: who in the world would be stupid enough to buy penny stocks or penile enhancement drugs from an anonymous somebody whose Internet address is jzqxkvw@goobledegook.com and the subject of their e-mail is "loquacious whitewash delirium fecal"? It beats the fecal out of me.

Lord Almighty, there were thirty e-mails in my queue—after I was done getting rid of the spam—and every one was from a card-carrying member of the Quilting Circle. In case you haven't already heard, the Circle was founded a generation ago by Winnie Bowe, Lulu Tiller, and yours truly. We had only two goals back then: to keep every child warm at night, and to make Ebb the nicest place on earth to live. Over the years, the idea caught on and most of the wives and divorcées in the county became members. Ebb is a woman's town now, and we're a force to be reckoned with. The majority of our elected officials are female and we own most of the businesses on Main Street. The Circle even holds a twenty-nine percent interest in Millet's Department Store, thanks to Mr. Moore.

We take particular pride in on our ability to keep the membership informed, but the deluge of e-mails that morning made me wonder if we had pushed the envelope too far, and that was before I discovered that there was more than rain on everybody's minds. Connie Kimball, the town florist, wanted Mr. Moore to stop by and see her mother, who was eighty-six years old and failing, the poor dear. Casey Jaworski wanted Mr. Moore to attend to a well that was going dry. Dana Yelm just had to remind me about the Bowes—again. The list went on and on.

I had no idea how to handle each and every request, so I sent the membership an e-mail saying that Mr. Moore was aware of the drought and I would be discussing their personal needs with him at my earliest opportunity. Then, because I knew I couldn't possibly discuss each and every one of their needs with Mr. Moore, I turned on my cell phone and called Loretta. I got beeped by two incoming calls while I was leaving a message.

I had no choice; I turned it off again. Me. For the first time in my life, I chose the laundry over the telephone.

That's how bad it was.

Chapter 5

. . . .

THE WHIMS OF THE HOI POLLOI

LATER THAT MORNING, Mr. Moore drove down to the River House, which is a large, ranch-style hunting lodge situated on a high bluff overlooking the Missouri River. Marie Delacroix, Clem's full-figured chef, lived with him there, and so did a practical nurse named Pearline O'Connor, who had been imported from Kansas to care for Clem during his chemotherapy. She was an older, cone-shaped girl with a flat chest and a religious streak who never drank, swore, or wore makeup. Because of her close proximity to my Fiancé in Perpetuity, she was inducted into the Quilting Circle at an emergency session of the membership committee, meaning in advance of Dot's usual background check. In other words, we buttered our own bread.

Pearline led Mr. Moore back to the master suite, which was lit by a single lamp on a bedside table. Despite the dimness, you could see that Clem's eyes were sunken and his skin was chalky and yellow-gray, like the yolk of a day-old, hard-boiled egg. He had lost weight because of the chemo, and he wore a knit cap to conceal the loss of his hair, even in bed. He said it was for warmth.

Pearline took up her position at the nurse's station in the hallway, just out of Clem's sight but within easy earshot. Mr. Moore sat down on a cane-backed chair next to the bed.

Clem pulled himself up to a sitting position, then hacked and cleared his throat. "Thanks for coming," he half-gargled. "Wilma was all aflutter when she told me the news last night."

"It's good to see you again. How are you feeling?"

"Like I was spun around on a top, run over by a bulldozer, and drowned in a tub of warm spit. I have some free advice for you, Vernon: don't get cancer. The disease is immune to money. If you don't catch it in time, a mountain of rubies won't do you a bit of good."

"So I've been told. What's the prognosis?"

"Medically speaking, I'm in deep shit." Clem coughed again, then resumed, "The skin cancer is gone, but it spread to other parts of my body before the doctors caught it. Next Saturday morning they're going to remove an unspecified percentage of my pancreas, lymph nodes in various and sundry locations around my body, and my prostate if they don't like what they see in there. Then they're going to clean up the infection in my leg and fill in all the holes with silly putty. If I survive, my oncologist says I have a twenty-five percent chance of seeing my sixtieth birthday, the bastard."

"I'm very sorry, Clem. Is there anything I can do?"

"Pardon me for bypassing all the touchy-feely bullshit, but there damn well is. Folks in Ebb are convinced that you can heal the sick. I may be in need of your services."

"Come on. You don't really believe that."

"Not exactly, but neither do the townsfolk. They believe you're one for two: that you lost my granddaughter but revived the mother of your child—twice by some accounts—and they have eyewitnesses. You may recall that one of them is extremely close to me."

"But . . ."

"No buts, Vernon. You double my chances of survival, even

if I discount you to one in three because I'm not your long-lost flame. I'd like to hire you to cure my cancer, and I'm willing to make it worth your while. Name your price."

Pearline O'Connor nearly peed in her pants when Clem offered what he did. I doubt that Mr. Moore had a similar urge, but water was a factor in his answer. "I took a walk around town this morning," he said. "Everyone I met wanted me to pray for rain."

"I'm aware of the goddamned drought, but I have a more pressing need. If you turn me down, I could be pushing up daisies within the week. I'm not ready to be ground into bone meal just yet, thank you very much. I have more to do."

"You do? Like what?"

"Have you ever faced death, Vernon? I don't mean a nickel-and-dime scare like a near-miss traffic accident; I mean nose-to-nose with the Grim Reaper himself."

"Yes. Once."

"Did it alter your way of thinkin'?"

"In a hundred different ways, but you're the one facing death today, not me. I take it that the perspective has changed you, too."

"You're damn right it has. From the day I took control of the National Bank of the Plains to the day I went on chemo, I never had a goddamned minute to myself. I want to get well, and then I want my old life back."

"You sound as if you're surprised, Clem. Did you expect that chairing a major bank would be a walk in the park?"

"Hell no, of course not."

"Then why did you do it?"

"You need to ask? Because it was my job; that's why."

"Your job?"

"I thought you knew me, Vernon. I'm a Tucker. Like my father and his father, and his father before him, I dedicated my life to the Tucker Trust. Not only that, I beat the crap out of all of them. I was the best damned custodian in family history, but now I'm ready to cash in."

"Are you sure? You've never been a man of leisure. What will you do with all the extra time?"

"Well, I'd like to put a few more heads on the dining-hall wall, that's for sure, and I'd like to get my golf handicap back down to single digits. I want to return to Europe, too, and spend more time with Wilma. I might even write my memoirs; I haven't decided yet. All I can say for certain is that I need more time."

"But you could've done all that years ago. Why didn't you?"

"Are you having trouble with your hearing today, Vernon? I'm the seventh Tucker in a direct line stretching back to 1815 and the fifth to control the Tucker Trust. It was my destiny. I fulfilled my goddamned destiny."

"Destiny is a myth," Mr. Moore asserted, almost coldly. "It doesn't exist."

"What did you say?"

"You were deluding yourself if you believed you were fulfilling some kind of destiny. There's no such thing."

Clem cleared his throat. "I don't normally like to think of myself as delusional, Vernon."

"Perhaps, but destiny makes no sense. It would rob us of two of our greatest gifts: uncertainty and free will. A benevolent God would never take either away from us."

"Whoa there, cowpoke. Did you just say 'God'? What the hell has He ever done for anybody?"

"How about the creation of heaven and Earth? On the surface, that would seem to be a fairly significant gesture."

"Okay, I'll give you that. I'll even give you Jesus, but what's He done in the last two thousand years? He never did a thing for me, that's for sure."

"So you believe that God abandoned us. Is that what you think?"

"You're damned right I do. I've been making my way around this planet for nearly sixty years, and I've never seen even a shred of evidence to the contrary."

"Then I'm confused. If God deserted us, who determined your destiny? Who turned the dials; who twisted the knobs; who kept you from straying off the chosen path?"

When my fiancé failed to respond, Mr. Moore carried on. "You're stuck, Clem. You believe that God has ignored us for two millennia, but you also believe in destiny. That's a clear contradiction, which is rarely a sign of a healthy belief system."

My fiancé laughed, which caused him to cough again. "You can't be serious. All I remember from Bible school is one contradiction after another. We can argue about it all goddamned morning if you want, or we can discuss my offer. Are you interested or not?"

After a pause, Mr. Moore said, "I am, but I'm still stuck at contradiction. If God is gone, then how can you believe that I might be able to save your life?"

"Are you kidding? Have you ever met Lulu Tiller? That woman can talk to the animals; I've seen her do it. Mark Breck, Wilma's grandson, can multiply two four-digit numbers in his head, just like that. And then there's you, of course, and that's just the local talent. Go anywhere else and you'll find people who can pick up a musical instrument for the first time and play it like a virtuoso, people who can read minds, people who can talk to the dead, and people who can heal the sick by the laying on of hands. The list is endless, but the common denominator isn't God; it's people. Tell me if I'm wrong, but you're a person, you're right here in my bedroom, and you're widely reputed to provide the exact service I need. Why in the world would I pray to a runaway God when I can pay you?"

Mr. Moore mulled over Clem's tirade, then he replied, "Fair enough. In light of your condition, I'm willing to make a counterproposal."

"A counterproposal? Now we're making progress. Let's hear it."

"If you and I can agree on price, I'll ask for your life instead of rain. How's that?"

"You said my life *or* rain. Why not both?"

"That's my business. Do you want the deal or not?"

The room was quiet for a while, then my fiancé said, "Do you have a price in mind?"

"No. I need to do a little research first."

"Research? What the hell for? Are you writing a term paper? In case you haven't noticed, I'm not exactly up to my chinny-chin-chin in spare time."

"You're right. I'll have a price for you in the morning. How's that?"

"It's a deal. I'll see you tomorrow at the same time." As Mr. Moore stood to leave, Clem added, "I'd invite you to stay for lunch, but I can't seem to hold anything down anymore. If you can squeeze in an early word, I'd give an arm and a leg if I could keep some of Marie's scrambled eggs in my stomach long enough to actually digest them."

"An arm and a leg? For scrambled eggs?"

"Don't get any bright ideas, Vernon. I expect a fair price from you."

"And you shall get one," Mr. Moore replied. "See you tomorrow."

• • •

IN CASE YOU HAVE never met any, the rich are not like you and me. The rest of us keep telephones close by because we want to hear from our friends and family, but rich folks have a different point of view. To them, telephones are for calling others; not vice versa. That's why Clem quit carrying a mobile phone when he became chairman of the National Bank of the Plains, and why he wouldn't allow a telephone in his bedroom either. He claimed that they made him a slave to the whims of the hoi polloi, whoever they are.

As soon as Mr. Moore left the ranch, Clem instructed Pearline to fetch him the house phone. She was only able to hear half the conversation that followed, but I've been able to piece the rest of it together since. I may have had to fill in the odd gap, too, but that's something all of us writers have to do from time to time. I hope you understand.

The first thing she heard was, "Buford, this is Clem Tucker."

Once upon a time, Buford Pickett was Clem's number two man. Some say he was Clem's hatchet man, but he became the general manager of the local branch when Clem took over the National Bank of the Plains up in Omaha. That's another way of saying that they grew apart. He replied, "It's nice to hear from you, sir. How are you feeling?"

"Like shit, Buford. How the hell else would I feel? You'll never guess who just came by the River House to have a chat."

"Vernon Moore."

"You got the news?"

"From Lily last night. He had dinner with the colonel of the state police up in Lincoln. Did you hear about that?"

"No, but I'm glad they're getting along. Since you're so well informed, do you know why I called?"

"No, sir. I don't."

"Then listen up. I need you to drop whatever you're doing and take another stab at finding out who Vernon Moore really is."

"Excuse me, sir, but how can I do that? I lost my research associate when the bank was absorbed by NBP. They've got a whole department up in Omaha. Why don't you call them?"

"Pay attention, Buford. You have experience with this matter; I want you to handle it. John Smith will help. He's good at fieldwork."

"But sir . . ."

"This isn't a discussion. If you're too busy, I can send one of those MBA whiz kids down from Omaha to run your shop for the rest of the week. How would that be?"

Buford Pickett is a balding, middle-aged man with a belly the size of Arkansas and the most pitiful taste in clothes you ever saw, but he is no country bumpkin, and only a country bumpkin would be stupid enough to refuse his boss's boss's boss's boss. He said, "Can you at least tell me why you're doing this, Mr. Tucker?"

"Confidentially, I just made Vernon a proposition that could end up costing me a boatload of money. Before I go through with it, I need to know who he really is, once and for all. And don't give me any bullshit about World War II, either. I want hard, verifiable facts."

"Hard facts have never been easy to come by when Mr. Moore is concerned. It sounds like the state police won't be much of a help this time either."

"Then you'll have to get creative, Buford. I'll expect a progress report tomorrow night. Are we clear?"

"Yessir, Mr. Tucker. Since I have you on the line, can I ask a question?"

"As long as you keep it neat. Shoot."

"How much do you think the Bowe place is worth?"

"Rufus Bowe's place?"

"Yessir."

"Why in God's name are you asking me? I've been out of the business for three years. When have you ever needed my help with a valuation anyway?"

"The auction closes on Friday, sir, but we have only two bids and they're way too low. Neither will cover the mortgage balance."

"Can you spell 'drought,' Buford?"

"Yessir, I can."

"How about 'aquifer depletion'? Can you spell that?"

"My spelling isn't the problem, sir. If I can't find another bidder, the branch will have to book a loss on the loan."

"Okay, so now we're down to brass tacks. How many more of your mortgages are in the same boat?"

"I'm sending out a dozen foreclosure notices at the end of the month, rain or no rain. I'll probably mail another twenty at the end of August."

"If that many of your farms are in trouble, how much profit do you expect to net this year?"

"None, sir, obviously."

"Well, then. If I was you, I'd be thinking about cutting my losses."

"But I am, Mr. Tucker. That's why I thought you might be interested in picking up the Bowe place. I'd break even on the roll-over if you paid seventy percent of fair market."

"Jesus, Buford! I'm on death's goddamned doorstep. Even if I wasn't, I'm a banker now. I'd rather buy scabs and boils than one more acre of friggin' farmland. In case you haven't noticed, nobody else wants it either; not in the middle of a goddamned drought. You need to start cutting your losses, and right now. Do you get my meaning?"

"Yessir, I do. What you're saying is very clear."

"Good. Are we done?"

"Yes, sir. It was a pleasure to talk to you again, just like always."

Chapter 6

. . . .

THE WISHBONE DEFENSE

E BB IS USUALLY such a colorful little town, but it was all
shades of brown during the drought: the land, the trees,
the buildings, the people, even the air. Dust particles stuck to everything, especially pant-legs and shoes, and they were so darned
fine that they had the confounding ability to pass through shut
windows and doors. I had to dust and vacuum nearly every day.

Beryl Williams came to the front door while I was vacuuming
the Persian carpet in my parlor. The years had been kind to that
old rug, but not to her. Her spindly gray hair had passed thin
and proceeded on to sparse, deep lines marked her cheeks and
forehead, and purplish age spots dotted the paper-thin skin on
her hands. Even in the summer, she wore a lavender, hand-me-
down cardigan over hunched, tired-out shoulders.

Long ago, Beryl's son fell out of the bed of his daddy's pickup
truck while they were turkey hunting in the Sand Hills out west.
The fall knocked him out cold and made him vomit afterwards,
but her husband wouldn't go to a doctor until he got a turkey to
bring home. By then, the poor boy had suffered permanent brain
damage. He spent Thanksgiving and Christmas in the hospital
and never returned to school. After his parents split up, a cousin
gave him a job at his auto repair shop, where he acquired the

nickname "Flathead." In later years, he drove the town snow-
plow and did odd jobs for the fire department, but he never left
his mother's care.

"Can you come in for some tea?" I asked.

"Oh no," Beryl replied. "I mustn't stay. I dropped by to have
a word with Mr. Moore. Is he in?"

"Not at the moment. Can I give him a message?"

"I was hoping he could see my boy. Do you think he would?"

"It's not up to me to say what Mr. Moore will or won't do, but
I'd be happy to inquire on your behalf. Would that be alright?"

"That would be very nice, Wilma. Thank you." Just before
she turned to leave, Beryl reached into her sweater pocket and
pulled out a pretty red apple, which she handed to me.

That was so sweet, but all I could see in my mind's eye was a
line of Beryls and Connies and Danas and Caseys that stretched
two-by-two from my front door to Main Street. One of Dot's
deputies was directing traffic around the procession, and street
concessionaires were selling lemonade and cotton candy and big
straw hats to ward off the sun.

I closed the door and turned on the phone just long enough to
call Hail Mary Wade, the Queen Bee, but she wasn't even remotely
interested in Beryl and my sad tale of woe. She had just heard about
Mr. Moore's "Clem-or-rain proposition" from Lily Park Pickett,
who had heard it from Marie Delacroix, who had heard it directly
from Pearline O'Connor. Since I'd been out of touch all morning,
it was a fierce shock to me. After Mary filled me in, we determined
that I would confirm Lily's report with Mr. Moore, and then we
would let the Circle board of governors decide what to do.

Mr. Moore showed up in my kitchen while I was slicing apples
for two crumble-crust apple pies: one for Beryl and one for my
guests. I put down my paring knife and said, "I am so relieved
to see you. We have to talk."

He gave me a kiss on the cheek and sat down at my table. "Relieved? About what? Have your friends stopped calling about the drought?"

"It's just the opposite, Mr. Moore. I can't turn on my phone or check my e-mail anymore. People are even coming to my door. They all want to talk to you, and not just about the weather. Most have other problems, too. What can I tell them?"

"I apologize for being so much trouble, Wilma. Would you like me to find a room elsewhere?"

"Good heavens, no! You're right where you belong. I just need a little direction, that's all. What do I tell these people?"

"Perhaps I'm the one who needs direction. What would you like to say?"

"I know you can't fix everybody's particular problem, but can I at least say that you're going to pray for a good, old-fashioned gully-washer? That couldn't do any harm, could it?"

Mr. Moore thought it over for a while, then he said, "I'd rather you didn't."

"Why?" I asked innocently.

"Because I made a deal with Clem."

I laid my hand across the top of my bosom and exclaimed, "A deal? With my Clem? What kind of deal?"

"I promised that I would ask for rain or his life at the end of the week. The decision could go either way, so I can't say for sure that I'll ask for rain."

I shook my head, which I've done a lot around Mr. Moore over the years. "My gracious Lord. Clem made you an offer, didn't he?"

"Yes."

"How much? How much money did he offer to pay you?"

"We didn't discuss specifics, but I agreed to consider his request."

"I can't believe you'd take Clem's money, Mr. Moore. That's not like you. That's not like you at all."

Mr. Moore frowned. "I haven't agreed to take a penny, Wilma, but his money could prove to be a factor in my decision. Besides, I thought you wanted me to help him."

"I do, but not this way. Can't you just forget about the money and pray for rain *and* Clem's life?"

He replied, "Do you ever keep the wishbone from a chicken?"

That's like asking a country girl if she takes a pocketknife on a first date. "Lo and I have a home-and-home series, but you know what? Ever since you brought her back, she seems to get the big piece all the time."

"Then why risk losing, Wilma? Why not pull both ends of the wishbone yourself? Aren't you sure to get your wish?"

"But, but . . . It's not the same thing, is it?"

"You're right; it's not. Uncertainty is the spice of life, and a deal is a deal."

"You won't change your mind?"

"No."

"Oh dear!" I moaned. "What am I to tell the Circle?"

"Tell them what I'm going to tell Clem: to have faith."

"I'm supposed to tell them to have faith?"

Mr. Moore became reflective for a minute, then he said, "Clem believes that God abandoned him somewhere along the way. That's no way for anyone to feel, especially a man who may be terminally ill. Between now and the end of the week, I'm going to try to sell him some faith. Perhaps you can sell some faith to the Quilting Circle, too."

"The women of the Circle have plenty of faith in God, Mr. Moore. It's their faith in you that has me worried."

"Don't. If their faith is in God, which is where it belongs, then I'm off the hook."

Some people are good at starting conversations and others are good at ending them. It is my impression that I have a talent for the former and Mr. Moore is a kung fu black belt at the latter, so I did what any good hostess would do: I fixed him a ham sandwich. While he ate, I rolled the dough for the pie shells and we talked about Winona, my younger daughter. She lives with her husband and two daughters in Council Bluffs, just across the river from Omaha, but her marriage is more like an uneasy détente than a loving alliance. I wonder how much longer it can last.

Near the end of his lunch, Mr. Moore said, "Have you seen Silas the Second lately?"

I believe I mentioned that Silas II built the Come Again after the Civil War and has haunted the place on a irregular basis ever since. "He stopped by last spring when I had the air-conditioner replaced, but I haven't seen boo of him since. Maybe he doesn't care for the heat."

"I'm sympathetic. Is there some way we might be able to induce him to visit?"

"I can't say, Mr. Moore. As I recall, you tried a note last time, but that didn't work. Silas is normally more interested in the Come Again itself, as if he is keeping track of his investment. If I was to add a bathroom or put up new siding, I'm sure he would show up."

"I don't suppose you can think of something a bit less substantial?"

"Not off the top of my head, but maybe your widow friends will draw him out. Every Tucker in the line has fancied himself a ladies' man. Maybe old Silas will take to them."

"Maybe so," Mr. Moore agreed. He thanked me for his meal —he has always been the politest person—and then he went off to see Laverne and Loretta. After he was gone, I put the pies in the oven and phoned Hail Mary to corroborate Lily's report. I should have seen it coming; she called an emergency meeting of the Quilting Circle board of governors.

LORETTA WAS WEARING blue denim jeans and a pink knit top that revealed an inch of midriff when she met Mr. Moore at the door of the Angles House. I swear: Calvin Klein patterns his jeans after her bottom. It's a tad irritating.

"Hello, Lo," my famous lodger said cheerily. "Can Laverne come out and play?"

"In this heat? Don't be silly. Come on back. She's having an after-school snack in the kitchen."

Laverne was eating a peanut butter sandwich at a little, green turtle table next to the kitchen counter. When she saw her other father, she jumped up and yelled, "I said you were coming but Mommy made me finish my sammich!"

Mr. Moore picked her up and gave her a huge hug. "She just wanted me to herself for a minute. How was school today, sweetheart?"

"It's only preschool. Can you stay? Mommy has a *meaning*."

"I got a call from Hail Mary Wade not two minutes ago," Loretta explained. "She's convening an emergency meeting of the board. I don't suppose you know why."

"I don't, but I'd be thrilled to sit with Laverne, even grateful."

"Nice try, Vern, but you're not getting off the hook that easily. The meeting is about you. According to Hail Mary, you've made some sort of pact with the devil. Is that right?"

"Hmmm. I did reach an agreement in principle with Clem, but it's personal. I can't see why it would be worth an emergency meeting."

"That's not what I heard. I heard that you agreed to ask for rain or Clem's life at the end of the week. That's from two separate and unimpeachable sources, by the way. The same two sources say that Clem offered you a king's ransom, and not for rain."

"That isn't quite right, Lo. Clem and I discussed money, but only briefly. No sums were mentioned."

"But the rest of the story is true."

"Yes. Why?"

"Why? You were never a slow-witted man, Vernon Moore; don't start now. The people in this town have faith in you. If they hear about your deal with Clem, they'll be mystified. They'll be hurt; they'll be afraid you abandoned them when they needed you most."

"How about you, Loretta? Is that how you feel?"

"Well, you can file me under 'mystified,' darlin', that's for sure. I have no idea why you'd make a deal like that with anybody, much less a man like Clem Tucker. Even Wilma is baffled, and he's her Fiancé in Perpetuity. What do his illness and his money have to do with the county's need for rain?"

"They just do. That's all I can say."

"Well, it's a heck of coincidence, that's for sure."

"A coincidence? How?"

Loretta never went to college, but she reads incessantly and she has the vocabulary of two English professors. She said, " 'Clement' is a word, Vern. It means 'fair' or 'mild,' as in the weather, but we need rain, which is 'inclement' weather. This deal is a clash of perfect opposites: Clement, or inclement. Was that intentional, or not?"

"They're just words . . ."

"Can we play, Daddy?" Laverne pleaded. "I have a big, pink castle in my room. You can take it apart and put it together again, like a puzzle."

Mr. Moore gave his daughter another squeeze. "There's nothing I'd like better, sweetheart. When will you be back, Lo?"

My best friend heaved a deep sigh, then she said, "It's an emergency meeting. It could last one hour or six. I'll give you a call if we haven't adjourned by five."

"No problem."

"Laverne can have juice while I'm gone, but no pop or junk food. Is that clear, soldier?"

Mr. Moore saluted. "Yes, ma'am. You can count on me, ma'am."

Loretta bent down and gave Laverne a kiss. "See you later, alligator."

My little goddaughter replied, "After a while, crocodile."

She is the sweetest child.

. . . .

Chapter 7

THE CIRCLE PURCHASES AN
UMBRELLA POLICY

THE HEAT IN NEBRASKA is generally accompanied by intolerable humidity, but that was not the case during the season of the drought. The downtown air was as dry as old bones, and deathly quiet because the bugs and birds had migrated to Mississippi. It was the only summer in living memory that you could drive down a Hayes County road without getting bug juice all over the windshield. Instead, your car got covered in dust.

My panama hat notwithstanding, I practically melted into a puddle on my walk to the Abattoir, where we hold our Quilting Circle meetings. If you have ever had a job in the meatpacking industry, you might be aware that "abattoir" is a pretty French word for slaughterhouse. We bought the place for pennies on the dollar after Old Man Jenkins declared bankruptcy and remodeled it for our purposes. The general meeting area is where the main floor butchery once was. A conveyor belt used to run across the ceiling and some of the old hardware is still in place. We hang Christmas lights and ornaments from it during the season.

Both bathrooms are for women now, although we left a urinal for the janitor. For all their hunting prowess, some men cannot hit a toilet from two feet. Old Man Jenkins's corner office was converted into our boardroom, complete with an elliptical, oak-veneered conference table, eight matching chairs, and a side-board made of genuine, aged oak. In my opinion, the sideboard makes the other furniture look cheap, but I wasn't on the decorating committee when it was acquired.

Hail Mary Wade, the Queen Bee, and Dottie Hrnicek were already seated when I arrived. Mary is a diminutive, fast-talking woman who dresses in expensive Ann Taylor suits and high heels. She took a quick glimpse at my limp hair and sweat-soaked armpits and said, "There's a new invention, Wilma. It's called a horseless carriage. These days, they come with another cool invention called air conditioning. I recommend both this time of year."

"You drove here from the county courthouse? It can't be five blocks."

"It's more like ten when you factor in the heat index, and I'm in heels. I rode over with Dottie. Hang on; Lily is bringing lemonade." Lily Park Pickett is Buford's wife. She has been the treasurer of the Quilting Circle for eight years running, and she represents the Circle on the board of Millet's Department Store along with Hail Mary.

"Where are Loretta and Bebe?" I asked. Bebe Palouse is the general manager of Millet's and the best-dressed woman in the Circle, Hail Mary included.

"They're on the way," Dot answered. "While we're twiddling our thumbs, what's this I hear about some acquaintances of Vernon's coming to town? I thought he worked alone."

"They're widows. Mr. Moore says they want to meet his friends."

"Widows, huh? No disrespect intended, but they'll be able to meet his friends in a phone booth if he prays for Clem instead of rain. I heard that your fiancé told Buford Pickett to look into your lodger's identity. Is Mr. Moore aware of that?"

"He didn't mention it, but Clem has been to that well twice before. Mr. Moore even tried to help him, but he came up dry anyway."

"So his identity is still a mystery."

"Either that, or he is who he says he is."

"Which is what, exactly?" Dottie asked.

"A retired salesman."

"Uh huh, and I'm Shania Twain. I wonder: where'd I put my diamond-encrusted guitar?"

A tick or two later, the three missing board members filed into the room. Lily had a country-sized pitcher of iced lemonade in one hand and a stack of red plastic tumblers in the other, Loretta was carrying sliced zucchini bread on a red plastic platter, and Bebe had paper plates, paper napkins, and plastic forks.

Loretta looked me over from head to foot. "You walked, didn't you?"

"I like to walk. It's the best exercise a woman can get, and I wore a hat."

"That nasty old hat won't do you a bit of good when it's four hundred degrees outside, darlin'."

Lily handed me a glass of iced lemonade, which I chugged part way. While she and Loretta served everybody else, Hail Mary called the meeting to order. "This is an emergency session of the Quilting Circle board of governors," she declared. "According to the bylaws, we're required to dispense with normal business and cut to the case at hand."

Lily raised her hand. "I'd like to bring another matter before the board if I may."

"That's against the rules, Lily. What's it about?"

"Buford."

"Your husband? That can't be good. Is it urgent?"

"Sorta. It's about the Bowe place."

"The Bowe place? I'd love to talk about it now, but it's one farm and we have the makings of a countywide catastrophe on our hands. Can we put Buford on the back burner for now?"

"Sure," Lily pouted. "It can wait, I guess."

"You're a dear. Now, just to make sure that we're all on the same page, would you please repeat what Mr. Moore said to Clem Tucker this morning."

"I don't see any way to sugarcoat the situation. Pearline O'Connor says that he's going to ask for rain or Clem's life at the end of the week."

"And what did he say to you at lunch, Wilma?"

I swallowed a bite of zucchini bread and wiped the corners of my mouth. "The same exact thing."

"You're sure he used the word 'or,' not 'and'?"

"He was very clear, Mary, and he said a deal is a deal. He can't go back on it."

Lily added, "That's not the worst of it. Clem offered to pay Mr. Moore for his life. Is that what he said to you, Wilma?"

"More or less. He told me that money was mentioned but no figures were discussed."

I finished my lemonade and motioned to Lily to pass me the pitcher. While I refilled my glass, she said, "You're Clem's fiancée, Wilma. How much can he afford to pay Mr. Moore?"

"A zillion dollars, give or take, but I don't see why it matters. Mr. Moore has never been interested in money. He seems to have plenty of his own. Isn't that so, Loretta?"

Dottie interrupted, "I'd have to agree. The man won't even file a missing vehicle report when his brand-new car disappears. But before we get into Vernon's motives—whatever they may be—we need to address a more pressing problem."

"A more pressing problem? What in the world could that be?"

"Think about it, Mary. What will happen if information

about this deal leaks to the general membership? We'll have a revolt on our hands. The mob will take to the streets. The Come Again will become the Bastille of the Plains."

"Aren't you letting your imagination go a little overboard?" Lo said. "As I recall, no political prisoners were left in the Bastille when the crowd arrived. The jailer invited them in for tea."

"Uh huh, and as I recall, the mob wasn't placated," Dot retorted. "I would've offered them beer myself. That would've done the trick."

In my mind's eye, the double-wide line from my door to Main Street was converted from a column of patient, mild-mannered petitioners into a swarm of angry French peasants waving pitchforks and teensy cups of espresso. The irony of a tea offering was instantly obvious.

Hail Mary intervened. "Dottie's right. As of now, only Pearline, Marie, and the six of us know what Vernon and Lord Clem are talking about. Is that true?"

Everybody nodded in the affirmative so she continued, "From this moment forward, every aspect of this deal must remain confidential to the board. That means no gossip, girls, and I mean no gossip. Zero. Lily, you need to call Marie and make sure that nothing leaks out of the River House. Wilma, you need to make sure that Vernon doesn't tell anybody else, especially Louise Nelson. That woman will talk the ears off a cornstalk."

"She's at the River House every day, Mary. She's going to find out anyway."

"Then tell her yourself, and make sure she keeps her mouth shut. Tell Mona to keep an eye on John, too. If there's a problem . . ."

Lily looked at the rest of us like she was about to blow a gasket. "*If* there's a problem? If there's a problem? Am I the only one who's suspicious here? I never got close to Mr. Moore like some of you did, but my alarm bells went off the day that man walked into Millet's. What if he's a crook? What if this is some sort of swindle?"

Loretta smiled sweetly. "You have me, Lily. I faked a coma for six weeks while the evil Vernon Moore plotted the second phase of his plan, which was to deprive the town of a vicious religious sect. And don't forget the dastardly Wilma. She has to be in on it, too."

"Fine! But nobody knows diddly-squat about the man except that he shows up out of nowhere every two years, he stays for exactly six days, and somebody dies or doesn't. We also know that Clem Tucker is about to cross swords with the Angel of Death—which can't be a coincidence—and he has more money than Kuwait. Doesn't that sound like motive, means, and opportunity, Mary?"

"Maybe, but no crime has been committed, so they're irrelevant, at least for now. The bottom line is that we have no idea what Mr. Moore intends to do this week."

"That's not so," I replied. "He's going to sell Clem some faith."

"He's going to do what?" Hail Mary demanded.

"He's going to sell Clem some faith. He said we need to have faith in him, too."

"Faith in him—because he's asking for rain or Clement Tucker's life at the end of the week? That's the strangest thing I ever heard."

I opened my mouth to differ but Loretta was faster on the draw. "You're right, Mary. When it comes to Vernon Moore, the word 'stranger' takes on an entirely new aspect. Nevertheless, we all believe that he might be able to make it rain, don't we?"

Under her breath, Lily muttered, "Bullshit." I interpreted that as a dissenting vote.

Dot grumbled, "We all believe it's a possibility, Lo, or we wouldn't be here. But if we don't quit beating around the damned bush, it'll die of thirst. Why don't I invite Vernon over to the courthouse for an interview? He won't have any trouble finding the way."

"That's a good idea," Loretta said. "While you're at it, throw him in jail. That should get him to open up."

"I was thinkin' about a little chat in my office, that's all. Do you have a better idea?"

"I do. He's always been willing to talk to Wilma and me. Instead of beating on him with a rubber hose, I propose that we invite him to dinner."

"He's not your beau any more, Loretta."

"You're uncommonly observant today, Lily, but Vern and I are still friends and I'm still the mother of his child. He's sitting for Laverne as we speak."

The realization that Mr. Moore and Loretta were still close seemed to take the wind out of Lily's sails. I said, "Would it be possible to put an official Buzzword out to the membership? My phone won't stop ringing, I'm getting a thousand e-mails an hour, and Mr. Moore can't go anywhere without being accosted by the membership. Beryl Williams came by my house this morning, for heaven's sake, and I hadn't seen her since the Christmas fete. If we don't do something, half of Ebb will be lined up outside my door by tomorrow morning."

"Wilma's not the only one. I had to turn my phone off last night because Laverne couldn't get to sleep. That's not right."

"Why isn't it?" Lily protested. "All they want is what you got."

Loretta and Lily had a little frowning contest. Hail Mary said, "I've had a few calls myself. It seems like half the families in the county have a problem requiring Vernon's special talents. What can we do?"

"Why not have an old-fashioned revival right here in the Abattoir?" Lily quipped. "If we do it tomorrow, Vernon can cure the sick and the stricken in one fell swoop and we can be back to complaining about the drought by sundown."

"He won't even admit he saved Loretta," I replied. "He would never agree to such a thing."

"Put a cork in it, you two," Mary commanded, using her district attorney's voice. "We need to get this situation under control. The question is how."

"I have an idea," Bebe announced. "Let's send a message to the membership and Mr. Moore at the same time." In case you haven't noticed, Bebe is the least talkative woman on the board. Given the company, that is not a media-worthy achievement.

"What?" I asked.

"Mr. Moore wants us to have faith. Okay; let's show him we have faith—in his ability to call in the rain. Let's send an umbrella to every member in the Circle."

"You're talking two-hundred-plus umbrellas, Bebe. Do you have that many in the store?"

"No, but here's a surprise: there's a surplus in this part of the country. I can't be sure, but I believe it's related to the lack of rain. I can have two hundred trucked in from Lincoln by noon tomorrow, as long as they're Cornhusker red."

"That's unbudgeted overhead," Lily grumbled. "How much will it cost?"

"Five dollars each in quantity, six tops. I'll sell them to the Circle at my cost."

Loretta chimed in, "I second Bebe's proposal. Considering the return on investment, I think the purchase of an umbrella policy is dirt cheap."

After we voted four to two in favor of Bebe's proposal, Hail Mary reckoned, "We still have to decide what to do with all the people who want Vernon's personal attention."

"Send out a Buzzword, Mary," Dottie said. "Tell the girls to pipe down or Vernon will head for the hills. That's what I'd do if half the county wanted me to cure their irritable bowel syndrome or whatever."

"Okay. If that's what it takes, I'll send out a Buzzword. Maybe it'll buy us enough time to find a real solution. I have one last matter to table before we adjourn . . ."

"What about Buford?"

"Just hang on a minute, Lily. As I recall, the board convened about one emergency meeting per day the last time Vernon was in town. I'd like to avoid repeating that mistake. Let's schedule the next one in advance. I suggest Wednesday morning, early, say seven thirty. That's a day and a half from now. Can Buford's latest scheme wait until then?"

It took some cajoling, but Lily caved in. After we adjourned, she huddled in the corner with Mary, Dottie, and Bebe to talk about e-mails, budgets, and umbrellas. Meanwhile, I lost at rock, scissors, paper to Loretta, which meant that dinner would be at my house.

It was my turn to clean up after the meeting — with Lily, who wasn't in her chattiest mood. As we were heading down the hall toward the exit, I asked, "Is everything okay?"

"My husband runs the local bank," she replied. "I have two wonderful sons, a Nicaraguan nanny, and a new SUV with a DVD player. My life is picture damned perfect."

"Do you want to talk about it?"

"No. It's the last thing I want to talk about." That may have been a sincere answer, but it was impermanent. When we got to the front door, Lily stopped and said, "If you had to do it all over, would you marry your first husband again?"

"I would if it was the only way to have my daughters."

"What if you could've picked them up at Kmart or a place like that?"

"Then I would have kicked the bastard in the jewels and fled to Idaho."

"Is that why you never married Clem?"

"Indirectly. I learned from my first go-round that a fiancé is sweet and surprising, but a husband is dour and disappointing. I'll take a fiancé every time, thank you very much. Even now, after four years of engagement, Clem still surprises me sometimes . . ."

"No shit," Lily said abruptly, then she pushed open the door and walked out by herself.

I've seen so many marriages go down the chute over the years, including my own and my eldest daughter's, that I've become an expert on the indicators. Lily tried to put Buford on the agenda, even though it was against the rules. Since nominations for Drone of the Year—excuse me, I meant Spouse of the Year—weren't due for three months, that was probably an indicator. Lily was also testy throughout the meeting, particularly toward Loretta, the woman who married her former boss. Lily had a crush on Calvin for years, so that was an indicator, too.

Then she asked about my failed marriage. That was indicator number three.

Chapter 8

. . . .

LADY BE GOOD

M R. MOORE WALKED BACK to the Come Again from the Angles House despite the scorching heat. He should have been sweating like a cigar thief in a Cuban jail when he arrived, but he was as dry as desert sand. I looked up from my cutting board, where I was preparing vegetables for a pot roast, and observed, "You have a high tolerance for the swelter, Mr. Moore."

"It's hot, Wilma, but I've been in worse, and for a lot longer. Loretta told me about dinner. I'm sorry that Calvin and Laverne can't come."

"They have a night to themselves every week," I fibbed. "It's a bonding thing." Calvin had called to say that he would be late, so Lo was dropping Laverne off at Virginia Allen's until he got home. "How was your afternoon with my perfect goddaughter?"

"Wonderful! We played checkers; we watched cartoons on TV; we shared some cookies and juice—but don't tell Loretta about the cookies. Laverne is very good at checkers."

Mr. Moore is a renowned game player himself. "Did you let her win?" I asked.

"No, but she grasped the principles quickly. Is that a pot roast?"

"It is." I pointed to the two apple pies sitting on a grate at the other end of the counter and added, "You can do me a favor, though. One of those pies is for dessert; the other is for Beryl Williams. It should be delivered while it's fresh, but I don't have any time. Would it be a terrible imposition if you took it over?"

Asking a lodger to take care of a chore is a violation of B & B protocol, but Mr. Moore is not your average, everyday lodger, is he? "I have to warn you," I added. "Beryl knows you by reputation. She dropped by earlier today to see if you might help her son."

Mr. Moore eyed my pies, which were in clear glass dishes and stacked high with apple slices and my mother's crumbly crust. "What kind of help does he need?"

I stopped chopping carrots long enough to recount the whole sorry tale about Beryl and her boy. When I was done, he said, "I'd be happy to deliver an apple pie for you, Wilma. Where do they live?"

I gave him directions to her house, which is on the south end of town near the old railroad tracks. It may be a cliché, but that's where it is. I thought he would come straight home but he was gone for hours. At first, I figured that he had been waylaid by townsfolk wanting rain and whatnot, but the usual reports of Mr. Moore sightings failed to accumulate in my voicemail. Later on, I learned that he had spent the rest of the afternoon with Beryl and Flathead. I suppose I shouldn't have been surprised, but I was.

In the meantime, John Smith stopped at the bank to see Buford Pickett. Like Clem, Buford preferred to do his suffering in the dark. The curtains were drawn in his office and the ceiling lights were turned off. The only illumination came from his desktop computer which, according to John, gave his face an eerie, yellow-green glow. Directly behind him and partially concealed by shadow, there was a long list of places and dates written in blue marker on a whiteboard.

John said, "His highness Lord Clem has instructed me to help you with an investigation into Mr. Moore's background."

"So I was told. Shut the door and take a seat. I'll have a list of places for you to start in a few minutes."

"Are you searching the Internet?"

"Yeah. I'm on my seventh search engine. The dates and locations on the whiteboard refer to one Vernon Moore or another."

My son-in-law looked the list over as well as he could in the dark. "Those are all Vernon Moores?" Coming from a man named John Smith, that was a pretty odd question.

"Every one."

"Okay, but a few of the dates you have up there are a hundred years old. What does the 'd' mean?"

"Deceased."

"The date Vernon died?"

"The date a Vernon died; that's right."

"I take it that you're eliminating the dead Vernons from the list."

Buford looked up from his computer with a glint in his eye. "No, I'm not," he replied. "When I tell you the story, you'll understand why."

Four years ago, Buford Pickett discovered that an Army Air Corps bomber named the *Lady Be Good* disappeared in the deep Sahara Desert after an aborted World War II mission over Naples, Italy. Eight of the nine crew members survived the crash, only to endure days of blistering heat, unrelenting thirst, and a slow, painful, agonizing death. Over the next fifty years, the remains of the entire crew were found, usually by accident, with one exception: a young radio operator named Vernon L. Moore, from New Boston, Ohio.

Buford concluded, "Guess what? The middle initial of the Vernon Moore who is staying at Wilma's is 'L,' and he's from New Boston. Four years ago, I eliminated the possibility that the radioman on the *Lady Be Good* could have been any other Vernon Moore born in the state of Ohio after 1900."

"That's an interesting theory, but it's hardly conclusive. Didn't you get the state police to run a fingerprint check on Mr. Moore two years ago?"

"You need to ask? You were the bagman on the job."

"But I never got the results. What were they?"

"Inconclusive. To be specific, the state police told us that they identified nine people who matched his fingerprints going back to 1954."

"Nine? Were they all named Vernon Moore?"

"I don't know. They refused to tell us."

"Why?"

"The investigation was compromised. That's all I was told except that we're on our own this go-round, and Mr. Tucker will expect quick results."

John said, "But you've tried before, Buford, and you've come up empty-handed. What makes you think you'll find anything new this time?"

"Not a darned thing. I still believe that our Vernon Moore is the sole survivor of the *Lady Be Good*. There's no other rational explanation."

"You call that rational? He can't be a day over forty-five, fifty tops. Are you saying that he's not a normal human being like the rest of us?"

"I wouldn't be the first to suggest the possibility. By the time we're done, you may be in the same camp."

Bless his heart, my son-in-law replied, "No I won't, Buford, not again. Whatever Mr. Moore is or isn't, he's an honorable man and a friend of my family. I won't sign on to any mission that could run contrary to his interests. You're on your own."

"I'm on my own? Did you tell Mr. Tucker?"

"I made the decision about two minutes ago. I'll tell him in the morning."

"But he'll fire you in a heartbeat."

"He doesn't have that many heartbeats left. If he wants to use one of his last to fire me, then I'll find a way to live with it. The question is whether he will."

"Don't count Clem Tucker out, John. If he lives, you won't want to be on his bad side."

John Smith is long and lithe; the closest thing I have ever seen to a cougar dressed in black. Buford is more closely related to the marshmallow, at least in a physical sense.

John stood, which meant he towered over the smaller, rounder man. "I pick my sides without fear," he said. "You should try it sometime."

LORETTA PARSONS MILLET hasn't knocked on my door since Methuselah's bar mitzvah. She just wanders back to my kitchen like it's her house, which is exactly how it should be. I had finished with the vegetables by then and the pot roast was safely in the oven, so I was slicing bananas, oranges, and mangoes for a fruit salad. Here's another hint: add orange juice to your fruit salad when you're done making it up. It will keep the bananas from turning brown for hours. You might add some grated coconut, too. It doesn't do anything special; it just tastes good.

Loretta gave me a hug with one arm and filched a banana slice with the other. "Where's Vern?" she asked.

"I sent him over to Beryl Williams's place with an apple pie. He should have been back two hours ago."

"You sent him to see Flathead?"

"Beryl asked. I didn't see how it could do any harm. Do you?"

"I'm not so sure. I worry that Vernon won't be able to cope with all the attention he's going to get this week."

"I have the same concern, but it's not like we have a choice in the matter. Speaking of attention, how is Calvin dealing with Mr. Moore's return?"

Lo pushed a chair aside and plopped her enviable bottom on my kitchen table. "He says he's okay, but he's conflicted about it."

"Because Laverne is Mr. Moore's daughter?"

"And Vern is my former lover. That man has spent a whopping twelve days in Ebb in the last four years, but Cal sees him everywhere he turns: at home, at the store, at the bank, in the eyes of his wife and daughter. It must be hard for him."

"I see him everywhere, too," I whimpered.

Loretta didn't bother to agree but I knew she did. Instead, she said, "Do you suppose Vern needs a rescue? Should I give Beryl a call?"

"Let her keep him a little longer," I suggested. "You can set the table and we can figure out what we're going to say over dinner."

"That's a good idea, Wilma. We need a plan, a devious plan."

Mr. Moore returned about an hour before dinner, but he went straight upstairs without saying hello. It seemed unfriendly to me at the time, but I didn't find out until later that he had gone to see Clara, my permanent third-floor boarder. They couldn't have said much to each other, but it must have been an amiable reunion. He was in a cordial, almost conversational mood by the time he came down for dinner, which I served buffet-style on the sideboard.

After we had gotten our food and seated ourselves, Loretta asked, "How was Beryl?"

"We had a lovely chat," Mr. Moore answered. "You two have something in common; did you know that? She's a voracious reader."

"I didn't. What does she like to read?"

"Mysteries, history, travel books. Beryl has never been farther from Ebb than Denver, Colorado. Her dream is to see an ocean before she passes on."

"I'd like to see one myself," I whined. "Clem and I have talked about his time in Europe so often, but the closest I've ever come is the Venetian in Las Vegas. He's been too wrapped up in his business and so have I. Now . . ."

Loretta touched my arm without ever taking her eyes off of Mr. Moore. "Did you meet Beryl's son?"

"Jimmy? I did. He sat on the couch while we talked." Jimmy is Flathead's real name, but Beryl is the only person in town who uses it anymore. He even has fire-retardant overalls from the fire department with the name "Flathead" stitched in orange on the chest.

"Did he talk?"

"No, but we shared a box of Cheerios. It was very sweet."

"Did Beryl ask you to help him?"

"It wasn't necessary."

"Is there anything you can do for the poor boy?" Loretta asked. I would never have brought that up myself, but she has always had more brass than a Marine band.

With his usual clarity Mr. Moore replied, "I'm not sure. Why?"

"The last we heard, you were going to ask for rain or for

Clem's life. I was just wondering if you had to make one of three choices now."

"I don't think so, Lo. I'll let you know if I change my mind, though."

"Can we discuss it now, Vern? Beryl is only the beginning. Wilma and I have gotten dozens of requests, and not just for rain."

I added, "They're coming out of the woodwork, Mr. Moore. It's Circle girls with family sickness and financial troubles mostly, but they all want to see you. What do we tell them?"

He pondered our predicament for a minute, then inquired, "Can you make me a list?"

"A list? Of everyone?"

"Yes, all of them."

"But there are so many. You won't possibly be able to see them all."

"I don't intend to try."

"Then why do you need a list?"

"I'm not the only fish in the sea, Wilma. Maybe there are others who can help."

"Like your widow friends?"

"Possibly. If you and Loretta will be kind enough to make me a list, I'll see what I can do. How is Hail Mary? Was she at the Abattoir today?"

Loretta shrugged. "She sent her best. So did Lily Park Pickett and Bebe Palouse. They're all looking forward to seeing you. Dot said hello, too."

"I understand that I was on the agenda, or was it my deal with Clem?"

"The latter, mostly. Just out of curiosity, have you told anybody else about it?"

"No. Why?"

"We're concerned that news of the deal might leak. If it does, I doubt that the people of Ebb will appreciate your position, probably because none of us do. We're afraid we could have a small uprising on our hands. Do you understand?"

"I do, Lo. You can report to the board that my lips are sealed. In return, all I ask is that you and the other members have a little faith in me."

"That's not fair, Vern. We're women; we're the faithful gender. But none of us can figure out why you have to make a choice between Clem and the weather. You didn't with me."

"As I recall, there was no shortage of rain when your heart stopped beating. Besides, I played no role in your recovery. That was either your pluck or divine intervention. I just happened to be venting my anger in the vicinity."

"Nobody buys that, Vern. The people of Ebb believe it was you."

"Then their faith is about to be tested, Lo. Yours, too. A deal is a deal."

That sounded like another kung fu conversation ender to me, but Loretta replied smoothly, "Uh uh, darlin'. You can't test my faith because I know two things for certain: you're going to do something extraordinary this week; and you'll disappear when you're done. Between now and then, Wilma and I will stand behind any decision you make and we'll do whatever we can to keep the people of Ebb from assaulting you at every street corner. But in return, you have to reciprocate. You have to have some faith in us, too."

"But I do. I have complete faith in both of you."

"Then why don't we know anything about you? If you have faith in Wilma and me, then answer three questions about yourself. Just three easy questions. We won't tell anyone what you say; not Cal, or Clem, not anybody in the Circle. No one."

"Just between us?"

"We won't tell anyone; not a soul."

Mr. Moore put down his knife and fork and wiped his hands on his napkin. Then he pushed his chair back from the table, crossed his legs, and said, "Okay."

Before he could change his mind, Lo asked, "Where have you been in the last two years?"

"In the western half of the United States, plus England, Italy, Japan, and North Africa."

"Do you help people in those other places like you help us here?"

"From time to time, but only in the U.S. as a rule."

"Do you work with your widow friends? Are they involved?"

"Yes."

There it was, and without a word of explanation. I couldn't help it. "They are?" I said. "How?"

Mr. Moore scooted his chair up to the table and picked up his fork. "That was question number four," he remarked, and then he plopped an orange slice into his mouth.

Like my goddaughter said, it was darned frusterating. But after four years of nothing, a country girl will take three of something.

Chapter 9

THE DROUGHT CYCLE

I DON'T KNOW HOW it was in the old days, but there is a cycle
to modern drought that is defined by the constant, up-to-
the-minute availability of bad news. At night, right before bedtime, you turn on the Weather Channel to see if the forecast has
changed. It never does in a drought—that's why they call it a
drought—so you say a little prayer and go to bed depressed. In
the morning, you turn the Weather Channel on again to see if
the forecast was revised overnight. After you learn that it wasn't,
you head downstairs to get the newspaper. When you open the
front door, you are hit by a blast of tepid morning air and you
see nothing but a translucent yellow haze stretching across an
empty, cloudless horizon, so you take the paper to the kitchen
and open it to the weather page, where you hope for a change in
the long-range forecast. When there isn't any, you say another
little prayer, and then you hunker down for another day of re-
lentless heat.

It couldn't have been an hour after sunup on day one hundred
and nineteen, but Mr. Moore's car was already gone by the time
I got downstairs. After I fixed myself a cup of coffee and read the
same-old, same-old weather report in the newspaper, I moseyed
into the den fearing the worst. For the second day in a row, I had

more e-mails than spam, which is a mite depressing when the spammers only want to steal you blind but the e-mailers want miracles. I found the official Buzzword from Hail Mary Wade about halfway down the screen. It read:

Dear Bees:

As you have no doubt heard, Mr. Vernon Moore is visiting us in Ebb this week. I want everyone to know that he is aware of the drought and working closely with your board of governors. You can help by routing any requests for a visit with Mr. Moore to Wilma Porter, but by e-mail only.

You can also show our support for Mr. Moore by stopping at Millet's after noon today to pick up a free umbrella, courtesy of the Quilting Circle. Please carry your official Quilting Circle umbrella everywhere you go. It could rain at any time.

Mary Wade, Queen Bee

I thought it was well written, all in all, and it gave me hope that I could turn on my telephone again some day. Just as I was beginning to feel better about our prospects, I noticed a second Buzzword at the bottom of the screen:

Dear Bees:

On a day when we have so many reasons to be hopeful, I'm sorry to report that Herb and Barb Knepper disappeared from their farm last night. They will be sorely missed. Let's keep them in our prayers.

Mary Wade, Queen Bee

The Kneppers owned a small bean and alfalfa spread that had been in the family for more than a century, and Barb had been a member of the Circle for fifteen years. She must have gotten the word that Mr. Moore was in town, but they didn't try to stick it out.

Maybe they were worn out; maybe the Bowes were, too. A lot of farmers in this neck of the woods were on the brink long before the drought—from year after year of being battered by dry weather, deaf banks, dumb government, greedy commodities traders, and bottom-dollar foreign competition, all at once. Even when they succeeded in getting a crop to market, only a few made more than a living wage. That's not much upside for backbreaking, fifteen-hour days, especially when the downside is next door to poor.

I'm all for capitalism, I really am, but I will never understand why we pay the people who feed us so little and the people who entertain us so much. That can't be smart in the long run.

Chapter 10

THE SCOREKEEPER'S LOT

OUISE NELSON, THE TOWN NURSE, met Mr. Moore at the
door of the River House that morning. She's a perky gal
who hails from a small town in Tennessee. "Welcome back,"
she announced with a big smile. "Pearline's off today, so it's my
shift, and I am so glad to see you! Now everything's going to
be okay."

"The pleasure is mine, Louise, and congratulations on your
marriage to Deputy Samoa. I'm sorry I couldn't be there."
Luther Salevasaosamoa, who is Louise's husband and Dot's chief
of county corrections, is normally referred to as Deputy Samoa
when he's in earshot and Deputy Giant when he's not. He is six
foot seven and used to play football for the Cornhuskers, but
Louise has since slimmed him down to a reedy three hundred
pounds, plus or minus.

"I guess you didn't get the memo, Mr. Moore. We eloped to
Samoa and got married on a beach in front of four hundred of
Luther's looniest relatives. His father roasted a pig in a sandpit
and we danced until dawn. It was so pretty and everyone was so
sweet, and so large. My Lord, they were large. I didn't want to
come back, but Luther said we had a duty to the county.

"How are you?" she continued, barely taking a breath. "Are

you well? You look like you haven't aged a day. Have you been watching your diet and getting plenty of exercise?"

"I'm fine, Louise, thank you."

"Well, you certainly look fine, and I have to thank you. Luther is terrible at cards but he just loves to play. I've never been tempted to use those special skills you taught me. Speaking of skills, I got an e-mail from Hail Mary Wade last night. It says I'm not supposed to talk to you about the weather, so I won't. If you need my help, though, all you have to do is give a holler. Would you like to see Clem now?"

"How's the old man feeling?"

"Not well, I'm sorry to say. He's been vomiting off and on since daybreak and he got bad news to boot."

"Bad news?"

"He should tell you himself."

Clem was asleep when they entered his room. Louise turned on the bedside light and touched his shoulder. "Mr. Tucker. You have a visitor."

Mr. Moore took a seat on the chair near the head of the bed.

Clem was still groggy when he rolled over. "What? Who is it?"

"It's Vernon Moore. He's come to see you." Louise wiped a drop of spittle off Clem's chin with a hanky and helped him sit up. "Is there anything I can bring you, Mr. Tucker?"

"Yeah. You can fetch the Japanese sword set from my office. Give Vernon the long sword; I'll take the short one. If I throw up one more time, I'm cutting my goddamned guts out. Vernon will behead me once the deed is done."

Mr. Moore put his hand on Clem's forearm. "Give yourself a little time. You should feel better later today."

Clem jerked his arm away. "What was that, the laying on of hands? Did I just get an early dose?"

"No, but your color is better and you look rested. It could be a better day."

"Bullshit! The day has already been crap. Would you excuse us please, Louise? Vernon and I have business to discuss."

She nodded and took up the nurse's station just outside the door. Meanwhile, Clem continued, "I guess you haven't heard the news. John Smith walked into my bedroom this morning and resigned, just like that."

"I'm sorry to hear it. Why?"

"Because I asked him to help Buford Pickett look into your background again, that's why. I told him you wouldn't mind but he quit anyway. He thinks you're a goddamned saint."

Louise couldn't see what was going on, but she could hear every word. She said Mr. Moore sounded almost sarcastic when he replied, "How unfortunate."

"I can't afford to lose a man of that caliber, Vernon; not now. I don't suppose you could get him to reconsider. Tell him it could be an extremely short mission. Maybe that'll help."

"No problem. I'll drop by and have a word."

"You're a gentleman and a scholar. I suppose that brings us to the business of the day. Would you like some iced tea or lemonade? Louise would be happy to get it."

"I'm okay, Clem. How about you? I know you're hurting, but how are your spirits?"

"My spirits? Screw my goddamned spirits! Did you ever meet Buzz Busby, my golfing buddy? He fell off a ladder back in the nineties and had to have back surgery. Do you know what he said when I visited him a few days later?"

"No."

"He said he felt better than two dead men. I thought it was funny at the time, but I sure as hell don't now. I feel better than two dead men myself, and barely at that. When I can muster up the energy, I get mad. When I can't, I'm just scared shitless."

"Everyone who faces death is scared, Clem. Everyone."

"Maybe, but I have a helluva lot more to lose than everybody else."

"You do? That's quite a statement, even from you. Why?"

"Was I the only person in the room yesterday? I had the perfect life until I took over that goddamned bank up in Omaha. Now I want it back. It's that simple."

"Then let's discuss it. How much does a perfect life cost these days?"

"What? Why do you give a rat's ass what my life costs?"

"You've offered me an unspecified sum to extend your life. In order to price myself fairly, I need to get an idea of how much your perfect life costs. I can make an educated guess, but I'd be surprised if you didn't have it down to the decimal point."

"Confidentially?"

"Not a word will pass my lips."

Louise could hear Clem squirming around in his bed, like he was trying to get comfortable. "I won't bother you with all the grimy details. You've seen the staff, the plant, et cetera. It costs me upwards of a million per year, after taxes."

"You pay taxes?"

"Move on, Vernon."

"Fair enough. If you retired tomorrow on a million per year, you'd need what—twenty million dollars in the bank? Twenty-five million at the most?"

"I suppose I could scrape by."

"Good. We've established a baseline. Now, how much are you worth?"

"What did you say?"

"It's a simple question, Clem. How much money are you worth? I don't need a precise number; round figures will do."

"Jesus! I'm not telling you that. It's highly confidential."

"Okay. Let's try a different approach. My guess is that you're worth between three hundred and four hundred million dollars."

"That's ridiculous!"

"Save your strength for an argument you can win. I did my homework. I know how much stock you own in the National Bank of the Plains, how much you've divested since the takeover, and at what price. Thanks to the SEC, it's public information."

"Your calculations aren't worth a tinker's damn, Vernon. That isn't my stock and it's not my money. They belong to the Tucker Trust."

"Your sister reviewed my figures."

"What? You saw Clara? When?"

"Last night. She couldn't tell me how much of the trust you own, but she confirmed that you hold a bit more than she does, and her share is thirty-one percent."

"How could you talk to Clara? She only says yes and no, and that's on a windy day."

"It's amazing how much you can learn from a friend if you ask the right questions, regardless of the limits of their vocabulary. Now, if I peg your trust ownership at thirty-three percent and value your holding in the National Bank of the Plains, inclusive of disposals over the last two years, I get a net worth in excess of two hundred and sixty million dollars, before accounting for any personal holdings outside the trust. How am I doing so far?"

"If you're headed down the path I think you are, you can forget it."

"I can? Great! I'm perfectly happy to forget the whole deal. In fact, I'm relieved. Everyone else in the county is desperate for rain."

"So I heard. How much are you going to charge them?"

"How witty, Clem! As you know, the majority of farmers in this county are already deeply in debt. How much do you think they can come up with? By the way, I noticed that NBP's stock price is down a third in the last sixty days. Is the drop attributable to the drought?"

"We're still profitable as hell. What do you think?"

"So, how much has the drought cost the Tucker Trust so far? Oops! I happen to have that number on hand. Your end of the loss is around sixty million dollars, isn't it? That's a million per day and counting. From where I sit, you should be paying me to make it rain — but you aren't. Why not?"

When my Fiancé in Perpetuity didn't reply, Mr. Moore said, "It's because you're dying, isn't it? Therefore, we can conclude that you value your life more than your portion of the Tucker Trust's sixty million dollars in losses. So, what's the present value of thirty million dollars per month?"

"I never put any stock in that present value bullshit, Vernon. It's all funny money, and the goddamned drought isn't going to last forever."

"Probably not. What's your theory about death? How long does it last?"

After another pause, Clem said, "How much do you want?"

Mr. Moore answered instantly, "One hundred million dollars." For the second day in a row, a Circle girl nearly peed in her pants in Clem Tucker's hallway.

"A hundred million? You call that a fair price? You're a thief and a goddamned charlatan. I'll dial 1-800-Kevorkian before I'll pay you a tenth of that!"

"Make the call. After you're done, tell me what you're going to do with all the money you saved. You won't need it to support your rustic, million-dollar-per-year lifestyle. You've got that covered by a factor of ten—assuming you beat the odds and survive. If you die, the money will go where, to the heir of the Tucker Throne? How is your daughter, by the way?"

"I have no idea. I haven't seen her in years."

"I'm so sorry, Clem. I had hoped . . ."

"Save it. She ran out on me just like her mother did. End of story."

"Then who will inherit your fortune?"

"That's none of your goddamned business, and I'm not writing you a check for a hundred million bucks. You can forget it."

"I won't need a check. A promissory note will do, but I'll have to have it by the end of the week."

"You expect me to sign a hundred million over to you *before* I go under the knife?"

"I leave Friday noon, and you still haven't answered my question. What are you going to do with all that money if you don't give it to me?"

No response was forthcoming, so Mr. Moore said, "It's hubris, isn't it? It's pride."

"What do you mean by that?"

"How many animal heads are mounted on the wall in the dining room?"

"Twenty. Why?"

"How many did you put there?"

"Eight. It would've been more, but I've been under the weather lately."

"Is that more or less than your father?"

"My father preferred waitresses to big game, but my granddaddy put six heads on that wall. I put him in second place."

"It's the same with the Tucker Trust, isn't it? You've spent half your life running up the score against your father and your grandfather and all the Tucker czars who preceded you; against your high school and college buddies; against everyone you've ever met on the golf course. Now you've won big, and you're not about to give up your margin of victory. Good for you! You face a fate shared by thousands of your fellow scorekeepers: you're about to die a big winner, prematurely and anonymously. I wonder: will there be enough grievers to carry your casket?"

"I can find six pallbearers for a shitload less than a hundred million."

"Then tell them to bury you in all the money you saved."

"Or I can write you a check. Is that your alternative?"

"No, Clem. It's your alternative. You wanted my help, remember? Now I've agreed, conditional on price. You should be dancing a jig."

Clem hesitated, then countered, "Dancing a jig? I'm half dead from cancer, you son of a bitch. I'll pay you twenty-five million."

"I appreciate the sentiment, but it's wholly inadequate."

"Inadequate? Twenty-five million? You can kiss my ass, you greedy bastard."

"Don't hold your breath, Clem. There's no way that I'll attach my lips to an ass that has been kissed by so many, but I do want to thank you, though."

"Thank me? Why?

"For being so predictably intractable. Now I can pray for rain with a clear conscience, but I'll be rooting for you on Saturday. Is there anything I can get you before I go?"

"Yeah. You can sit down for a goddamned minute and let me think." After a bit, Clem stated, "I'll give you fifty million, but that's the limit."

Mr. Moore replied, "It's ironic, isn't it? I think you're worth twice as much as you do. Since it's also a price you can easily afford, I see no reason to change my original proposal, but not for very much longer. The offer expires in sixty seconds. Take it or leave it."

The room became so quiet that Louise could hear the grandfather clock ticking in the foyer, halfway across the house. It didn't really tick, though; it was more like a *thock*. After maybe fifty-nine thocks, my fiancé said, "Seventy million; not a penny more."

"Make it eighty and we have a deal."

"Seventy-five, Vernon. That's my final offer, and it's conditional."

"On what?"

"I'll give you a promissory note, but it won't be due for a hundred and eight days. That will get me past my sixtieth birthday."

"I can't wait that long. I'll take fifteen million in cash or equivalents on Friday and the rest in the promissory note. Can you live with that?"

"I can, but maybe you won't be so goddamned sarcastic about the second condition."

"Which is . . . ?"

"I'll have the note drawn up on Friday, but I won't sign it until Monday. If I'm dead or a reasonable facsimile thereof, you won't get a dime."

"Then the deal's off. I'm leaving Friday afternoon."

"We're talking seventy-five million dollars, Vernon. You can't stay a few extra days?"

"No."

"Fine. Then I'll need a guarantee."

"A guarantee? Yesterday, you had me pegged at one in three. Now you want a guarantee?"

"That was before you gave me a price equal to the goddamned trade deficit."

"No problem. If you want a guarantee, get it from your other supplier."

"My other supplier? What other supplier?"

"My point exactly. Are we done?"

It must have been a difficult position for Clem. He was used to being in complete control, not on Death's Doorstep. I have no idea what was going on in his head at the time, but he cogitated for a while, then answered, "There's one more condition."

"You're the customer. What do you want?"

"As you are well aware, I believe that God left us in the lurch long ago, and I've never seen a speck of proof otherwise. If you won't give me a guarantee, then I'm not going to pay you a plug nickel unless you can convince me that He's still on duty, and He's on your side."

"What if I can convince you that He's on everyone's side, including yours? Wouldn't that be better?

"Maybe, maybe not. Do you have a plan, or are you going to wing it?"

It was Mr. Moore's turn to think a bit, then he said, "Wing it, mostly. You're asking me to solve an ancient puzzle called the Deist's Paradox."

"The what? What's a goddamned Deist?"

"You are. A Deist is a person who believes that God has abandoned us."

"Okay, so I'm a Deist. Take me off your Christmas list. Why should I give a shit about this paradox of yours?"

"The Deist's Paradox is a simple expression of your belief. It presumes that a benevolent God created Earth and can be stated as follows:

A benevolent God would intervene in the affairs of men
from time to time;
But God has not intervened in the last two thousand
years;
Therefore, He has abandoned us."

"Makes perfect sense to me. So what?"
"There are a lot of Deists out there, Clem. Do you know why?"
"Nope, but I bet you're about to tell me."
"Because the paradox has never been solved."
"Really? Then it'll be a pleasure to watch you in action. But
there's one little detail I forgot to mention: I don't want to hear
a word of religious bullshit out of your mouth."
"Don't worry. If the Deist's Paradox could have been solved
with conventional theological thinking, it would have happened
centuries ago."
"I'm serious, Vernon. If I hear 'God moves in mysterious
ways' out of your mouth even once, we're done."
"You can relax, Clem. You'll never hear an excuse like that
from me. I believe that everything He does makes perfect sense;
we just have to figure it out."
"Hold on there, cowpoke. Did you just say 'we'? What do you
mean by 'we'?"
"I have a theory in the back of my mind, but it's never been
tested. I'll need your help to talk it through, say a half hour to
an hour per day. Can you give me that much time?"
"Look around, Vernon. There's a chance that I can squeeze
you into my otherwise hectic schedule. Will you need any visual
aids? Flip charts? A white board? Kneepads?"
"Thanks, but I'm not much for props. I'll see you tomorrow
morning."

"Tomorrow? Why can't we start today?"

"I would, but a few friends of mine are arriving this afternoon."

"You have friends? No shit! I thought you worked alone."

"Nobody works alone, Clem. Get some rest. You should feel better later today."

Louise is quick on her feet. By the time Mr. Moore left the master's suite, she was already on the line to Dottie Hrnicek, who reports directly to Hail Mary Wade, who had left her cell phone in her car—in my parking lot.

Chapter 44

....

A TEAL AND TURQUOISE SEA

OVER THE YEARS, a lot of folks have asked me what it takes to run a bed and breakfast. There are differing opinions on the subject, but I believe that just about anybody can do it—as long as she or he (which I am legally obligated to mention) can decorate like a decorator, clean like a maid, cook like a chef, handle money like an accountant, and converse like a talk show host with lodgers of all persuasions, all day, seven days a week. You can study hospitality at college and there are a lot of good books on the subject but, in my experience, the one-stop shop for B & B education is motherhood, hands down. It will teach you a thousand little lessons about housekeeping, stretching a dollar, and caring for helpless, thankless guests that you can never learn in a classroom or a book.

I finished up the cleaning while Mr. Moore was at the River House, and then I put my chef's hat on and occupied myself with meal planning and food inventory. When I closed the refrigerator, I found Hail Mary Wade standing silently in my kitchen, holding a long-stemmed white rose and a greeting card. I would have fainted on the spot if she had been any taller than an eleven-year-old boy, and not because I never receive flowers, thank you very much.

"I knocked, but nobody came to the door," she said sheepishly.

The brass knocker on my front door is the size of a ham hock. On a clear night, it can be heard in Kansas, or so I thought. "My head was in the refrigerator," I hypothesized. "It's probably soundproof for safety reasons. Is the rose for me?"

"It's for Vernon, from Connie Kimball. I found it on the porch."

"Did you read the note?" I inquired, as if I needed to.

"It's a request to visit her mother."

"I'd see that poor woman myself if I thought it would do a particle of good. Leave it on the counter there; I'll make sure he gets it. Would you care for tea?"

"No thanks. I'm late for a deposition, but I wanted to stop in and see how your dinner with Vernon went last night. I tried to call but all I got was a recording."

"The phone is on auto. Otherwise, it rings all the time. Did you try Loretta?"

"I stopped by on my way over. She said that Vernon has asked you two to prepare a list of all the people who want to see him. Is that right?"

"It is. Do you need to add some names?"

"Keep me out of the loop, if you don't mind. I've had a few e-mails, but they were copied to either you or Lo. In your judgment, how long will this list be when you're done?"

"Fifty names, maybe more."

"Hmph. Maybe Lily was right. Unless we assemble the membership, Vernon will never be able to reach them all."

"That won't work, Mary; not with Mr. Moore. Anyway, he has another plan."

"He does? Did he tell you what it is?"

"No, but I suspect it's related to the list. In case you haven't noticed, Mr. Moore is not entirely forthcoming about his plans."

Hail Mary is a prosecuting attorney by trade, and a darned

good one. She peered into my eyes like I was a witness for the defense and said, "Is that so? Did he tell you and Loretta that he is planning to ask for rain?"

"We tried our best, Mary. He promised that he would keep quiet about the deal, but he wouldn't budge otherwise. Isn't that what Loretta said?"

"Word for word. I'm disappointed in your lodger, I have to say. I'm very disappointed, but there are two parties involved in this transaction, aren't there?"

When a woman states the obvious, she is usually being vague. I replied cautiously, "Mr. Moore and my fiancé."

"You're uniquely positioned, Wilma. You're closer to Clem than anyone. Are you going to the River House today?"

"I go down every day."

"Is he well enough to discuss business?"

"Are you kidding? Clem will be talking business a week after he's passed on. Why?"

"What if he changes the deal? What if he offers to pay Vernon, but only if he asks for rain and his life?"

"Hold on a minute! You want Clem to change the deal?"

"He's Clement Tucker, isn't he? When did he ever let somebody else define the parameters of a business deal? Besides, what I'm proposing is a win-win. I don't see why he wouldn't go for it."

"Did you run this by Loretta?"

"Uh huh. She couldn't see any harm in it either."

"No harm? You're asking my fiancé to change a deal. That's not dipping your tippy-toes into the shallow end of the pool; it's leaping headfirst into the deep end. In my opinion, we'll be better off if we step aside and let Mr. Moore do his work."

Hail Mary shook her head. "That's so, so easy for you to say. You win either way, but hundreds of others could lose everything they own. Did you check your e-mail this morning?"

"Of course, and I was as sorry as anybody to see the Kneppers go. Barb was a fine person and a heck of a needlepointer, one of the best I've ever seen . . ."

"Who's next, Wilma? How many more will disappear in the dead of night before we get rain? Vernon is our last hope. You have to talk to Clem. He'll listen to you."

"Shouldn't you bring this before the board first?"

"I could but the clock is ticking, and it's not like I'm asking for thirteen hundred dollars—for umbrellas, in a drought."

I shouldn't be giving away a secret like this, but you can always tell when a country girl is out of arguments. It's when she says, "It's not like I'm asking for the moon," or the rhetorical equivalent. It was time for me to decide. "Okay. I'll run it by him, but only if he's up to it. Otherwise, it'll have to wait another day."

"Thank you, Wilma. The women of Hayes County owe you a great debt."

"And may God bless us all," I added. "If we're getting in bed with my fiancé, we'll need all the help we can get."

Mary gave me the most peculiar look you ever saw, which is when I caught the irony of my own words. What's a girl to do? I shrugged and walked her to the front door, where we both stopped dead in our tracks. Sitting in my parking lot next to her dust-encrusted black Buick was a vehicle the size of a boxcar. Upon closer inspection, it looked more like an extralarge, ocean-blue bus, except it was missing a bunch of windows. On the side, under an eye-high layer of dust, you could make out a large mural of silver bottle-nosed dolphins jumping and spinning in a teal and turquoise sea.

"What the f——?" Modesty forbids me from spelling out Mary's remark.

"My Lord! Is that Mr. Moore's conception of an RV?" I said to myself.

"An RV?"

"He said his widow friends were arriving in big RVs. Good heavens!"

We stood there like two schoolgirls who had been paralyzed by alien gamma rays, but somebody in the bus or RV or whatever must have noticed. A neckless, potato-shaped man with shoulder-length hair and sunglasses stepped out and ambled across the lot. In my mind, I had expected a rickety old chauffeur with a black suit and teeny, billed cap, but Mr. Potato was wearing blue jeans, a white tee shirt, a black leather vest, and a red bandana. His forearms were the size of a woman's thighs and covered with black and blue tattoos.

He removed the bandana when he got to the doorway. "My name is Raymond," he said. "I'm s'posed to greet the lady of the house for my boss, the Widow Marion Meanwell. Would one of you be Ms. Wilma Porter?"

With a tinge of anxiety, I said, "I would, and this is Mary Wade, the *county attorney*." I admit it; I emphasized the "county attorney" part for my own safety. "Mr. Moore told us you were coming. Welcome to the Come Again. Would you care for a drink?"

"Thank you, but I'm not allowed. Maybe you'd like to meet Ms. Meanwell on board the coach. Most folks wanna see inside."

Hail Mary, who was late for a meeting, replied instantly, "We'd love to."

"Follow me, ladies."

When we got to the bus, Raymond retrieved a little metal footstool and assisted us up the steps. It was air-conditioned inside and the dashboard looked like an airplane cockpit. You have never seen so many dials and gauges. Behind the driver's seat, there was a beautiful booth trimmed in blue leather with an expensive burled table. A stainless-steel refrigerator and range were opposite the dining area, then the aisleway arced around a bathroom into what I can only describe as an expanse of deep-blue carpet, light-blue leather furniture of the sort you might see on an expensive yacht, and another half acre of burled maple polished to a high sheen.

"Have a seat," Raymond suggested. "Ms. Meanwell will join you in a minute."

While Mary walked around the room inspecting the decor, I plopped down in a captain's chair and prepared myself to greet anything from a biker's moll to a baroness. The Widow Meanwell came sweeping into the room moments later in a glossy green knee-length frock, heels, and a matching flat-topped hat with blue feathers and a fishnet veil that covered an inch or so of her forehead. The ensemble was styled after the fifties, but she looked fifty-odd herself, which struck me as a tad incongruous.

I felt compelled to stand. She came straight over, held out her hand, and gave me a smile that would melt an iceberg, assuming there are any left. "I'm Marion Meanwell," she announced in a voice that sounded a smidge like Angela Lansbury in *Murder, She Wrote*. "You must be Wilma. Vernon has told us so much about you."

I resisted an impulse to curtsy. "It's a pleasure. This is my good friend Mary Wade."

You'd have thought she was meeting Perry Mason. "Hail Mary Wade? Why, I've heard about you, too. It's so nice to meet you. Can you stay?"

"I'd love to, but I have an appointment at the office. How long will you be in town?"

"Oh, I never know for sure. A few days, if it's okay with Wilma. Perhaps I can stop by later in the week."

"That would be lovely, Ms. . . ."

"And please call me Marion; everyone does."

Hail Mary made her apologies and Raymond led her out. In the meanwhile, the Widow Meanwell took a chair opposite mine. "This is unlike any bus I've ever seen," I observed. "It must be a wonderful way to see the country." In my mind, I was wondering where the heck it came from, how much it cost, and what kind of miles per gallon it got.

"It's a lovely coach, isn't it?" she replied. "Vernon had one built for each of us."

"For each of you?"

"One for me and one each for Birdie and Eloise. It was the sweetest gift. I have no idea how much he spent, but they have one downside: the mileage isn't very good. Vernon says it's like pushing a giant brick into the wind. Next year, he's going to have them refitted with more efficient, low-sulfur diesel engines. Won't that be nice?"

I knew nothing about diesel engines except that they could run on biofuel, which would be good for the farming community. "Are Birdie and Eloise your widow friends?" I asked.

"Yes. They're arriving later in the day. By chance, is Vernon here?"

"He isn't. I believe he's at the River House seeing Clem Tucker."

"Clement Tucker? Your fiancé? I'm so sorry to hear that he's ill, Wilma. How are you? Are you holding up?"

I was holding up fine, more or less, but I was getting a mite fidgety in my chair. "Clem is the one who's sick, not me, and half the state is in the grip of a dreadful drought. I have nothing to complain about."

"It never seems to do any good anyway, does it? Do you have any idea when Vernon will return?"

"None whatsoever. I never do."

Marion clapped her hands together. "Me either. Isn't he a scamp? Would it be an imposition if I asked for a tour of the Come Again? Vernon says it's such a lovely place. I understand that your fiancé's sister lives on the top floor. Does she receive guests?"

"Not since Bush senior was in the White House, but I can ask."

"Would you, please? I'd love to meet her."

The phrase "home invasion" flashed before my eyes. "Has Mr. Moore told you about Clara? She isn't much of a conversationalist."

"Oh, don't worry about that, Wilma. She probably won't agree to see me anyway."

For one split second, I felt like I was talking to Vernon Moore in drag. That was exactly what he would've said.

Just as we were about to exit the motor coach, Hail Mary came running up to the steps and said breathlessly, "Wilma, we have to talk. In private."

"Right now?"

"This second. Alone."

"But I was about to give Marion a tour of the Come Again."

Hail Mary looked up at the Widow Meanwell. "I'm very sorry. We have an emergency and I need Wilma right away. Will you forgive us?"

"Of course, dear. I can tour your house at another time."

"That's very gracious. Thank you."

I stepped down and Mary practically dragged me past her Buick, which was still running under the porte-cochere with the driver's side door open. When we got into the parlor, I said, "Has the sky fallen? Has something happened to Mr. Moore?"

"The sky has fallen on us, Wilma. Your Fiancé in Perpetuity

just offered your famous lodger seventy-five million dollars to
save his life!"

All of a sudden, I could see myself drowning in a teal and
turquoise sea, and I wasn't even putting up a struggle. My eyes
were wide open and tiny little bubbles of air trailed out of my
nostrils as I sank listlessly into the murky depths. "How much?"
I burbled when I hit bottom.

Hail Mary repeated the number slowly. "Seventy-five million
dollars."

"That much? It can't be!"

"Dottie just got the word from Louise Nelson. We're screwed
to the friggin' wall, Wilma. Again, and by you-know-who."

"Dear Lord! My dear, dear Lord. Are you calling an emergency session of the board?"

"One's already scheduled for tomorrow. We'll need confir-
mation between now and then. When can you get down to the
River House?"

"I'll grab my pocketbook." I started toward the den, then
stopped. "We can't tell Clem what we just learned; Mr. Moore
either. They'll clam up and that will be the end of it."

"That's right, Wilma, but find out what you can, and make
sure that everybody keeps this deal under wraps. If we thought
we were going to have a revolt on our hands before . . ." Hail
Mary gave me a hug. She had never given me a hug before. "Call
me as soon as you hear something," she added. "Please?"

"Please" wasn't in her normal lexicon either, but women tend
to become more solicitous under stress. The same cannot be said
for men!

Chapter 12

THE WIN-WIN ILLUSION

I BOUGHT MYSELF a brand new Oldsmobile station wagon years ago, but the windshield wipers refused to budge the first time I tried to drive in the rain. Safety-conscious woman that I am, I took my brand-new car back to the dealership in Lincoln as soon as the rain stopped. But when the serviceman turned the little knob next to the steering wheel, the darned things worked just fine. After I received a mannish lecture on the care and operation of modern windshield wipers, I drove all the way home to Ebb, only to discover that the wipers didn't work the next time it rained. I went straight back to the dealership as soon as it stopped, but you know what happened: the little doodads swept across my windshield in perfect rhythm, like they were hooked up to a metronome. I explained to the serviceman that they worked fine in the dry but never in the wet, so he kindly suggested that I drive the sixty miles back to Lincoln the next time it rained, as if I could navigate my way there by radar.

That old Oldsmobile was on my mind when I drove down to see Clement that morning, and not because I was thinking about buying a new car. It was because I would have gladly taken it in trade for the very weather that had caused me so much grief.

Isn't it funny how a different perspective will change your way of thinking?

As usual, I checked in at the kitchen when I arrived. Marie, who eats under duress, was sitting at the big, butcher-block table, whipping up a two-gallon bowl of tuna salad. Louise was standing in the corner next to the freezer, doing knee bends and muttering to herself.

With as much cheer as I could muster I said, "Afternoon, y'all. How is my affianced today?"

Marie replied, "He's healthier but poorer. Didn't you get the news?"

"If you mean about the seventy-five million . . ."

When Nurse Nelson is upset, the monosyllables fly out of her mouth at machine-gun speed. She stopped moving and said to me, "You have to talk to Clem. You have to talk to Vernon. You have to stop the deal. We have to stop the deal. We have to stop it right now."

"Settle down, Louise. First off, that information has to stay in this room until the Circle decides what to do. If it leaks, we'll have panic on our hands. Do you understand?"

She began to pull her knees up to her chest, one at a time, then let them down. "I understand," she exhaled after a few reps. "I won't say a word."

"Good. Before I see Clem, I need you to sit down in a chair and tell me every little detail of Clem's meeting with Mr. Moore. Don't leave a syllable out. If I know my fiancé, there's more to this arrangement than meets the eye."

Louise sat at the butcher-block table and reported every word she heard, and then I had her repeat it all. Meanwhile, Marie ate tuna fish salad straight from the bowl. She makes a memorable tuna salad, but I turned down a heaping, wooden spoonful on two occasions.

After Louise was done, I said, "So Mr. Moore has to convince Clem that God is going to help him. That's a tall order. As far as I'm aware, Clem has been to church three times in the last twenty years—for funerals. What happens if Mr. Moore fails?"

"He has to reduce the price for his services."

"By how much?"

"He didn't say, Wilma."

"So that's the ace up Clement's sleeve. On Friday, he's going to say that he still doesn't believe, and that will force Mr. Moore to cut the price."

"But if he tries to cut too much, Mr. Moore will just ask for rain."

All I could do was shake my head. "So the deal is contingent both ways. Can you imagine? They'll be trying to outfox each other for the next three days. If I wasn't a civil woman, I'd snatch them both bald-headed."

With a half-full mouth, Marie commented, "Clem's already bald, from the chemo. What's Plan B?"

"I was speaking metaphorically. How's Old Baldy feeling today? Better? Worse?"

"We'll get an indication in a bit," Louise answered.

It had never occurred to me that cancer kept a timetable. "What the heck does that mean?" I asked.

"Vernon told your scurrilous but deathly ill fiancé that he would feel better this morning, and then he touched his arm. Clem said it was the laying on of hands; like a down payment. He had Marie fix him a plate of scrambled eggs on toast. If he holds it down, he'll be better."

"What did you put in it, Marie?"

"Salt and pepper, plus a pinch of havarti to make it smooth and tasty."

"No cyanide; no crushed glass?"

"Good heavens no!"

"Don't be so defensive. If he wasn't so sick . . . Oh, never mind! When did you take it in?"

"Half an hour ago," Louise answered. "He should be getting pretty close if he's going to puke it up. Do you want me to check?"

Marie stopped chewing long enough to ask, "Is 'puke' a medical term, Louise?"

I replied, "It's a lay term, like gizzard or pea-shooter. You all enjoy your lunch; I'll check in on the dark-hearted scourge myself. If I need assistance, I'll call."

"Are you sure you wouldn't like a tuna salad sandwich first? I can make more."

"I already ate," I lied, "but don't go anyplace. The first of Mr. Moore's widow friends arrived at the Come Again an hour ago. You'll want to hear about how she travels."

"It's old news," Louise remarked. "We picked up the story on the grapevine half an hour ago. Even Mr. Tucker was interested."

"You told Clem?"

"While I was taking his vitals. It's not like I could bring up the seventy-five million dollars, could I?"

Clem was sleeping soundly when I entered his room. A dinner plate with a few specks of yellow lay on a tray at the foot of his bed, which led me to believe that he had enjoyed his eggs on toast. He can be crankier than a teething baby when he is awakened from a deep sleep, so I picked up a copy of the *Economist* from the bedside table and took the cane chair. Clem swears by that magazine. He says it's his bible, but it isn't even written by Americans. Come to think of it, I guess the real Bible wasn't either.

It's hard to believe sometimes, but people in other parts of the world must have their problems, too. I was reading an article about this economic calamity or that when Clem awoke. As near as I could tell, every single one of them was caused by evilhearted men.

My fiancé opened his eyes and squinted into the lamplight. "Wilma? Is that you?"

"It is, honeypot. How are you feeling?"

"I'd feel a hell of a lot better if you were to slide in here with me. How about a snuggle? Are you in the mood?"

"Clement Tucker! You're in a fragile state. We'll cuddle all you want when you're better, but not till then. Can I bring you anything; a glass of iced water maybe?" Involuntarily, the idea of crushed glass entered my mind. Wasn't that awful?

"Naw, not right now. What time is it?"

"Just a tick after one p.m."

"Is it hot outside?"

"The citizens of Ebb are grilling steaks on manhole covers. Automobile tires are melting in the streets. Chickens are dropping in the henhouse, already fried. Wouldn't we be in a pickle if Mr. Moore hadn't come to save us from the conflagration?"

Clem paused for a second, like he was thinking about fried chicken, then he turned the tables on me. "What the hell is going on with your son-in-law? Did you hear? He quit on me this morning, without a day's goddamned notice."

"Um hmm. I did hear. I heard the reason, too."

"You did?"

"He's married to my daughter, Clement. In my opinion, you need to call off the dogs. Excuse me; I meant Buford."

"That's business, Wilma. We never discuss business. That's the rule."

I hate rules, especially men's rules. "Well, we have to discuss business this morning, honeypot. Things have gotten terribly mixed up, but you can help."

Clem belched. A person could never tell if his belches were involuntary or not, even when he was healthy.

"Are you okay?" I asked.

"Actually, I think so," he replied. "When you say things have gotten mixed up, I assume you're referring to a certain lodger of yours."

"He's part of it," I sighed. "You're the other part. We need you to change the deal."

"You want me to change a deal? What deal?"

"Last night, Mr. Moore told me that he's going to ask for rain or your life at the end of the week; not both. Is that right?"

All of a sudden, Clem's countenance became darker. It was as if someone had cast a shadow over the bed. "That agreement is between Vernon and me, Wilma. It's highly confidential. I'm damned disappointed that he even mentioned it to you."

"He wouldn't have, but Loretta and I cornered him over dinner. He either had to lie or he had to tell us about the deal."

"Then he should have lied. It's business."

I had heard that tone a jillion times. It was his "CEO tone," and I wasn't in a humor for it. "Just listen to me for a darned minute. This deal isn't just between you and Mr. Moore. It affects the whole county."

After a moment of reflection, my fiancé seemed to have a change of heart. I know what you're thinking: when did Clem Tucker get a heart he could change? "Okay," he said. "You wanted a minute. For one minute, lets pretend that discussing a business deal with a third party isn't a blatant breach of protocol."

"I'm not a third party; I'm your fiancée."

"In perpetuity, and a board member of that infernal Quilting

Circle, apparently for the same term. Even though it's an obvious conflict of interest, I just agreed to discuss the damned deal—for one minute. Now, what in God's name do you want?"

"Mr. Moore said you offered him money to ask for your life instead of rain."

Clem sat up. "Run that by me again," he demanded.

"Okay, that wasn't exactly what he said, but he admitted that money might change hands."

"Did he mention a figure? Did he say how much?"

"No, but it's your life and you have a lot of money, so we put two and two together and guessed that you might be offering him a lot of it."

"What's your preference, Wilma? Would you rather that I paid him ten dollars? Exactly how much is my life worth to you?"

"It's not the money, honeypot; it's the either/or part. That's what has people so scared. Can't you think of a way to pay Mr. Moore for both? That would be a win-win, wouldn't it?"

Clem pursed his lips, then said, "When you were a little girl, did you ever want something that would cost your parents a lot of money? A bicycle maybe?"

"Sure. I can remember asking my daddy for one like it was yesterday."

"Did you ask for a bicycle, or did you ask for a bicycle and a color TV?"

"Clement Tucker. I would never . . ."

"Why? What would have happened if you'd asked for both?"

"I don't . . ."

Clem didn't wait for me to finish. "The county will be here after the drought, Wilma. I may not see another Sunday, and Vernon Moore is the only hedge I've got. I'm not changing the deal; I don't care if hell freezes over." After a second, he added,

"And don't be fooled by all that win-win crap. Every business deal is a competition: somebody wins and somebody loses. One guy gets a fat wallet, and the other gets a fat lip."

That is just what I needed: another manly lecture! I was about to excuse myself to go sulk in the john when Louise came into the room carrying the telephone. "I apologize for interrupting, Mr. Tucker, but you have a call. I thought you'd want to take it."

"Who is it?" Clem growled.

"John Smith."

"Fine," he groused. "Leave the phone but take the tray. You can stay, Wilma."

As usual, I only heard Clem's half of the conversation, but I managed to reconstruct the balance later on. My newest and most favorite son-in-law said, "Vernon Moore just stopped by and asked me to reconsider my resignation. Is that what you want?"

"You're a good man, John; a pain in the ass, but a good man. I'll make you a deal: don't hold me up for a raise, and I won't ask you to investigate Mr. Moore. How's that?"

"It's not enough, Mr. Tucker. I won't split my loyalties. If you want me back, then you have to scrub the mission."

"You're firm on that?"

"Yessir."

"But that's it? That's all you want?"

"Yessir."

Clem didn't hesitate. "It's a bargain."

John was caught off guard. "I'm serious, Mr. Tucker."

"You think I'm not? How long have you been working for me?"

"Three years, sir."

"Have you ever seen me break a promise? Can you name one instance?"

"No, sir."

"That's because I keep my word, John. In return, I expect you to keep to yours. Do we have a deal?"

After a second or two, John said, "Yessir."

"Good. Will you do me a favor, please? Will you stop at the bank on the way down and tell Buford to give me a call? I'll need to talk to him, too."

"No problem, sir."

Clem hung up the phone and announced triumphantly, "John is back in the fold. And you can tell your friends at the Circle that I'm calling Buford off, just like you wanted. The investigation into Vernon's identity will cease and desist as of today."

"Are you feeling okay?" I asked. "You never give in like that."

"I've seen the Reaper, Wilma, and I'm a smarter man for it. I have no problem sacrificing a pawn here or there—so long as the king is still standing at the end."

Chapter 13

THE MULTITUDE

I RECEIVED A CALL from Loretta while Louise was giving Clem his afternoon medications. At the time, he was choking down twenty-three pills per day, but he never complained, not even once. He said his grievance was with the disease, not the cure.

Loretta asked, "How's your dark-hearted fiancé this morning?"

"He has cancer," I reminded us both, "but he's better than he's been in weeks, almost frisky. Maybe Louise slipped some Viagra into his chemo."

"You don't suppose that Vern . . ."

"Who knows? Either way, he's been running on at the mouth like his old self."

"Did you ask him about changing the deal?"

"I did, and straight out. Here's a shocker: he'd have none of it."

"You're right, Wilma. He is his ornery old self."

"You're not worried?"

"Heck no. Clem is Clem, which means money, and Vern is Vern, which means miracles. In a contest, I'll take miracles every time. When should I tell everybody you'll be home?"

That caught me by surprise. "Everybody?"

"I'm at your place, darlin'. The other two widows have arrived and Vern was right: they have a gift for making an entrance. Side-by-side, those are three of the biggest vehicles I've ever seen. A multitude is forming out front."

"A what?"

"There's maybe twenty people milling around in your driveway. Most are Circle girls, and every one is sporting a red umbrella. Pokie's keeping the crowd at a respectful distance and Dottie's in the kitchen making lemonade with Virgie." Pokie Melhuse is Dot's right-hand man. She runs the watch desk at the county sheriff's office, and she knows Mr. Moore. Besides yours truly and John Smith, she was the other eyewitness. She saw him stand in the pouring rain and call in the lightning bolt that brought Loretta back to life.

"Where's my famous lodger?" I asked, following my own train of thought.

"He and Lovey went for ice cream. He didn't say where, but I'm guessing Texas. He should've been back by now to greet his friends."

"Have you introduced yourself?"

"To the widows? Nope. They haven't seen fit to appear before the throng as of yet. Maybe they're awaiting their hostess. When can we expect you?"

"I'll be there just as soon as I can make my apologies to Clem. Hold the fort."

"That man should be apologizing to you, Wilma, and to everybody else in the county. He better be careful if he comes into my salon. We keep sharp instruments in our drawers, and we're not afraid to use them."

DUSTY CARS AND pickup trucks were parked cheek-to-jowl in my driveway when I got home, and there was wasn't enough space in the parking lot for a shopping cart. The three giant motor coaches used it all. One of the new arrivals was bright white and had a mural on the side of seagulls frolicking over frothy ocean waves. It reminded me of some Japanese art I had seen once in a museum. The other was candy-apple red with twin-winged dragonflies drawn in thin, smooth strokes of silver and gold, like filigree.

Mysteriously, there were no umbrella-toting onlookers to be seen, so I parked behind the house and went in the rear door, where I discovered that the multitude had not dispersed; it had relocated. Half a dozen women were gabbing and drinking lemonade in my kitchen, and red umbrellas were strewn everywhere: on the table; on the counters; on the stairs; leaning up against the wall.

Dottie yelled from beside the sink, "Come on in, Wilma. You're throwing a reception. Grab a cold drink and I'll usher you into the parlor."

Virgie Allen handed me a glass and slurred. "You were running low on lemonade mix, so we added a little zing to it. We're in great shape now."

Jenny McCallum walked up to me while I was eying the three empty bottles of vodka on my counter. Jenny is the town piano teacher and the organist at the Protestant church, but she broke her neck in a car crash and never quite recovered. She has to wear a foam brace to prop up her chin now and then, and she rarely teaches anymore. She says her lust for music was shattered in the wreck.

"Did you get my e-mail, Wilma?" she asked.

"Uh huh."

"Have a lot of people requested an audience with Mr. Moore? I get the impression from talking to the other girls that they have."

"We've received fifty e-mails so far, maybe more."

"Oh my! That's what I was afraid of. Their problems must be worse than mine."

"Don't sell yourself short, Jen. You'd be surprised at what some of these girls think they need."

"Thank you for saying so, Wilma, but I'll understand if Mr. Moore can't stop by."

Dottie grabbed me by the arm while I was trying to think of something nice to say and started pulling me toward the dining room. "You can't hide in here all day, Wilma," she said. "You have to meet the widows." Then, just before we passed through the swinging door, she stopped and whispered, "I need to fill you in on a few items before we go any further."

"What?"

"First off, Hail Mary told me to run a quick check on the Widow Marion's chauffeur. For your edification, his name is Raymond 'Road Rage' Duke. He used to ride with a biker gang in Flagstaff, but he had a problem with drivers who wouldn't get out of the left-hand lane so he could pass. The boy has eleven convictions for assault, vandalism, and property destruction."

"Eleven! Remind me to pull over if I see him in the rearview mirror."

"The other two chauffeurs don't look real savory either. Pokie's at the office checking their records as we speak." I started to turn, but Dottie grabbed my arm and stuck a cell phone in my hand.

"What's this?" I asked.

"A phone. I thought you might have seen one before."

"I have, but . . ."

"Hail Mary's tired of not being able to reach you. Me, too. Nobody has the number to this phone except Mary, me, Pokie, and the board. You can give the number to Mona, but nobody else. Okay?"

"That's very nice, thank you."

"You're welcome. Let's meet the widows."

I pushed through the door and was greeted by a gaggle of lubricated Circle girls, each sporting a furled red umbrella. Loretta jumped up from a side chair and grabbed my free elbow. "Come with me," she said. "The widows are waiting."

Dottie refused to release her hold on the other arm, so they marched me into my parlor like I was a disobedient student being hauled before the school principal. Two women I didn't recognize were sitting at opposite ends of my antique, purple-and-white striped sofa and Marion was in the center. She stood as I approached and said, "Hello again, Wilma. Loretta invited us in for refreshments. I hope you don't mind."

Every girl in the room stopped gabbing at once and turned an ear in our direction, just like in that old E. F. Hutton ad. "Not a bit," I replied. "You're all welcome in my house."

"Thank you for being so kind. Allow me to introduce my very best friends and traveling companions, Eloise Richardson and Bertha Fabian."

Eloise was the youngest and tallest of the three widows. She wore a plain tan dress with brass buttons down the bodice and a wide, black patent belt at the waist. "We've looked forward to meeting you for such a long time."

I jerked my arm away from Dottie so I could take her hand. "It's a pleasure to meet you," I answered.

The third widow was short and portly with white hair. She wore coarse wool slacks and a white, long-sleeved blouse that didn't fit quite right, like it was a hand-me-down. "And call me Birdie," she said. "What happened to the big tree out front? Did it catch on fire?"

"Two years ago, the poor thing. It was a town landmark. I can hardly remember a sadder day."

"My, my. What an awful shame."

Ever the sheriff, Dottie testified, "It wasn't a shame; it was arson. Thanks to Vernon, we brought the miscreants to justice."

Marion smiled. "Isn't that just like him? I've never met a man who could get so involved in so many people's affairs so quickly. Have you?"

I shook my head. As far as I knew, Mr. Moore was the champ. He beat everybody I've ever met, and I have the acquaintance of some world-class busybodies. I know what you're thinking, but I don't want to hear about it. It's my job.

The Widow Marion sighed audibly and added, "Return visits can be so difficult for that poor man. He has a tendency to get in over his head. He can't cope."

"Can't cope with what?"

She turned and waved her hand slowly around the room in a semicircle, directing our attention to the throng in my parlor and dining room. "With all of this, Sheriff. That's why he calls us."

"He calls you?" Loretta asked.

"Not always, but yes. That reminds me: Vernon phoned to say that you and Wilma were preparing a list. By chance, is it finished?"

"What list?" Dottie demanded.

Lo said, "Vern asked Wilma and me to make a list of all the people who want to see him." She turned to Marion and continued, "It'll be finished this afternoon."

"Would you be kind enough to give it to Vernon when you're done? He can review it with us later this evening."

"Sure," I answered, "but do you mind if I ask what you're going to do with it?"

"Not at all, dear."

That was another déjà vu. "Okay. What are you going to do with it?"

"As you can see, Vernon can't possibly visit everyone himself, but he doesn't want to disappoint anyone either, so the three of us are going to divide it up." Patsy Mancuso, who was sitting six feet away, said out loud, "Can you raise the dead, honey? Oops! Don't answer that. Just stay away from my husband. He's right where I want him." Did I mention that she's a widow, too?

"She's right," Loretta remarked. "The people on that list will be expecting Mr. Moore. What can you tell them?"

Patsy appeared in our little circle before any of the widows could reply, swaying slightly, like a willow in a fresh breeze. "Excuse me. Which one of you is the Chief Widow?"

"We're friends, not Indians," Birdie answered. "There's no 'Chief Widow.'"

"Okay, but you all know Mr. Moore, right?"

"Yes. He's our very close friend and traveling companion."

"Terrific. What the hell is he: a man, a ghost, a guardian angel, what? Everybody in the Circle wants to know. They're just afraid to ask outright."

The Widow Marion said, "He's a man, dear, but an exceptional one, don't you think?"

"No shit. Where's he now; out saving the world?"

"My understanding is that he's spending the afternoon with his daughter. He intends to save the world later on."

"Well, tell him to hurry up, will ya'? We need some friggin' rain." Patsy held up her vodka lemonade in salute and took a large swallow, then she headed toward the kitchen, stopping occasionally to steady herself on a chair or the shoulder of a fellow Circle girl.

As we watched her go, Dottie commented, "Remind me to pick up her keys."

Loretta smiled and steered the conversation back to my

parking-lot guests. "Vern hinted that you all work together, but he wouldn't explain how. Now I get it. You're his bailers, aren't you? You bail him out of trouble."

"Not as a matter of routine," Marion replied. "More often than not, it's our job to get Vernon into trouble, not out of it."

Dottie rolled her eyes at Lo and me. "I don't suppose you'd care to explain that."

"That would be against the rules, Sheriff, particularly in a crowd with such well-trained ears. If you wish, though, I'd be happy to stop by your office tomorrow."

"You must be a mind reader, Marion; I was thinkin' the same way. We have a meeting at the Abattoir first thing but I should be back in the office by ten. Come any time afterwards."

"At the Abattoir? Isn't that where your Quilting Circle is located?"

Dottie frowned. "Forgive me for sayin' so, but you all seem to be real well informed."

"Oh yes, Sheriff! Vernon is quite thorough. Will all three of you be attending tomorrow's meeting?"

"You're looking at half the board of governors. We'll all be there."

Marion smiled and spoke to Loretta. "Might Birdie and I drop by your house tomorrow afternoon? We'd so like to meet Laverne."

"Uh, okay. Sure. How about three o'clock?"

"Tea time? That would be marvelous."

"Shouldn't Wilma be there, too?"

Eloise turned to me. "I was hoping that you could introduce me to your fiancé in the afternoon. Perhaps you'd like to ride down to the River House in Seagull, my motor coach. It's very comfortable."

Loretta's eyes were the size of saucers by then and Dottie

looked like she was about to draw her pistol. "I should speak to Clem first," I said. "He's not much for entertaining, even when he's chipper."

"I understand, Wilma. If you're unsure, feel free to speak to Vernon, too."

Eloise caught Marion's eye and pointed to her watch. Birdie interjected, "Please accept our apologies. We have to go, but could I ask one last question?"

"Of course," I answered smugly, just like Mr. Moore would have.

Birdie wasn't impressed. "We just love your red parasols. They're the perfect remedy for the sun. Can we pick them up at Millet's?"

I felt like smacking myself on the side of the head, and I wasn't alone. In unison, Dottie and Loretta stammered, "Parasols?"

. . . .

Chapter 14

THE OLD SWITCHEROO

I N ALL HIS YEARS of servitude to my fiancé, Buford Pickett had never been invited to the River House. On the evening of his inaugural visit, Lily said he fretted like a fifteen-year-old boy before his first date. He was as quiet as a monk at the dinner table by habit, but he talked a streak that night, and then he changed clothes afterward. Buford likes to wear polo shirts in the summertime, but they have never been kind to his physique. In yellow, which was the color he chose for the occasion, he looked like a giant-sized lemon on two cracker barrels.

Marie answered the door at the River House and escorted him to the master suite, where Clement was watching CNN while he finished a bowl of homemade chicken noodle soup with garlic butter croutons. In case you're wondering, that was no mistake. Marie makes her chicken soup from scratch, including the noodles, which she hand rolls. I kid you not.

Clem clicked off the TV. "Hello, Buford. Have you two met before? Marie here is the best chef in the state, period."

Marie blushed. Buford answered, "We've seen each other around town."

"I thought you might. It's not like we live in New York, is it? Have you had dinner yet?"

"Yessir, Mr. Tucker. I'm afraid I have."

"Would you like some of Marie's chicken soup anyway? It'll be worth the discomfort."

"No, sir, but thanks for the offer."

"You heard the man, Marie. I'd appreciate it if you could take this away."

"Would you like anything else, Mr. Tucker?"

"Maybe I would. I don't suppose you've got any tapioca pudding in the fridge?"

"I don't, but I'd be happy to make you some. Are you sure you can hold it down?"

"The way I feel right now I could hold down a pound of nachos with your homemade salsa. I'll settle for the tapioca, though. Vanilla, if you don't mind."

"I'll bring you a bowl as soon as it's ready," Marie said, then she took Clem's dishes and went off in search of Pearline, who had to eavesdrop while Marie was making the tapioca. When Pearline arrived on station, Clem was saying, "Did you take my advice and put together a lay-off plan for the bank?"

"Yessir. Would you like to see it?"

"Nope. Just send it up the line. Do it tomorrow; don't wait for Omaha to call."

"I appreciate the tip, sir."

"You're welcome, but that's not why I invited you over tonight. I want you to terminate your investigation into Vernon Moore's background."

"You what?"

"You're an important man in this town, Buford. You shouldn't be spinning your wheels on a fool's errand like that."

"I, . . . I agree, sir. Thank you."

"Have you heard about the three widows who are staying at the Come Again?"

"Everybody has. You should see their motor homes. They're huge."

"I'm seeing one tomorrow, as a matter of fact. One of the widows is paying me a visit. The rumor mill says they're close to Vernon Moore. Is that what you hear?"

"Yes, sir. Everybody says so."

"That's what I thought. I want you to switch your investigation — to them."

The room went quiet, then Buford said, "You want me to investigate the widows?"

"Hell, yes. If we can't find anything on Vernon, let's triple our chances."

"But . . ."

"For just one minute, Buford, I want you to close your mouth and open the mind your parents blessed you with. I'm giving you a chance to prove your theory. For all we know, those women served in Cleopatra's court, or maybe they fought with Joan of Arc. If they did, then your *Lady Be Good* theory would look pretty damned smart, wouldn't it?"

"I guess so, sir."

Clem looked down his nose and said, "Uh uh, Buford. No, you don't. You may not guess anymore. That part has to stop, right here and right now. Get on top of those widows, and get me some hard, verifiable data by tomorrow night. Can you do that?"

"Yessir."

LIKE MOST FOLKS, I prefer being with family and friends to being with myself. It's healthier from a mental point of view.

There are exceptions, though, and one of them is the evening after I've had an impromptu reception for three incredibly strange
guests and a houseful of curious, over-served Circle girls. Once
the dishes were done and the widows had spirited Mr. Moore
off to dinner, all I wanted was to fix myself a bowl of popcorn
and collapse in front of the TV.

As a cook who takes pride in her skills, I am against micro-
waved popcorn on principal. You might as well nuke a steak or a
duck. Prepared properly, popcorn is a delicacy. I buy a premium
brand and heat it on the range in a special-made aluminum pan
with a crank in the handle that I can turn to keep the kernels
from burning, and then I add just the right amount of melted
butter and salt. They may not be the healthiest condiments, but
I doubt that popcorn would taste half as good if it was sprinkled
with hummus or bean sprouts.

I had just curled up in front of the TV with a fresh bowl of
steaming hot Orville Redenbacher's and an icy cold bottle of
root beer when my very own sheriff-supplied cell phone rang.
Since it was a gift, I felt obligated to answer it.

"Hello," I said.

"Wilma, this is Hail Mary. I just got off the phone with
Dottie. She says you had quite a party this afternoon."

"I did. You should have been here, if not to meet the widows then to sample Virgie's lemonade punch. I got asked for the
recipe twice."

"I'm sorry I couldn't make it, but we public servants are required to serve the public every once in a while. Otherwise, they
vote. Dottie says that the three widows work with Vernon in
some capacity. Is that true?"

"That appears to be the case."

"I also hear that they're well informed. Did you have a chance
to ask them about Vernon's nefarious 'Clem-or-rain' deal?"

"In the middle of a crowd of Circle girls? I don't think so. Why? Do you plan on asking them yourself?"

"I might. The umbrellas were good for morale, but they're a pitiful gesture against a seventy-five-million-dollar bribe. We need a plan."

"What kind of plan?"

"If I knew, we wouldn't need a plan; we'd already have one. Since you're Clem's fiancée, I need to remind you before tomorrow's meeting that the Circle's goal remains the same: we want Vernon to ask for Clem's life and rain; not one or the other. Do you understand?"

"No, Mary. For a fact, I don't. I've never been so confused in my life."

"Join the club. You all have a nice evening."

My popcorn was lukewarm by the time she hung up, but it's not like I could violate my principles and nuke it. I popped a handful in my mouth and checked the TV schedule to see if any old-fashioned movies were playing. The first one I found was *The Grapes of Wrath,* starring Henry Fonda! Did the station manager think we needed a history lesson?

I searched the cable directory for *Singin' in the Rain* with Gene Kelly, or *The Rainmaker* with Burt Lancaster, or even *Finian's Rainbow* with Fred Astaire, but they were nowhere to be found, so I settled on *The Flight of the Phoenix* with James Stewart. It was fine escapist fare, if a tad ironic from a topographical point of view.

Just before I went to bed, I stuck my head through the front drapes to check on the widows. Marion's motor home was still gone, but the other two were parked side-by-side just as they had been earlier in the day. A short, wide man in a yellow knit shirt and a black cowboy hat was standing about five feet from the rear of the white RV with a flashlight trained on its license plate. I would've called 9-1-1 right then and there, but I could see his Cornhusker-red Cadillac parked under the streetlight at the base of my driveway.

It was Buford Pickett snooping on the widows. He was darned lucky he didn't run into Road Rage.

Men are such boys.

Chapter 15

· ·

THE PRINCE CHARMING MYTH

LIKE MOST TEENAGED GIRLS of my day, I fell for the Prince
Charming Myth hook, line, and sinker. It's not like I blame
Walt Disney, not by himself anyway. I knew going in that Al,
my husband-to-be, had faults, but they seemed small enough
through the misty lens of my love (although a few of his physical
assets remained ironically large). I was even fond of his rough
spots. They made him fun and even a mite dangerous, and I was
sure that I could polish him up as we raised a family and grew
old together.

What a silly young fool I was! Al changed after we got married, but in the opposite direction I expected. Instead of maturing
into a devoted husband, he reverted to the peevish, self-centered
child he had been before we met. But don't be fooled; I do not
take my delusions lightly. A woman never can, especially when
there are children in the picture. I clung to the tatters of the
Prince Charming Myth for upwards of thirteen years before I
finally put myself and my girls out of our collective misery and
got a d-i-v-o-r-c-e.

I may have given up my virginity before my marriage, but I
lost something of far greater consequence after it was over: my
capacity to adore a man. In its place were skepticism and dis-

trust, which evolved over time into a form of detachment driven by self-preservation. Even when I accepted Clem's proposal, I knew that I could never adore him, but at least I wasn't foolish enough to believe that I could change him either. That's the upside and downside of detachment right there, like two peanuts in a shell.

Then Clem got sick, which put my detachment to the test, and then he tried to buy off Mr. Moore, which was more of a test than either my head or my heart could stand. The upshot was that I couldn't get to sleep that night, no matter how hard I tried, and I tried everything. I counted sheep but quit at a thousand or so. I recalled what it was like to sit through Algebra II class in high school: "If one man drives to the store at twenty-five miles per hour . . ." When that didn't work, I turned on the TV and watched the Weather Channel, where I learned that the entire eastern seaboard was getting pelted with rain! Finally, in the depths of my desperation, I dragged myself out of bed and took a hot, steaming bath with perfumed salts in it.

That was not a good decision. I woke up like a spring-loaded, size twelve, albino raisin at seven fifteen, convinced beyond a shadow of a doubt that Mr. Moore had left my premises without so much as a cup of tea, and that was before I remembered that I was due at the Abattoir at oh-seven-thirty. Luckily, I was soaking wet and stunk like a Texas whorehouse.

I took the fastest shower in the history of womankind, dried and brushed my hair, threw on a running outfit, and dashed upstairs to tell Clara that I had a Circle emergency so I could not fix her oatmeal until I got back. That's not the sort of news a rich recluse likes to receive, but it's easier to deliver when you're pretty sure that you won't get any backtalk. I groveled for a minute anyway, and then I sprinted down to the main floor—to find an empty household. Mr. Moore was gone. The giant buses were gone. If I had dropped a Q-tip in my kitchen, my daughter Winona would've heard it in Council Bluffs.

That was when my special phone rang. It was Bebe, wondering if a certain person had forgotten a certain meeting. I promised that I would get to the Abattoir as fast as I could and then, since I am a woman of my word, I got in my car and drove over. As it turns out, I could have walked. Hail Mary and Dottie had arrived only a minute or two before I did.

After I had taken my customary seat next to Lo, Hail Mary announced, "This is day one hundred and twenty of the drought and we have a full agenda." Lily Pickett began to interrupt, but Mary would have none of it. She looked across the table and said, "I know you're chomping at the bit, Lily, and we'll get to you in a second, but I'd like to start with the news from Hereford Haven Ranch. Will you fill us all in, Sheriff?"

Dottie reported, "I got word this morning that Hereford Haven has laid off four hands and they're liquidating a thousand head. For all practical purposes, that means they're shutting down for the season, and we believe it's just the tip of the iceberg . . ."

Lily couldn't hold herself in any longer. "Buford said we passed the 'tipping point' at dinner last night. He said it could rain cats and dogs tomorrow and fifty farms in the tri-county area would still go belly up."

"Fifty? My dear Lord."

"That's the upside, Wilma. He believes it'll be a hundred or more if we don't get rain in the next thirty days, but that's not the part that scared me the most."

Lily paused for effect, as if we needed any. "Excuse me," Dottie declared, "but what in the world could've scared you more than that?"

"He told me that we need to look at this situation the way Clem Tucker would: as an opportunity."

"Jesus H. Christ! Did I hear you right? Did you just say that Buford sees the drought as an opportunity? Did he tell you that himself?"

"Yes, and he's willing to put our money where his mouth is. The bids on the Bowe place are below fair market, so he's planning to pick up the mortgage himself. He's looking at the Knepper place, too."

"Long live the king; the king is dead," Hail Mary moaned. "Buford Pickett has anointed himself successor to the Tucker throne."

"Clem isn't gone yet, the bastard," Lily protested. "We can't count him out."

I was every bit as distraught as my comrades-in-arms, but I couldn't sit there and let them talk about my cancer-stricken Clement like that anymore. "He's not a bastard, Lily," I said with a little extra authority. "He's a sick bastard. We all need to remember that."

"I apologize, Wilma. I shouldn't have been so unkind. Did you know that my husband drove down to see your sick bastard of a fiancé last night?"

"He did? Was Marie able to listen in?" Mary asked.

"Pearline did the dirty deed. Clem told Buford to switch his investigation from Mr. Moore to the widows."

"I should have figured as much," I observed. "I saw Buford flashing a light on the license plate of one of widow's motor homes just before I went to bed last night."

Lily shook her head and muttered, "I swear to God; if Clem told my feedbag of a husband to squeeze through the eye of a needle, he'd butter himself up and give it a try."

I tried to blot it out. I did my best to think of pretty pink sunsets, cute newborn puppies, and sweet, funny songs from *My Fair Lady*, but a wide-screen, Technicolor picture of a short-armed sumo wrestler dressed in nothing but melted butter appeared in my head anyway.

"That's not all. Buford left his briefcase in the front room when he went to the River House last night. It was sitting out in the open, and the boys had gone to bed, so I thought I'd make sure he hadn't left any unpaid bills in it."

We all nodded our approval. A Circle girl is expected to keep her husband's briefcase neat and tidy. It's a matter of hygiene.

Lily went on. "I found the first draft of a staff reduction plan in it. Buford is going to lay off nine people at the bank on Monday."

"He, . . . he's what?" I stuttered. "The drought is barely four months old and those people need their jobs. Why does he have to lay them off so soon?"

Bebe shrugged. "He's not alone, Wilma. If we don't get rain, I'll have to let some people go at the store after Labor Day. How's business at the salon, Lo?"

"Dried up. Mona and I began to cut everybody's hours back two weeks ago."

Mary smacked the tabletop with such force that it vibrated. "Goddammit!" she cried. "This town will not come apart at the seams while I'm the Queen Bee! We're the Quilting Circle, for heaven's sakes! Did you see your fiancé yesterday, Wilma?"

"Uh huh."

"Did you talk to him about changing the deal?"

"Yes, but I was wasting my breath. I would have done better if I had asked him to make out a check to the Democratic Party."

"I'm sure that everyone in the room is as stunned as I am. What was his excuse?"

"Clem doesn't believe in win-wins, Mary. He believes he has a better chance to win if the rest of the county loses."

"That makes no sense to me whatsoever."

"It doesn't make any sense to me either. I guess that's why he's Clem and we're not."

"Is there any chance he'll change his mind?"

"None. His mind is set in stone. He likes the deal he has."

"Which means that Vernon Moore stands to collect seventy-five million dollars. How in God's name can we possibly compete with that?"

"We can't," Lily griped. "Who else has that kind of money?"

"Clara," Loretta volunteered casually, like it should have been obvious to everybody—which it should have. "And she can be extremely generous, when she comes out of her shell."

"And when was the last time that happened?" Mary inquired. She wouldn't have needed to ask except that she was a relative newcomer to Ebb, having been with us only three years.

"At the end of Mr. Moore's first visit," I replied. "She came down from her aerie to help him save Millet's from Clem. Not only that, she uttered a complete sentence. It was just one, but it had a noun, a verb, everything."

"Can she be trusted?"

That was an eyebrow raiser. "Who would she tell, Mary?"

"How about Vernon?"

"Okay," I answered. "That could be a problem. He saw Clara last night."

"He did? You don't suppose he told her about his deal with Clem."

"I have no idea. She hasn't said boo to me, but then she wouldn't, would she?"

Mary looked me square in the eye. "You need to set up a meeting, Wilma."

"A meeting? With Clara? For you and me?"

"Yes, as soon as possible."

"I can give it a try, but could I ask a question before we take on Mr. Moore, Clem and his millions, and the drought all at once?"

"If it'll advance the cause. What's on your mind?"

"Do we really want to bet on Clara? Pardon me for saying so, but it sounds like we're putting all our eggs in one basket case."

"Do you have another basket case to put our eggs in? Given the going rate for miracles these days, who else can possibly help us? Does anybody have another idea?"

Dottie winked at Hail Mary like she knew that question was coming, then she replied, "I have one. You two ought to see Clem's sister, but we should invite Vernon over to the courthouse for a little chitchat, too."

"We've been over this before . . ."

Hail Mary cut in, "You and Wilma had your chance, Lo. Now it's our turn . . ."

"To do what exactly?"

"To see if we can get him to change the deal; what else?"

"How? How are you going to do that?"

"I'm a lawyer . . ."

"Oh, dear God! You're not going to beat on him with a phone book, are you?"

Mary answered, "No, Loretta; that's Dottie's department. I'm trained in the art of persuasion. My job is to persuade people to do the right thing . . ."

"You. You're going to persuade Vernon Moore to do the right thing."

"Yes."

"I can't speak for anyone else in the room, but that strikes me as a teeny bit presumptuous. Did it ever cross your mind that he's doing the right thing already?"

"By asking for Clem's life instead of rain? Please! How can that be the right thing?"

"I don't know, Mary, but I can add. Vernon Moore has saved this town twice before, and you haven't."

"So your strategy is to leave him be. Is that it?"

"My strategy is to have faith in the man with the track record. Before you and Dottie throw him in the hoosegow, you might consider doing the same."

"Oh, I will, Loretta; I will—after he agrees to ask for rain." Then she looked at me and added, "And Clem's life, of course."

Save for a few housekeeping items, Hail Mary's halfhearted promise to remember my fiancé concluded the meeting. Lo and Bebe had cleanup duty, so I walked to the exit with Lily again. When we got outside, she opened her red umbrella to protect us from the sun and said, "I'm married to an insensitive, over-weight, scourge wannabe, Wilma. What should I do?"

At that moment, I couldn't imagine why a girl would want to talk about anybody except Clem or Mr. Moore. "You're asking me?" I inquired. "About Buford?"

"You're the expert. Who else in this town has as much scourge experience as you do? Oh crap! There I go being insensitive again; I mean sick bastard experience."

"It's a fair point, I suppose. Are you happy?"

"No."

Tell me if I'm wrong, but I didn't get the sense that she had even a pinch of adoration left, assuming she had any to start with. "But you have two fine boys, right?"

"Uh huh."

The picture of a naked, buttered Buford reappeared involuntarily in mind. I shuddered and went on, "Then his job is done,

but I wouldn't throw Prince Charming out the door just yet. I'd
wait till the weekend at least."

"Why?"

"Because Vernon Moore is in town, Lily. *The* Vernon Moore.
We can sit around the Abattoir all day plotting this or that, but
it won't amount to a hill of beans come Friday afternoon. He is
going to do whatever he is going to do, and it won't be what anybody expects; not you, not me, not Lo, not Clem, and certainly
not Hail Mary Wade. None of us have a clue."

"Are you sure, Wilma?"

"Heck no, but it'll all be over in three days. What have you
got to lose?"

Chapter 16

. . . .

GOD'S DILEMMA

JOHN SMITH WASHED Clem's black limousine in the front
courtyard of the River House every Wednesday and Saturday,
come hell or high water, or nearly no water. He customarily
wore black from head to foot, but he removed his shirt for the
purpose of washing a car in the blistering sun. As a consequence,
the ladies of the household became familiar with his pectorals
and abdominals, but from a purely admirational point of view.
He kept himself in fine physical condition, I have to say.

When Mr. Moore pulled up to the house in his blue Mustang,
John put down his hose and walked over to open the door.

My famous lodger emerged and said, "It's good to see you,
John. Given your presence, would I be correct in assuming that
you and Clem have ironed out your differences?"

"We did, Mr. Moore. Thanks for your advice."

"You're welcome. Would I also be correct in concluding that
Clem is ignoring the ban on washing cars?"

"Laws like that are made for little people, not Tuckers, but
if using a few extra gallons of water is the worst he ever does, I
expect I'll be able to cope. Are you here to see him?"

"Yes. How's he doing today?"

"He's officer material, that's for sure. He's been running

around the house all morning, barking out orders and causing trouble everywhere he goes. If Pearline can get him back in bed, he gets on the hooter and starts swearing at somebody."

"So he's better."

"A lot better, and he credits you. He says you gave him his strength back."

"It sounds like I may have given him the wrong end of his vocabulary back, too."

"I'm afraid so, sir. Would you like me to walk you in?"

"Thanks, but I can find the way. If I were you, I'd finish the limo so I could get out of the heat."

"I don't mean to diminish the county's need for rain, Mr. Moore, but this isn't hot. Hot is North Africa in the summertime. Have you ever had the pleasure?"

"Once upon a time, long, long ago. Have a good day, John."

The young man returned to his chores while the older man let himself in and walked back to the master suite, where Pearline was checking the sick man's blood pressure.

Clem was sitting at the head of the bed in Wedgwood-blue silk pajamas with white piping and buttons, which I gave him for Christmas one year. They complemented his white terrycloth robe, which was long and hooded, like a boxer's.

"Come on in, Vernon," he said as he rolled down his sleeve. "Have a seat. Pearl is just finishing up." He looked up at her and inquired, "Well? Am I going to live?"

"It's amazing, Mr. Tucker. Your temperature is back to normal, your pulse and respiration are fine, and your blood pressure is down fifteen points. But you need to quit hopping up and down and get your rest. Should I leave the phone?"

"Naw. Take it with you, please. I'm expecting a few calls, but take messages until Vernon and I are done. Okay?"

"Yes, sir."

After Pearline had excused herself, Clem said to Mr. Moore, "I hear your friends arrived at the Come Again yesterday afternoon, and they're all widows. Is there a reason you like to hang around women with dead husbands?"

"Let's just say that I've learned to prefer them to women with living husbands, generally speaking."

"That's pretty sound reasoning, now that you mention it. Why'd you invite them here?"

"I didn't. They wanted to see Ebb for themselves."

"So they're not here to help you call in the rain or exorcise my cancer?"

"Not at all. They're just good friends, and a little nosy."

"I heard that, too. Wilma's bringing one of them down to see me later today. Heloise, I believe her name is."

"Eloise, or El. She's very nice. You'll like her."

"Eloise; I'll try to remember. Why are you sending her out here? Are you looking for a second opinion?"

"It wasn't my idea, Clem; it was hers. If you're up to it, you might enjoy a tour of her motor home."

"Maybe I will. I am feeling better; a hell of a lot better thanks to you, and don't deny it either. I'm happy with the theory I have. What's on the program this morning?"

"The Deist's Paradox. Do you remember it?"

"You'll have to forgive me, Vernon. It must have been the excitement of the day. I forgot to commit it to memory."

"No problem. It goes:

A benevolent God would intervene in the affairs of men
    from time to time;
But God has not intervened in the last two thousand
    years;
Therefore, He has abandoned us."

"Okay, but why is that a paradox? It sounds to me like a simple statement of fact. God took off. He flew the coop, just like I've been saying all along."

"But what if He didn't? What if He's still here, but He chooses not to intervene?"

"Are you saying that He's nothing but a spectator, Vernon; that He just sits up there and watches us, like we're on TV?"

"Why not? It's a possible solution to the paradox. If you were to try on His shoes for a few minutes, then maybe we could determine whether He does or not."

"Hold on a minute, cowpoke. Did I hear you right? Did you just say that you want me to step into God's shoes? What size does he wear: a twelve zillion triple E?"

"Don't be modest, Clem. If anyone can fill His shoes, you can. Aren't you the chairman of the largest bank in the state . . . ?"

"Three states."

"Then let's move you up a rung. Let's put you in God's shoes and see if we can discover whether you, as God, would be a spectator, or you would intervene on Earth. Do you think you can handle it?"

Clem thought it over, then answered, "No problem. If playing God is what it takes, then I can play God. Would you like to say a little prayer to me now?"

"Maybe later. For now, I'd like you to relax: close your eyes, let your shoulders drop, breathe deeply. Imagine that you're all-knowing and all-powerful. It can't be much of a leap."

"I hope you're not expecting me to eat humble pie today, Vernon. I'm God. I've got my infinite shit together."

"More importantly, you're omnipotent and omniscient. Under such extraordinary circumstances, what would you want more than anything else?"

"A big-chested woman with no vocal cords and no emotional

baggage. If Wilma had my sister's vocabulary, she'd be two words short of perfect."

In case you're wondering, I didn't make that up. It was reported exactly as recorded; I swear to God.

"Is that all you want, Clem? Over the course of history, kings and caliphs have kept hundreds of wives and concubines, and they're merely royalty. Isn't there something more elusive you would want, something beyond mortal reach?"

"Jesus, Vernon, I don't know. Give me a hint."

"Remember, you're omniscient. You're aware of everything that has ever happened, is happening now, and ever will happen. What's the one thing you crave more than anything else?"

After a pause, Clem replied, "I apologize for being so thickheaded, but I'm still leaning toward my first choice. Maybe you'd better explain the error of my ways."

"It's simple, really. If you were omniscient, you would know everything about the past, the present, and the future, forever. You could never be surprised or amazed; there would be no mysteries or revelations. You couldn't even have an idea; you'd have already had them all. If you were an omniscient God, wouldn't you be bored to tears? Wouldn't eternal life be a curse of infinite proportion?"

"So what am I supposed to do: make myself stupid?"

"Would you rather be stupid, or would you rather be surprised?"

"You just lost me, Vernon."

"Think about it, Clem. If you knew everything, wouldn't you crave uncertainty? Wouldn't you value surprise and excitement above all else? In fact, weren't you in a similar position a few years ago? Isn't that why you parlayed the family bank into a coup d'etat at the National Bank of the Plains? Weren't you just plain bored with the same old job at the same old office in the same old town every single day?"

My fiancé opened his eyes. "That was a brilliant business maneuver, if I say so myself. It made me wealthier than even you can imagine."

"Maybe, but to pull it off you had to consolidate the trust's wealth in the loan portfolio of a small, rural bank. Was that a brilliant maneuver, or was it the reckless act of a terminally bored businessman?"

"Okay, so I was bored, but I'm not real fond of the word 'terminal' right now, if you don't mind. I'm happy to assume that God was bored, too. That's why He took off and left us behind—because we're a boring goddamned species. What do you say to that?"

"I'd say you were jumping ahead of me. You're an all-knowing God, so you suffer from God's Dilemma: you're infinitely bored. However, you are also all-powerful, so you can make anything you want. What do you make?"

"I suppose a chesty woman is still the wrong answer."

"Oddly, you're on the right track, but instead of one woman, why not build a planet full of women and millions of other species, and maybe even a few men? Since you're omnipotent, why not build billions of galaxies, each with billions of stars and planets of their own? If you had the inclination, I bet you could finish the job in a few days, maybe even less."

"Yeah. I suppose I could."

"Good. Now what's the most important feature that you would build into this giant universe of yours?"

"I take it I'm supposed to say 'uncertainty' instead of 'boobs.'"

"That's right! If you were God, you could build an uncertainty engine the size of a universe. While you were at it, you could embed the principles of uncertainty into everything from the actions of subatomic quantum particles to the impenetrable emotions of lovely, large-chested women, to the behavior of the very stars themselves. Then you would be surprised and mystified and pleased and excited, and even disappointed, every single day."

"Check the org chart, Vernon. You're not God; I am. I've had enough disappointment for one life so my universe isn't going to have any."

"You'd eliminate disappointment? Really?"

"Absolutely."

"How?"

"I'm God. I'd remove the prospect of disappointment. It would be a piece of cake."

"Would you allow your subjects to eat the same cake?"

"That depends. Am I a benevolent God or a prick?"

"You're benevolent."

"Okay, then I'm an equal-opportunity God. Nobody gets any disappointment."

"Fair enough. Suppose a dozen of your humans place bets on a single turn of a roulette wheel. In order to eliminate the prospect of disappointment, wouldn't you have to let them all win, every turn of the wheel? How could you do that?"

"I'm omniscient, Vernon. I'd figure it out."

"Suppose you did. Would the excitement of the game be preserved? How could it be if every player won every time?"

Clem didn't reply, so Mr. Moore continued, "What about free will? Wouldn't you have to eliminate that, too?"

"Why?"

"What was the most disappointing day in your life?"

"July fourth; the night my granddaughter died on my porch. She was my last heir."

"It must have been heartbreaking. How about the second most disappointing day?"

Clem thought for a moment, then answered, "It's a toss-up;

either the day my wife ran out on me, or the day my daughter ran out on Calvin Millet and my dying granddaughter."

"So, in order to eliminate disappointment, you'd have to prevent your human subjects from leaving their loved ones behind. In other words, you'd have to inhibit free will. Would He do that, or would a truly benevolent God leave our free will intact?"

"Okay, Vernon. I get free will, and I've been bored enough in my own lifetime to understand that excitement requires an element of risk. So what?"

"You're still God, Clem. What would happen if you intervened in anything on Earth: the birth of a child; the outcome of a baseball game; the illness of an old man; the path of a tornado? What would happen?"

The room was silent for a long while, then Clem said, "Uncertainty would be kaput."

"That's correct. In effect, you'd be unraveling the tapestry of uncertainty you deliberately sought to weave, and not only for yourself, but for your little human subjects as well. You'd be destroying everyone's uncertainty, and the ramifications wouldn't stop there."

"What does that mean?"

"You're God. You take pity on the people of Ebb, so you decide to drop down to Earth and end the drought. How do the locals react? What do they do?"

"Now that you mention it, I've been in that position before. If I step in and bail everybody out, then they expect me to change their diapers, wipe their butts, and fix every other goddamned problem they have from that day onward."

"Right again. In a single demonstration of your power, you have not only destroyed uncertainty, you've destroyed self-determination. You've reduced your human subjects to less than parasites. You've turned them into whining, sniveling, inert little creatures with extraordinary expectations."

"I already have a bunch of those, Vernon; they're called relatives. I take it that's why God never answered my prayers. He didn't want to turn me into a relative."

After a pause, Mr. Moore said, "That would seem to be the inevitable conclusion, wouldn't it? Luckily, there's a wee flaw in my argument."

"A flaw? What are you saying? Are you saying that God could've answered my prayers?"

"More to the point, He still can."

"You're contradicting yourself, Vernon. If He answered my prayers, the outcome would be predetermined. You said so yourself. He'd be destroying my uncertainty; His, too."

"So it would appear, but there is a solution. Actually, it's more like a loophole."

"A loophole? No shit! I adore loopholes. What is it?"

"I'm sorry, but it'll have to wait until tomorrow."

"Tomorrow? Why not now? If there's a loophole that will allow God to answer my prayers, then I'd like to find out what the hell it is before it's too goddamned late."

Mr. Moore stood up. "The loophole will have to wait, Clem. I have another appointment in thirty minutes."

"Another appointment? Who with? Those widow friends of yours?"

"No. It's just a little homework."

"More homework? Jesus Christ! What the hell are you doing; goin' to night school?"

"In a manner of speaking. I'll tell you all about it in a few days. Between now and then, anything I say would be speculative."

"So you're doing speculative homework."

"That's it exactly."

"You're a pistol, Vernon, and a bona fide pleasure to do business with. I swear to God, I couldn't have had a better distraction from the prospect of my own, hugely disappointing outcome. Regardless of what happens, I want to thank you for coming back."

"You're welcome, Clem. I wouldn't have missed it for all the tea in China."

"If I pay you anywhere near seventy-five million dollars, you'll be able to afford all the tea in China, you prick."

Chapter 17

. . . .

LOHENGRIN'S CHILDREN

THE SILAS C. TUCKER county courthouse is an elevated, three-story, redbrick building with six Greek columns out front. Like so many of its ilk, it is a city block unto itself, inclusive of the grounds and the parking lot. On the inside, there is a domed, marble-floored foyer that has the rare quality of being acoustically perfect, which means that a person can whisper a word on one side and a person on the other can hear it as clear as a bell. For a hundred years, little boys and girls have gone there to tell each other secrets.

When Dottie and Hail Mary walked into the foyer that morning, they found the Widow Meanwell sitting on a wooden bench under a brass plaque dedicated to the dearly departed Lucy Millet, Calvin's daughter. Marion's driver was leaning against the wall next to the elevator, reading a worn, paperback copy of *Zen and the Art of Motorcycle Maintenance*. After Mary made the introductions, Road Rage took a seat on the bench and the three women took the elevator up to the county attorney's office on the third floor.

Hail Mary sits in a cushy, black leather chair behind a polished mahogany desk in front of the window in her office. Her guests have the pleasure of choosing any one of four straight-backed, wooden chairs with iron-hard seats and cushions that are thinner than a tardy husband's excuse. Nobody except Mary has a hope of getting comfortable, but the view out the window is pleasant—except during a drought, when every living thing in sight is half dead or worse.

Once the three women had seated themselves, the Widow Marion remarked, "I don't believe I've been in the office of a prosecuting attorney before. Have you two put dozens of miscreants behind bars?"

"We're *Charlie's Angels* meets *Law & Order*," Dottie replied. "My deputies catch 'em and Mary puts 'em away. Do you have a particular miscreant in mind?"

"Oh no, dear, but I understand that you two have worked with Vernon in the past. Is that true?"

"It sure is. He was helpful with one case in particular, if a tad unconventional in his ways. Even today, people argue about what he did or didn't do. I don't suppose you could shed a little light on the matter?"

"Oh, I very much doubt it, Sheriff. Vernon is hardly the quiet type, but he rarely talks about himself. Instead, he seems to be selling something half the time. Does it seem that way to you, too?"

Hail Mary chuckled. "It seems that way to everybody. According to legend, he was a traveling salesman when he first came to Ebb. Was he a salesman when you met?"

"Oh, I don't believe so, but we weren't introduced in a professional capacity. Rather, it was when he was inducted into an association of travelers to which I belong. Birdie and Eloise are members, too."

"An association of travelers; like a travel club?"

"Yes. That's it precisely."

"Does your association have a name?"

"Naturally, dear. How else would we know what to call ourselves?"

After a pause, Dottie asked, "Could you tell us what it is?"

"We're Lohengrin's Children. It's rather catchy, don't you agree?"

"Never heard of it," Dot commented.

Hail Mary asked, "Lohengrin, as in the opera?"

The widow clapped her hands in delight. "Why, yes! Good for you! I take it that you've been." Marion pronounced the word "been" like "bean."

"At the Kennedy Center, when I was interning in Washington. As I recall, Lohengrin was a knight with special powers and a protector of the Holy Grail."

"Quite so, but he could only use his powers if his true identity remained secret. It's just a myth, of course, but the name seems to fit our mission."

"Your mission?"

"Yes. All of Lohengrin's Children share two goals: to see the world, and to help those in need. If my understanding is correct, the goals of your Quilting Circle are quite similar."

"Yes, very." Hail Mary cleared her throat and continued, "By every account, Vernon has fulfilled your mission wonderfully in Ebb, and twice at that. But his third visit hasn't been much of a charm, Marion. We're in a bit of a quandary right now."

"Isn't that the awful truth!" she answered. "So many good people are being hurt by this horrific drought."

"I'm referring to one person in particular. Have you heard of Clem Tucker?"

"Why, yes. Vernon has spoken of him on several occasions, but we learned of his illness only recently. We're all praying for his recovery, of course."

"Apparently, you won't need to bother; us either. Vernon is going to ask for Clem's life at the end of the week."

According to Dot, the Widow Marion didn't appear to be the least bit surprised. "I don't get your implication, dear," she replied. "It almost sounds as if you would rather that Vernon didn't pray for Mr. Tucker's life."

"Not at all. If I had my druthers, he would pray for Clem's life and rain, but he won't. He says he'll only pray for one and not the other, and he's decided to pray for Clem—for a fee of seventy-five million dollars! On the off chance, did Vernon happen to mention this little transaction to you or your friends?"

"We discussed it over dinner last night. Why? Does it worry you?"

"Hell no!" Dottie barked. "The drought is only sucking the lifeblood out of my county like a giant, vampire sponge. Why the hell would I care that the one person who can save us has been bought off by the fourth richest man in the state?"

"Oh my! What a curious point of view you have, Sheriff! I thought a woman in your profession would have learned to rely upon facts, but you seem to believe that Vernon has some sort of supernatural ability to make it rain. Does that make any sense?"

Dot didn't blink. "Vernon Moore has saved this town twice before, and in ways that made no sense to anybody. If anyone on this Earth can make it rain, he can."

Hail Mary continued, "And he was just bought off by Clem Tucker, so you can see why we're so concerned. Do you know what fraud is, Marion?"

"Not from personal experience, but I believe I could use it in a sentence. Why?"

"Because I will have no choice but to send Vernon to prison if he defrauds Clem Tucker of seventy-five million dollars."

"Really? I had no idea! Ever since I arrived, the women of Ebb have been telling me that Clement Tucker is the meanest, most miserly businessman in the state. How can a man like that be fooled into paying so much for a prayer, unless he believes that he's getting fair value for his money? Unless I'm quite mistaken, you believe it, too. If you didn't, why would you so desperately want Vernon to pray for rain?"

Hail Mary took a deep breath, then replied, "We all have faith in Vernon's extraordinary abilities, Marion. What we don't understand is the logic of this deal with Clem . . ."

Dottie interrupted, "Nobody in this county—and I mean no body—understands why he can't ask for rain and Clem's life. That's what's so damned frustrating! It just doesn't make any sense!"

"So faith and logic have collided, dear. It's a classic dilemma, but logic suggests, and rather strongly I believe, that Vernon could never make it rain in the first place, or heal Mr. Tucker for that matter. Since logic fails, it would appear that faith is your only rational resort."

"Did you just say that faith is our only rational resort? Isn't that a contradiction?"

"Heavens no, Mary! In His wisdom, God knew that we could never sort everything out for ourselves, so He gave us faith to fill the gap. But He made it optional, didn't He? So you can choose to use your faith, or you can choose to leave a great, gnawing hole in your heart by ignoring it."

"So I'm supposed to fill my gap with faith. Is that right?"

"Yes. That's quite right. It's what we're all supposed to do."

"And what about the reservoirs and rivers in Hayes County? Am I supposed to fill them with faith, too?"

The Widow Marion answered, "If you look into your heart, I believe you'll find that faith is the most prudent choice you have." Then she added, "It's been lovely, but I have such a long list of people to see. Do you have a last question before I go? I sense that you do."

"Yeah," Dottie declared. "I've got a bunch of 'em. I'd like to know where Vernon was born, and I'd like to have a date. I'd like to know once and for all if he has special powers, like that Lohengrin guy, and I'd like to know what he intends to do in my county for the rest of the week. Can you answer any of those?"

"Only what he's doing now, Sheriff. He's visiting farms on Wilma's list."

"He's what? I thought you and the other two widows had divided it up."

"And so we did, but Vernon decided to make a few calls himself."

"But why?" Hail Mary demanded. "The list is so long and they're all so needy! Isn't there a risk that he'll overextend himself?"

Marion smiled and replied, "Oh no, dear. There's no risk of that. Vernon always overextends himself. He wouldn't have it any other way."

After the usual expressions of mutual appreciation, Dottie escorted the widow downstairs to meet Pokie, Luther, and her other day-shift deputies. Meanwhile, Hail Mary got on-line and searched for "Lohengrin's Children," and then she summoned the sheriff back to her office.

Dot appeared in her doorway and announced, "The Widow Marion is holding court in the 'pit' downstairs. Deputy Giant is giving her the play-by-play of Vernon's salvation of Matt Breck, and Pokie is so eager to talk about Loretta's shocking recovery that she's about to bust a gut. If you don't mind, I'd like to get back to my people as soon as possible. That woman makes me itch."

"Me, too. There's no mention of 'Lohengrin's Children' on the Internet. I just checked."

"None at all? Are you sure you spelled it right? It's a foreign name."

Mary ignored her. "If their club charges even a dollar a year in dues, then it has to be registered somewhere. Look into it. Find out everything you can about Lohengrin's Children."

"Me? I can hardly spell my own last name." In case you forgot, Dottie's last name is "Hrnicek." Hardly anybody can spell it.

"Then put Pokie on it. She's a college girl. Are we all square?"

"I'm not so sure, Mary. We've been lectured twice today about having faith in Vernon Moore, and it's not even lunchtime. It seems to me that we're not getting the message."

"Here's the only message you need to get, Dot: the survival of the county is at stake and the devil's own spawn has offered Vernon Moore seventy-five million dollars to hang us out to dry. We're the elected representatives of the people of Hayes County. If we won't fight for them, who will?"

Chapter 18

··

MORE LOOPHOLES

I HATE TO KEEP DWELLING on the drought, but it was surely dwelling on us. That Wednesday was the hottest July day in Hayes County history: the temperature reached a hundred and nine in the shade. Hardly a woman could be seen on the streets, but the few I met on the way home from the Abattoir were carrying red parasols to ward off the sun. I guess things don't always work out the way people plan, even when Mr. Moore isn't involved.

I had a little time to myself before I hitched a ride to the River House, so I sent an e-mail to Clara requesting an audience for Hail Mary, and then I cleaned up the kitchen and made sure that the bathrooms had plenty of toilet paper, hand soap, and whatnot. I stuck my head into Mr. Moore's room, too, but it was neat as a pin: his clothes were put away; the newspaper had been placed in the trash bin in the bathroom; and his towels had been hung on the rack to dry. He had even made his own bed, and better than I could. There wasn't a wrinkle in it.

A modern psychologist might take the position that Mr. Moore was mildly obsessive-compulsive. In my opinion, he was just a tidy man, which was what you would expect of a man who had served his country in the U.S. Army. That was Buford's theory, and I liked it better than the newfangled one for about seventy-five million reasons.

In general, I believe that we should take the positive view until proven otherwise, but that was a hard row to hoe when it came to Nicky Molineaux, the Widow El's chauffeur. He did his best to dress the part, but he was a thin, rat-faced man with slicked black hair, opaque sunglasses, and a perpetual five o'clock shadow. According to Pokie, he had been convicted of forgery in California and served an extra "nickel" for knifing another inmate. If I had been on the jury, I might have voted for conviction based upon his appearance alone. Isn't that terrible?

Nicky the Knife knocked on my door at eleven a.m. on the dot. When I answered, he said in a nasal, northeast accent, "Hello, Ms. Porter. I'm supposed to drive Ms. Richardson down to the River House. She says you're coming and you know the way."

"Let me get my pocketbook. I won't be a minute."

When I returned, he led me across the driveway to the Seagull, Eloise's motor home. It was shaped exactly like Marion's on the inside, but the carpets were Persian in appearance, the appliances and walls were glossy white, and the booth and captain's chairs were upholstered in lipstick-red leather.

Nicky pointed to the copilot's seat up front and declared, "You're the navigator." I strapped myself in while he took the pilot's chair. Just when I had begun to theorize that conversation was not his forte, he put on a headset and added, "I'll call the Widow Richardson."

See. You shouldn't judge people.

Eloise appeared behind my seat just a tick or two later. I started to unhitch the buckle on my seatbelt, but she touched my shoulder and said, "Don't get up." The woman couldn't have been a day over thirty-five, which meant she was my junior by more years than a body would care to admit, but she spoke to me like I was a child. It was a tad discombobulating.

"Shouldn't you be sitting here?" I asked.

"I'll sit in the booth if the road gets bouncy. Enjoy the view."

Nicky turned the ignition on and let the engine warm up, then he pulled out of the parking lot and headed south to the River House. On the way, we passed acre after acre of brown, half-dead corn and soy, which made it next to impossible to talk about anything but the drought. I thought about mentioning Clem's deal with Mr. Moore, but it was just as depressing and I was afraid to bring up that much money in front of a convicted con artist.

As Nicky turned left on State Highway 159, Eloise pointed toward a field of dry, stunted stalks planted in long, straight, dusty rows and inquired, "Whose farm is that?"

"It belongs to Rick and Casey Jaworski," I replied. "They raise some corn and run one of the last family dairies in the county, but the local scuttlebutt says their well is running dry, and the only way they can afford to drill a new one is to sell off the dairy stock or a big chunk of farmland. It's Hobson's Choice. They lose either way."

"Can't they borrow the money?"

"If their last name was Tucker they could, but the farmers in this neck of the woods are generally leveraged up to their eyeballs. Most couldn't borrow a cup of laundry detergent without signing over a first-born."

"What a shame! They must feel so helpless."

"Oh, they do, Eloise. They most certainly do."

I DIDN'T KNOW IT at the time, but Mr. Moore had stopped by the Jaworski place on his way back to Ebb. Since the house never had any air conditioning, Casey served iced tea to her guest and her husband on the veranda off the kitchen, where there is a ceiling fan and some pretty wicker furniture with puffy floral cushions she made in a Quilting Circle class.

After the usual small talk, Mr. Moore said, "You requested that I drop by. May I ask why?" Casey is a fifth generation Nebraskan and a child born of the corn, no disrespect to Mr. Stephen King. She's as skinny as a stalk and as brown as the ground, with blue sky eyes and sun-bleached hair the color of tassels. Coincidentally, she happens to make the lightest, most scrumptious corn soufflé in the county. In case you're wondering, you serve it as a vegetable, not as a dessert, and you don't sprinkle any powdered sugar on it either.

"There's no other way to put it, Mr. Moore," she answered. "We're beat."

Rick, her husband, is a barrel-chested, red-faced man with short black hair that pokes straight out of his head like a porcupine's. During the season, he likes to wear blue, sleeveless work shirts, camouflage pants cut off above the knee, and work boots with floppy laces that he never ties up. "If we don't get rain in the next few weeks," he added, "and I mean a decent accumulation with more to follow, the corn's gone. It's dead. We have thirty-two milkin' cows, but I'm running out of hay and we're down to mud in the well."

"What about subsidies? Don't they help?"

"We get twenty dollars an acre in this part of the country, but it costs upwards of a hundred and fifty dollars in seed, pesticides, fertilizer, and fuel to till an acre anymore, not to mention the crop insurance. The government also guarantees me a minimum of a dollar and ninety cents per bushel, but that's way below market, assuming I have a bushel to sell in the first place."

"Hold on for a minute, Rick. Did you say crop insurance?"

"Yep. Every farmer with a mortgage has to have crop insurance. If the weather doesn't turn, it'll cover up to seventy percent of my losses come October."

"Won't that help you out?"

"It'll get us through the winter, but there won't be enough left over to plant next season; not unless I sell off the dairy. It won't get me a working well till November, either, assuming we can beat the frost, and I need water now."

"Forgive my naïveté, Rick, but I've never made a living off the land. As a businessman, it would seem to me that the bank would be interested in retaining its customer base. Couldn't you work out some sort of solution with them; a bridge loan, for example?"

"A loan? From a bank? We're upside down on the mortgage because valuations have gone to hell, our credit cards are maxed out, and we're leveraged to the hilt on the equipment. I haven't checked our credit rating lately, but I'd be surprised if it broke three digits."

"Would it help if I spoke to Clem Tucker?"

"The Clement Tucker? You've got to be kidding! I heard you two were tight, but that man was a conscientious objector in the war on poverty. Besides, I have to deal with Buford Pickett. Have you ever tried to negotiate with Buford, Mr. Moore?"

"No. I can't say that I have."

Rick held up his right hand, which was missing the upper half of his index finger. "I got this nub because I stuck my hand in the wrong end of a 1947 Massey Harris when I was a kid, but I tell you what: I'd cut the other four off with a meat cleaver before I'd get down on my knees in front of that self-servin' son of a bitch ever again. Have you heard the latest? The rumor mill says he's buying the Bowe place himself."

"I hadn't."

"Well, you have now, Mr. Moore. We're a cursed people. Just

when Clem Tucker is about to kick the bucket, Buford Pickett rises up from hell to take his place."

"Richard Milhous Jaworski! You take that back!" Casey exclaimed. "You should never speak ill of the sick. It's bad luck."

Rick muttered an apology, then Mr. Moore said, "What if the governor declared southeast Nebraska a disaster area? Wouldn't that qualify you for federal loan assistance?"

"You'll need to ask the governor, assuming he ever returns from China. I figure he'll be back in time to run for reelection, but not much before."

"Why?"

"Because he's got a different agenda, Mr. Moore. Nebraska is one of the few states with a law protecting family farms, but the voters don't have much of a say in Lincoln anymore. The balance of power has shifted to the big agriculture interests in Omaha and Minneapolis. They care plenty about farming, but not much for families, if you get my meaning."

"I believe I understand, but let me make sure. If the governor doesn't step in, then the corporations will be able to acquire failing family farms. Is that right?"

"You got it. That's the loophole. A farmer can't sell his place to a combine, but the bank can once they've foreclosed. How's that for a law to protect family farmers?"

"Not incredibly fair. What can I do to help?"

"Plain and simple: we need you to make it rain."

"Me? That's quite an expectation, Rick."

"It don't matter. If you can't make it rain in the next two weeks, then you need to give me the winning numbers for the lottery. Otherwise, the wife and I can bend over and kiss our hearth and home good-bye, and so can a hundred of our friends."

After a bit, Mr. Moore said, "Just for my edification, would you have to win the whole lottery, or would a bit less suffice?"

"Are you asking me how much I need?"

"You asked for my help. How much do you need? An exact number isn't necessary; an approximation will do."

Casey and Rick kicked some numbers back and forth, then they gave Mr. Moore a figure. She wasn't obliged to divulge it in her report since it was information of a personal nature, but it was probably more than seventy-five dollars and less than seventy-five million.

Mr. Moore listened carefully and asked a few more questions, then he said, "I'd like to thank you for your candor. It's been a very informative visit."

"Pardon me for sayin' so, but we weren't lookin' for an information exchange. Should we be praying for rain or buying lottery tickets?"

"Frankly, Rick, the odds are stacked rather heavily against us either way. I have a favor to ask, though."

"What's that?"

"Stick around. If I can find a way to help, you'll know within a week. Can you hang on for that long?"

"A week? Yeah, we can. Thanks."

"Don't thank me. I haven't done anything. I never do."

After Mr. Moore had gone, Rick jumped in the family pickup truck and drove down to the 7-Eleven in Falls City where he bought twelve lottery tickets, one for each of Jesus' apostles. It was good money spent in vain, except that the prospect of winning kept their hopes alive for a few more days.

As you get older, you learn that money can't buy faith and it can't buy charity, but hope is the exception. I suppose that's why rich folks have more hope than charity or faith.

Chapter 19

· ·

A QUESTION OF BLASPHEMY

WHILE NICKY PARKED the motor coach in the courtyard in front of the River House, I escorted Eloise back to the kitchen to meet Marie Delacroix. She was watching a cooking show on TV and stirring egg whites in a bowl, while Pearline, Clem's practical nurse, was playing a game of double-deck solitaire at the far end of the butcher block table.

After I had introduced everyone, Pearline said, "Where're you from, Ms. Richardson?"

"San Diego, although I rarely get home anymore. How about you?"

"Olathe, Kansas. I've been a midwestern girl all my life."

"And you?" Eloise asked Marie.

"I was born six blocks from the Café du Monde in New Orleans, and raised on beignets, gumbo, and bread pudding with chocolate sauce." That and her profession explain Marie's shape, which is generally ovoid, although she has lovely, milk-white skin.

"Nebraska's a long way from the French Quarter, but I get the sense that you moved here long before Hurricane Katrina."

"I was the victim of a prior disaster, ma'am. My first employer out of culinary school was a professional athlete with the taste

buds and disposition of a spoiled child. After two years of bar-
becued chicken wings and temper tantrums, I decided I'd rather
cook for a cranky, middle-aged banker whose favorite meal is a
double-decker BLT with fries."

"Life is so full of compromises, isn't it? But I bet you make a
mean BLT."

"You bet I do. I made one for the Old Man today, but don't
tell Nurse Nelson. The bacon was against doctor's orders. Come
to think of it, so was the mayo, and the fries."

Eloise smiled. "I've heard that Mr. Tucker can be a demand-
ing boss. Is that your impression, Marie?"

"He's grumpy but fair, sort of like Clint Eastwood. He likes
his guns, too. If you pass by the dining room, you'll see what I
mean."

The dead heads mounted on the dining hall wall included elk,
bighorn sheep, moose, mountain lion, and just about every other
critter that was bigger than a breadbox, had teeth, and could be
shot legally in the U.S. or Canada. Clem tried to explain it to me
a hundred times, but I could never understand why a man would
want to shoot all those magnificent animals.

Pearline looked up from her solitaire game. "We hear you're
a friend of Vernon Moore's. Is that right?"

"Why, yes. Word seems to travel quickly in this part of the
country."

"You have no idea, ma'am. Can he do what they say he can
do?"

I thought that was a tad pushy for a probationary member of
the Circle, but Eloise said, "That depends. What do they say he
can do, dear?"

"Raise the dead; heal the sick. Stuff like that."

"Between you and me, I have some reservations, but Vernon
has surprised me more times than I can count."

"But isn't it a blasphemy just to say so? Isn't it a blasphemy if a plain man claims he can heal the sick or make it rain?"

That ruffled my fetlocks again, but Eloise was as calm as the surface of a mountain lake on a windless day. "I'd normally refer a question like that to Vernon, but since he isn't here, I'll try to handle it myself." She put her finger to her chin in thoughtful pose, then concluded, "No."

"No? Why?"

"We live in miraculous times, Pearline. Trained medical professionals bring people back from the dead every day."

"Okay, but what about making it rain?"

"That's a different story. Have you met someone who claims to have that ability?"

"Yes, ma'am. Your Mr. Moore claims that he can do that, too."

"Really? He told me last night that he might ask God for rain, but he never claimed that he could do it by himself. Is that blasphemy, or is it prayer?" Pearl must've bit her tongue, so Eloise continued, "To be perfectly honest, I couldn't care less about blasphemy anyway. The only victims are thin-skinned believers, but shouldn't they be gracious enough to forgive?"

Game, set, and match, at least in my book. I said, "Let's go see the old man."

"You won't find Mr. Tucker in bed," Marie offered. "I served him his BLT in the great room. The last time I checked, he was watching TV."

The great room at the River House is the size of an indoor tennis court. A long time ago, Clem had it arranged into four, equal-sized rectangles: a business library; a multimedia entertainment center with four rows of easy chairs; a bar that has antique neon signs and an old-time jukebox; and a gaming area with a pool table, a pinball machine, and a card table. Each section is decorated so distinctly that you feel like you're walking from one room to another, even though you're just crossing a red carpet divider.

Eloise and I found Clem in PJs and his boxer's robe in the entertainment center, watching the Bloomberg channel on his widest screen television. His head was hatless, meaning it was as hairless as a cue ball and twice as shiny. Other than the glare, it didn't look bad. He was sitting in the center of the first row in his favorite recliner, which had a remote controller like the TV. Depending on the button you pushed, it massaged your sacroiliac, warmed your butt, kneaded your calves, or peeled your potatoes. That last part was a prevarication, but it was an amazing chair. If it had been mine, I would've given it a name.

Clem didn't exactly leap to his feet when he saw us coming, but he stood like a gentleman, and with no apparent discomfort. "How do you do?" he said to Eloise, as he held out his hand. "You must be the famous Widow Richardson I've heard so much about."

I gave him a kiss on the cheek while Eloise took his hand in both of hers, like Pastor Hooper does after church when he wants something. "You flatter me, Mr. Tucker. Please, call me Eloise. Wilma and I will pull up some chairs so we can visit."

"No need. I'll swivel around and you can take a chair in the second row. How would that be?"

I sat on the arm of Clem's chair and stroked his neck while Eloise took a seat. I was tempted to rub his shiny bald head, but it didn't seem proper in front of a widow.

"You have such a lovely home, Mr. Tucker. Has it been in the family for a long time?"

"Not by Tucker time. Silas the Fourth built it in the twenties. My grandfather, Silas the Fifth, taught me to hunt and fish here, and how to read an annual report. He even taught me to drive a tractor out back. What a hoot! I damned near drove it over the cliff and into the river."

"Wilma and I took a peek into your dining room. Do you still hunt?"

"Not lately, I'm sorry to report. I suppose Wilma briefed you about my condition."

"She did. How are you feeling? For a man on chemotherapy, you look remarkably well. Your color is good; your energy level appears to be high. Are you taking your meds?"

Clem chortled. "You must not have met Louise Nelson, my other nurse. If I hesitate to take even one measly little pill, she lectures me for an hour on my health and well-being, and then she tapes my eyes open and forces me to watch daytime TV. I can stomach the lectures, but those soap operas corrode the soul."

"She sounds like a kindred spirit. How is your blood pressure?"

"One-thirty over eighty this morning. Why?"

Eloise stood up and took Clem's wrist while she looked down at her watch. "Are you eating well?"

"Like a horse, thanks to Vernon."

"Vernon?"

"Who else? Frankly, I was sicker than a dog until he came along. Now, I feel like I could bring down a rhino with a fondue fork. Wilma tells me you're an old friend of his. Does he normally have that kind of effect on people?"

"I'm rarely on the scene when Vernon is out and about, but he seems to have a positive effect on almost everyone. However, I believe that you're the first chemotherapy patient I've ever met who was ready to take on a rhinoceros with a common kitchen utensil."

"What do you think, Eloise? Wouldn't a rhino look fine on my dining-hall wall?"

"Not with a fork in its ear, dear. By the way, your pulse is seventy-seven. That's a bit high, but probably attributable to the close proximity of your fiancée."

"Wilma's always been able to get my juices flowing," Clem replied, smiling like a cat who had just landed in a pound of catnip. "Do I say 'ah' next or pee into a cup?"

"Neither. Why?"

"'Cause I feel like I'm getting a physical. Are you from the insurance company?"

"Oh my, no! I'm so sorry. I'm a retired nurse. I just can't seem to help myself."

Clem glanced up at me, but only for a second. "You're awful young-looking for a retiree, Eloise."

"Thank you, but I was an army nurse. We can retire at an early age, you know."

"I guess so. Military pensions must be pretty damned good, too. I caught a glimpse of your motor home from the bathroom window."

"Mr. Moore paid for it," I answered.

Clem patted my arm like I was a pet retriever. "I understand that Vernon was in the army back in the day. Is that how you two met?"

"We never served together," Eloise answered, "but we joined the same travel club afterward. Vernon is quite the rolling stone, you know."

"Well, he sure as hell doesn't stick around here, that's for sure. What kind of travel club is it? Do you get discounts and free tickets, things like that?"

"Absolutely! We take trips together, we share pictures and stories, we keep lists of nice places to visit. It's lots of fun."

"I expect it is, but Vernon and I have a certain business arrangement. Out of curiosity, did he happen to share it with you and your friends?"

I nearly fell off the chair, but the young widow came through like a true Circle girl. "No," she lied, as deadpan as a riverboat gambler. "Vernon is a very private man."

Clem grunted, then said, "It's getting toward my nap time, Eloise, but I'd like to ask you one last question before I hobble off to my bed of pain."

"Yes, of course."

"Can Vernon Moore work miracles?"

I can be so thick in the head. It wasn't until that very moment that I figured out why he had jumped at the chance to meet Eloise.

He continued, "A lot of the townsfolk believe he can, includin' my Wilma here, but it seems to me that he uses his head more than anything else."

I got the distinct impression that Eloise had heard that question before. She replied, "A policeman carries a gun, Mr. Tucker. Does he use it every day, or does he try to use his head instead?"

Clem sat silently in his chair for half a minute, then he surprised me. "Assuming it's okay with my fiancée, how'd you and your widow friends like to have dinner at the River House tomorrow night? We'll invite Vernon, too."

"And the Millets," I added, excited by the prospect. "They should be here."

"Absolutely. How about it, Eloise?"

"Will you be up to it?"

"I'll be fine. Saint Vernon will see to it."

"In that case, I'm happy to accept. I'll have to check, but I'm sure that Birdie and Marion will want to come, too."

"Then I'll look forward to tomorrow evening, and thanks for stopping in. It's been a pleasure."

Eloise smiled graciously, like a queen who had granted an audience to a minor cousin. "The pleasure was mine, but you should take that nap now. You need your rest, and be careful of those fries. They can be very hard on the digestion."

AFTER THE WIDOW ELOISE and Nicky the Knife had departed for parts unknown, I gravitated back to the kitchen to warn the chef about the upcoming dinner party. When I walked through the door, Marie, Pearl, John, and Clem's housekeeper, a lovely Hispanic woman named Consuela Bocachica, were sitting in a row at the butcher block table, glued to the television news.

Fearing the usual, which is bad news, I said, "What happened?"

John turned and answered, "The National Weather Service has revised the weekend forecast."

"What could be worse than the weather we have now: tornadoes; typhoons?"

"Shush, Wilma!" Marie pointed the controller at the TV and turned up the volume.

Two men in shirts and ties were talking on the screen in front of a big brown map of the midwestern United States. The older one pointed to the map and said, "The jet stream has taken an unexpected turn to the south, which is allowing a large, slow-moving Canadian cold front to begin drifting down to Montana, North Dakota, and Minnesota. This may be the break we've been hoping for, Frank. For the last four months, the jet stream has been pushing all the moist air northward into Saskatchewan and Manitoba."

"That's fantastic news, Tom! When does the storm reach southeast Nebraska?"

"Assuming the jet stream stays where it belongs, we're expecting the front to cross the border late Friday. But it's a plodder. It won't reach us here in Lancaster County till Saturday."

"Is the system carrying a lot of moisture?"

"No more or less than we would typically expect this time of year. Of course, this isn't a typical year. Even a tenth of an inch would be a godsend."

"Everybody out there in Channel 23 country is on pins and needles, Tom. What are the chances that we'll get rain this weekend?"

"It's only a preliminary estimate, but the National Weather Service has pegged the odds at twenty-five percent."

"Twenty-five percent? That's all? Couldn't it go higher?"

"It could and it should. If the storm behaves normally, I would expect the odds to increase steadily over the next several days."

"But you can't be sure."

"It's the weather, Frank. Nobody can be sure."

The anchorman turned and looked into the camera. "Thank you, Tom. That's great news. We now switch to Courtney Stockton, our roving reporter, who's live on the steps of the statehouse. Courtney, are you there?"

A sweaty, red-faced young girl with tousled blonde hair and a microphone appeared on screen and replied, "Yes, Frank."

"What's the temperature out there, Courtney?"

"A hundred and six in the shade, but it feels like a hundred and sixty out here in the sun."

"Wow! That's hot! What's the governor's reaction to the weather forecast?"

"It's still the middle of the night in Beijing. According to an aide, he won't be briefed for another three or four hours."

"They're forecasting rain! It's headline news. Aren't they going to wake him up?"

"Not for several hours. I guess he had a hard night."

"Okay. How about the usual 'unnamed sources'? What are they saying?"

"They're split down the middle. About half believe that the governor is leaning toward a disaster declaration and the other half expect him to extend the trade mission to Japan."

"Japan?"

"I'm just a reporter, Frank. I'm not responsible for his itinerary."

"You do good work, Courtney. Come on back to the station. It's nice and cool here." The scene shifted back to the studio news desk, where the young anchorman faced the camera. "Well, there you have it, folks, straight from the capitol. Rain has been forecasted for the first time in four months, and the governor is taking a detour to Japan. Sayonara for now, but don't touch that dial! For the latest in news, weather, and sports, stay tuned to Channel 23!"

A slick advertisement for a high-yield, low-moisture corn hybrid appeared on the TV just as Marie hit the off button. "Hot damn!" she exclaimed. "The rain's comin'. Maybe we'll get lucky. Maybe we won't need Mr. Moore after all."

You know what I was thinking. I was thinking that Mr. Moore had caused the jet stream to shift to the south, but it sounded so outlandish that I didn't have the courage to say so. John Smith, my number one son-in-law, must have sensed my inner conflict. He grinned at me and said, "Rain on Saturday. Is it luck, or is it Mr. Moore?"

Just loud enough for everyone to hear, Pearline whispered, "It's a blasphemy."

Chapter 20

. . . .

A CANARY IN A URANIUM MINE

THE QUEEN BEE of the Quilting Circle called while I was
rooting around in Clem's giant-sized, double-door refrigerator for the pimiento cheese. Marie swore that nobody ate it
except me, but the container kept disappearing from the cheese
drawer. I had the same problem at home with my favorite hairbrush, which I accused Silas the Second of pilfering more than
once.

Hail Mary bypassed the usual niceties, as usual. "Where have
you been, girl? This is the third time I've called."

I couldn't admit that my head was stuck in the refrigerator
again, so I fibbed. "I was with my fiancé."

"Were you? How is the evil Lord Clem doing today?"

"He has a deadly case of cancer, thank you very much, but he
seems to be doing better."

"He's better? You don't suppose Vernon . . ."

"I have no idea. To what do I owe the pleasure?"

"I've got big news, Wilma. The weather forecast has been revised. Can you believe it? Rain is predicted for the weekend!"

"How did you hear about it?" I asked, keeping my suspicions
in check.

"Lily called Dottie; she called me."

"Did Lily get the information from Marie Delacroix?"

"Yeah." After another second, Mary added, "Oops!"

"I'm in the kitchen at the River House as we speak, trying to fix myself a cheese sandwich. Marie is on the house phone not six feet away. We watched the weather together."

"Well, I'll be damned! The system works!"

"Before we pull a muscle patting ourselves on the back, let's make sure that nothing was lost in transmission. Did Lily mention the odds of rain?"

"Twenty-five percent, and it doesn't arrive till Saturday. My AA marched into my office not one minute ago to inform me that Pastor Hooper has scheduled a sunrise service tomorrow morning. He must want God to up the odds."

"It sounds to me like he wants to get his two cents in before the downpour, but why the heck does it always have to be the crack of dawn? Lulu Tiller used to schedule sunrise meetings at the Abattoir all the time. She was as chirpy as a bird, but everybody else was crankier than an overdue mother with a water retention problem." In retrospect, I probably picked a poor metaphor because Hail Mary had never experienced the joy of childbirth. For all you wild-eyed fathers- and mothers-to-be out there, there is nothing quite like impending motherhood, especially when you are fifty pounds overweight, your lower back is killing you, and you are carrying so much excess water that you slosh when you walk.

"The time is inconvenient, Wilma, but the cause is worthy. I'd like everyone to show the flag, or the red umbrella as the case may be. Can you bring Vernon and the widows along?"

"I can ask, but why?"

"They need to see how desperate we are for rain. That reminds me: have you heard from Clara yet?"

"It's not like she could call, Mary, and I can't check my e-mail till I get home."

"Ask in person if necessary. We need to meet with her before the next board meeting."

"But the forecast has changed for the better. Do we still have to go?"

"The odds are only one in four, Wilma. Until the rivers and streams of Hayes County are overflowing with rainwater, we need to think like Pastor Hooper; we need to pursue every possible angle. Call me when you hear from Clara."

She just had to bring up water again, didn't she?

IF HAIL MARY had peered out her office window while we were yammering on the phone, she would have spied two extremely large motor homes pulling up in front of the Angles House. Laverne was nowhere to be found when Marion and Bertha rang the doorbell, so Loretta led them to the library and then excused herself so she could conduct a room-to-room search. Eventually, she found my cute little goddaughter underneath her Peter Pan bed, behind a hastily constructed wall of pillows and stuffed animals.

Lo kneeled down and peered into the dark recesses. To two little eyes, she said, "We have guests, Lovey."

A tiny voice peeped back, "I don't wanna go."

"Why not? They're Poppy's friends."

"I don't care."

"Come on, Lovey. Aren't Poppy's friends your friends?"

"No!"

"Why not?"

"'Cuz they make Poppy go away."

"What? How do you know that?"

"I just do."

"It doesn't matter, Lovey. I promised Poppy that you would say hello. You have to come downstairs."

"No, I don't. You go."

Loretta was a devotee of the escalation school of parenthood. "One," she said sternly. There was no discernible movement behind the wall, so Lo raised her voice. "Two-o-o!"

Like most little girls and boys, Laverne had no desire to find out what was on the other side of three. When mother and daughter appeared in the library, the Widow Fabian stood up and remarked, "My oh my! What a beautiful child you are!"

The beautiful child took cover behind her mother's leg.

The eldest widow put her hands on her hips in mock disappointment. "I heard from your other daddy that you're a very, very special little girl. Is that true?"

Laverne peeked out from behind her mother and replied, "He's not my other daddy anymore. He's my Poppy! He bought me ice cream."

"Really? What kind?"

"Pink."

"I like pink ice cream, too. Did he take you for a ride in his new car?"

"Uh huh."

"What fun! Where did you go?"

"To the ice cream store."

Don't you just love little children?

Everyone took a seat—Laverne in her mother's lap—then Birdie said, "Have you heard the latest weather forecast? My driver just picked it up on the radio."

"I got the call a few minutes ago," Lo answered. "I was expecting it, of course."

"Expecting it?"

"Sure, just as soon as Vern arrived."

Marion smiled and asked, "How about you, Laverne? Do you expect rain?"

"Uh uh. I like the sun."

"I like the sun as well, but in moderation. Are you in school now, dear?"

"Preschool."

"Is it fun? Do you enjoy going to school?"

"It's just preschool!" Laverne repeated.

Loretta chided her. "Marion and Birdie are Poppy's friends, Lovey. Be nice."

"We've been your Poppy's friends for a long, long time," Marion said. "Could you tell that we were coming to visit?"

Laverne glowered at the widows. "Poppy's leaving again. How come?"

Birdie and Marion made eye contact with each other, then Marion replied, "Because he has people to help, dear. Your Poppy is an extraordinary man, you know. There are others like him, but only very, very few."

Loretta's chin dropped to the floor. "There are others?"

"Oh yes, but the numbers are so small that a person could live a lifetime and never meet another like him. Even then, he wouldn't be *the* Vernon Moore. Vernon is exceptional, even amongst the extraordinary."

"How? How is he so extraordinary?"

"Perhaps we're not speaking of the same Vernon Moore, dear. I thought he'd been to Ebb twice before."

"Okay, point taken. Since Vern is so extraordinary, can I conclude that my daughter is half extraordinary?"

"Come, come," Birdie said. "Don't you already know the answer to that question, too?"

"What do you mean?"

"Let's try a little demonstration. Laverne, do you know what h-o-r-s-e spells?"

"Uh uh. I don't have all my letters yet."

"Then let me give you a clue. H-o-r-s-e spells an animal. I'm going to picture it in my mind. Tell me if you can see it."

Laverne leaped to the floor. "Mommy, Mommy! It's a horse! I can see a horse!"

Loretta nearly swooned in her chair, but I have no idea why. It's not like we hadn't seen it coming. We just couldn't admit it to each other.

"That's exactly right," Birdie affirmed. "Now, the horse I'm thinking of is b-r-o-w-n. Can you tell me what color it is?"

"It's pink! It's pink!"

Marion sat forward. "That was a good try, but you weren't quite right. Perhaps something else is on your mind. Is it your Poppy?"

Laverne began to jump up and down like she was on a trampoline. "He's coming! Poppy's coming, and he's going to buy me a cold drink!"

Loretta's hand came up to her mouth, then she regained enough of her composure to say, "What kind of cold drink, Lovey?"

"Pink, Mommy! It's gonna be pink!"

"Are you sure? Are you very sure?"

Laverne stopped jumping. After a pause, she replied modestly, "No."

Marion said, "That's exactly the way it should be, dear. Do you know why?"

Laverne shook her head.

"Because you can sense what other people are thinking, but people don't always think clearly, do they? They change their minds, they imagine, they make wishes or guess about the future; they even fool themselves. Do you understand?"

"Uh uh."

"That's a sensible reply; good for you. No one blessed with a gift such as yours has ever truly understood it—or its consequences."

"Its consequences?" Loretta gasped. "What consequences?"

"There are too many to list, but one is quite certain: you have a daughter who will sometimes see your thoughts."

At that moment, my best friend left the State of Denial and moved to Bargaining. "Dear Lord in heaven; you're right. What can I do?"

"Not to worry, dear. There's a simple protocol . . ."

"A protocol? You've done this before?"

"On occasion. There are five important steps you must take."

Loretta closed her eyes and rubbed the back of her neck. "Okay!" she replied. "I give! What am I supposed to do?"

"First, educate Laverne broadly: in history, science, languages, music."

"Music?"

"Most definitely," Birdie replied. "Have you considered lessons—the piano, for instance?"

"The piano? Look at her hands. They're tiny."

Laverne hid her hands behind her back. Birdie said, "Professional teachers have keyboards made just for a little girl's hands these days. Do you know Jenny McCallum?"

"Of course. She's a member of the Circle."

"I bet there's nothing she'd like better than to teach the piano to an extraordinary child. Would you like to play the piano, Laverne? Wouldn't it be fun?"

"No."

Marion smiled and continued, "Second, she must be taught very early on to respect the privacy of others."

"No shit, pardon my French. What else?"

"She must learn to choose her confidantes with care. It's best if she confides only in her parents and her godmother until she's much, much older."

"Okay. That's not much of an intellectual leap either."

"The fourth step is on you, dear. Until she gains a measure of maturity, Laverne will be unable to distinguish a memory from a daydream or an intention. In a moment of frustration, for instance, it won't be wise for you to visualize yourself planting a pick-axe in the back of your husband's head. It's not the sort of scene an innocent child should see."

"She's not seeing it now?"

"She's distracted, but Birdie won't always be here to help you."

Lo looked over at Birdie, who didn't appear to be distracting anybody. "I'm more of a scissors girl," she said, "but I get the gist. I'll try to be careful."

"Good. Finally, you must pay careful attention to whatever your daughter says. If she speaks of matters that ought to be far beyond her reach, you must call me without delay." Marion pulled a business card out of her purse and handed it to Loretta.

Loretta read it carefully, then said, "Could you give me an example, please?"

"Oh, it could be almost anything: astronomical phenomena, extreme geological or meteorological conditions, serious crimes, any phrase with the word 'nuclear' in it."

"Nuclear? Nuclear! Now you're scaring the shit out of me, Marion. You make my daughter sound like a canary in a uranium mine."

"And so she is, in a distant, symbolic sort of way. But remember: a child of her age has no ability to distinguish between fact, imagination, and intent. If you have any questions, any at all, pick up the phone and call me."

"Here's a fact, Marion: you can imagine me picking up the phone right now because I have a question on intent. What if Lovey decides to be a coal miner instead of a canary?"

"Then we'll pray that she's a good one, and that she survives its hardships to old age."

"So her future isn't preordained. She doesn't have a destiny."

Birdie frowned. "Oh no, no, no. No! Destiny is a myth, but opportunity is another matter altogether. Doors may open for Laverne that open only for a handful of young people. Your job is to prepare her."

"I can't quite put my finger on it, but I'm having trouble putting the word 'opportunity' and the word 'nuclear' in the same sentence. I wonder why that is."

The door bell rang just then. "Shall I get it?" Marion offered. "It's for us."

Loretta thought to herself, "Thank God." But she smiled weakly and said, "Sit, please. I can use the time to myself."

She found Road Rage Duke standing on the doorstep, bandana in hand. "Pardon me, ma'am. The Widow Meanwell asked me to knock at three thirty."

"Would you care to step inside while I get her?"

"No thanks. I'll wait in the coach."

Lo returned to the library to find the widows engaged in a hushed exchange with Laverne. "Your driver is here," she announced with a little extra gusto.

"Oh dear! Oh dear!" Birdie declared, as if she was the White Rabbit in *Alice in Wonderland*. "We're overdue; we have to go. There are so many to see and time is so short."

The widows stood to leave, then Marion touched Laverne's

cheek. "Will you remember what Auntie Marion said, dear? Do you promise?"

Loretta interrupted, "Why don't you watch some TV, Lovey? Mommy has to have a little talk with 'Auntie' Marion outside."

"Can't I come?"

"No. It's too hot. I'll put on *Dora the Explorer.*"

Birdie departed after a last good-bye, but Marion waited for Loretta and they left the house together. The Dolphin was idling by the curb with the door open. Lo said she could see the cool, moist air rolling down the steps into the heat, like mists of tumbleweed down a terraced hillside.

"What did you tell Lovey back in the library?" she asked.

"To confide in her mother and her godmother before all others."

"Is that all? I guess I wasn't expecting to hear the word 'auntie.' "

"Forgive me, dear, but it seemed so preferable to 'widow' at the time."

"You're forgiven," Lo said. "Can I ask a confidential question? I have no right . . ."

Marion touched her forearm and answered, "There was another; long ago in a distant, arid place. We were never introduced, but I can tell you that she was an intelligent, dark-skinned beauty with enormous intellect and spirit. Does that sound familiar?"

"Yeah. Thanks for building up my self-esteem. I had hoped that I was a poor country cousin to the one who got away."

"Come, come. Are we speaking of the same Vernon Moore? Which was more likely: was she the one who got away, or was he?"

"Did she bear his child?"

"No. If it makes you feel any better, you're quite alone in that regard."

"Will he ever return to Ebb?"

Marion took a step backward. "Think it through, dear. What do the people of Ebb expect from Vernon this week?"

"That's easy. They expect him to make it rain."

"If, indeed, it does rain, then what will they want next time?"

Lo's hand came up to her mouth for the second time. "Oh my God!" she exclaimed. "They'll want even more. He'll never get a moment's peace."

"Then what must he do if he wants to return to Ebb?"

"It's so clear! He has to fail, doesn't he?"

"So it would seem. I'm very sorry, but so it would seem."

When Loretta went inside, she found my cute little goddaughter sitting splay-legged on the rug in the entryway. Angrily, she pronounced, "Poppy's coming! For me!"

Chapter 24

....

THE FARMER'S RETIREMENT PLAN

CONNIE KIMBALL OWNED a florist shop on the south side of Main next door to the Corn Palace, the town watering hole. Long ago, she learned that she could do a brisk business by staying open until nine p.m. on Friday and Saturday nights so that late, overlubricated husbands could pick up some flowers for the missus on the way home.

Dean Kimball, Connie's father, was a farmer until he retired, by keeling over from a heart attack in the north forty on the day before his eighty-eighth birthday. That's how a lot of farmers retire in this part of the country, and their wives are barely better off. Marta was eighty-five herself when Dean passed on, wheelchair-bound and suffering from mild dementia. But the closest nursing home was forty miles away and as dear as a big city hotel, so Connie took her in.

Caring for a lonely, scared, feeble, confused, incontinent, and immobile parent is like caring for a small child, only ten times harder and complicated by the fact that they never go to school. Poor Connie could barely cope, and her business began to suffer because her mother required so much attention. That's why she hoped to see Mr. Moore.

Marta was asleep in the back office when Birdie Fabian entered the store. Connie was at the counter out front, trimming stems and humming to herself. "Can I help you?" she asked, as her customer stopped to admire a climate-controlled display of sunflowers and dahlias.

"I've heard such glowing reports about your arrangements," Birdie replied. "Could you make up a bouquet for a dinner party tomorrow night? It's a gift for the host, but I have no idea what might be suitable for the occasion."

Connie extended her hand over the counter. "We haven't met. I'm Connie Kimball."

"Everybody calls me Birdie. It's a pleasure to meet you."

Besides being a true artist, Connie is no slouch in the IQ department. "The buzz says that one of Mr. Moore's widow friends was at the River House today. Might that have been you?"

"It was my partner, Eloise, but we've all been invited back for dinner. Given our host's unfortunate diagnosis, I'd think the bouquet should be lovely and gay. Don't you?"

"Gay?"

"Happy, cheerful. Can you arrange a nice one for us?"

"Sure. Sure I can. How much do you want me to spend?"

Birdie reached into her purse, a worn leather item with a beaded strap, and pulled out a crisp, one-hundred-dollar bill. "Is this enough? I'd like it sent over tomorrow afternoon."

In Ebb, Benjamin Franklin is a dead inventor and a hundred dollars is made up of three twenties, three tens, a five, and five crinkled-up ones. Connie held the bill up to the light, then put it in the register. "Yes, ma'am. I'll take care of it."

"Good. Let your imagination run wild, and spend every penny. I understand that you asked Mr. Moore to visit your mother. Is that her in the back room? Is she asleep?"

"Yes. Why?"

"I'm sorry, dear. He wanted to stop by in person but he won't be able to make it. So many others have asked to see him, and his time is very short."

"So my mom isn't important enough for Mr. Moore. Is that what you're saying?"

"It's so exasperating, isn't it? Everyone he's been unable to visit in person has had the same question, and I can't think of a good answer. Do you have any ideas? What would you say if you were in my position?"

Connie mumbled, "Gee. I don't know."

"Maybe it would be easier if he didn't see anyone. Then no one would feel any more or less important than anyone else. Should I advise him to do that?"

There was no reply, so Birdie said, "What were your expectations, dear? In a perfect world, what would you want Mr. Moore to do?"

"I don't know."

"You don't?"

"He's Mr. Moore. I was just hoping that he could help my mom."

"Alright. Then perhaps your mother can point us in the right direction. What does she want more than anything else?"

After a second or two, Connie replied, "It sounds kinda weird, but Mom says that World War II was the best time of her life. She worked double shifts for a cannery in Lincoln and shared a small apartment with three friends. On weekends, they'd go to the USO and dance with the GIs. In a perfect world, she'd want to be young again, with her friends, dancing at the USO."

"Oh my! Is that what you expected? Did you expect Mr. Moore to turn back the clock?"

Again, Connie hesitated. "No, but he can work miracles, can't he?"

"That's the prevailing theory," Birdie whispered. "Between

you and me, he has a little trouble with time travel, though. It's not his best category."

"Then can he at least make my mom feel better?"

"How, dear? What would you have him do?"

"Oh my, there are so many ways. Mom refuses to eat half the time because she can't control her bathroom functions. I try to tell her otherwise, but the accidents embarrass her to death. She can't walk because of her hips; she can't even enjoy the TV because she doesn't hear anymore. I bought her a fifteen-hundred-dollar hearing aid last year but she lost it. Now, she won't let me buy another one because they're so expensive. In her mind, a car should cost that kind of money."

"I share your mother's respect for a dollar, but it's been a long time since a decent automobile cost only fifteen hundred of them. If she doesn't want a new hearing aid, what is she saying to you? Does she really want to get better, or does she want something else?"

Connie did her best to resist, but a lone tear escaped an eye and ran down her cheek.

Birdie said, "Take your time. It's just you and me. There's no rush."

"Mom's lonely," Connie said softly, fighting back a sniffle. "She loves me, but she misses Dad and she's outlived all her friends. In a way, she even misses herself. She wants God to take her so she can be with Dad and her friends; so she can be young again."

Birdie sighed. "Isn't life unfair? Either we die too young or we live to be so old that we prefer the black uncertainty of death to the loneliness and indignities of diminished capacity. Does your mother know who Vernon is? Is she aware?"

"Sure. Everyone does."

Birdie took one of two small white envelopes out of her purse and laid it on the counter. "He asked me to give this to your mother."

"It's from Mr. Moore? Why didn't you say so?"

"It's for your mother, Connie. How is her vision? Can she read?"

"It's odd that you would ask. Mom had corrective surgery when they removed her cataracts. Nothing else works in that beat-up old body of hers, but her eyes are perfect."

"Then let her see it first. Do you promise?"

Connie looked down at the sealed envelope, then replied, "Okay. I promise. Before you go, did you hear about the weather forecast?"

"I did, and I'm very hopeful."

"Would you thank Mr. Moore? For me? For everybody?"

"He's a hard man to thank, dear, and it hasn't rained yet."

"It will. I'm certain it will."

Connie did her best to be patient after Birdie left, but she had a devil of a time keeping her word. The second Marta awoke, she brought her the note.

"From Vernon Moore?" her mother said. "For me?"

She opened the envelope with care, as if it was made of old-fashioned rice paper. Inside, she found a simple greeting card with dancing yellow-and-gold monarch butterflies painted in watercolor on the front. The message read:

My Dearest Marta:

   You should fear death no more than a caterpillar fears a cocoon. Your days as a butterfly are still to come, and they are far from numbered.

                              Vernon L. Moore

As far as we know, Birdie never gave the second envelope to anybody.

Chapter 22

EDEN

A ROUND SUNDOWN, BUFORD PICKETT put in a telephone call to my Fiancé in Perpetuity. Clem was in the media room at the time, enjoying a Reuben sandwich with extra Russian dressing and onion rings on the side. All of a sudden, the man had a cast-iron stomach. He snatched the phone from Marie and said, "You're right on time. What have you got?"

"You're not gonna believe it, Mr. Tucker."

"Uh oh! This isn't more of that World War II bullshit, is it?"

"Well, yes and no, sir. None of the widows was with Joan of Arc like you said, but the story is just as unbelievable."

"Just as unbelievable? Jesus Christ, Buford! I was kidding about Joan of goddamned Arc! I want facts, not a bunch of bullshit. You're gonna put me off my onion rings, and then I'll be pissed as hell. I'm a sick man. I need to eat my vegetables."

"Would you prefer that I call again later, sir?"

"You're damned right I would. Call when you've got hard data. When will that be?"

"It's up to you, Mr. Tucker. We can talk again tomorrow, but the facts will be the same and another day will have passed us by. What do you want to do?"

"All right, goddammit! Give me what you've got, and straight from the hip, please. I'd like to finish my dinner before it turns ice cold."

"I'll start with Bertha Fabian . . ."

"Eloise Richardson came to see me today. Give me the poop on her first."

"The data on Ms. Richardson is more persuasive if I begin with Bertha Fabian."

"Start with Eloise anyway. What have you got?"

"Okay, sir. You're the boss. Richardson is a common name but Eloise is as old-fashioned as they come. Extensive Internet searches yielded only two viable candidates. Neither could be alive today, but one met an interesting end."

"Okay, Buford. I'll bite. How did she die?"

"She was killed in World War II when her plane went down in the Pacific, between Guadalcanal and Bougainville."

"Guadalcanal? Bougainville? I'll be damned! It's Vernon Moore, the sequel! What in God's name was a woman doing out there?"

"She was a nurse, sir."

The phone went dead, then Clem said softly, "An army nurse?"

"Yessir. That's all I could find."

"When did she die exactly?"

"May eighteenth, 1944."

"Wasn't that about the time that Vernon's plane went down?"

"The *Lady Be Good* went down in April of 1943, sir, but Mr. Moore's body was never recovered. Lt. Richardson's wasn't either."

"Is that a coincidence, Buford, or is it a recurring theme? My gut is telling me that it's the latter."

"As usual, your intuition is on the button, sir. Shall I move on?"

Clem grabbed an onion ring and took a bite. "Shoot."

"Bertha Fabian was culled from the same herd. A four-hour search on half a dozen Internet engines produced exactly one hit."

"I'm on the edge of my chair. What have you got?"

"She and her secondhand store perished in the San Francisco fire of 1906. The records are unclear, but it appears that her body was never recovered."

"Did you say 1906? This is goddamned interesting, Buford! It's like the dating game for ghosts and ghouls. And who, pray tell, is in casket number three?"

"Marion Meanwell. Only one verifiable candidate showed up after hours of searching. She was a third-class passenger on the *Titanic*."

"The *Titanic*! Don't tell me. She drowned and her body was never recovered."

"On or about April 14, 1912. That's correct."

"Okay. So Vernon hangs with dead people. That has to be good news."

"Good news, sir?"

"It sure as hell is. The part I can't understand is why a man of his considerable capabilities would keep the company of three dead women."

"Mr. Moore isn't a man, sir. He's probably more like the widows than us."

"Then how did he father a child?"

"It beats the heck out of me, but I don't see how he could call in a lightning strike either."

"So you believe he works miracles. Is that right, Buford?"

"Yessir, I do. Everybody does, but now I believe that the widows are part of it, too."

"You think they're on some kind of team? If that's so, then

what do the widows do?"

"I don't have a clue, sir. It's just a theory."

"A theory? How's this for a theory? The widows work the miracles and Vernon's just a cipher. Did you ever think of that?"

"No sir, but it wouldn't make any difference. Miracles are miracles."

"So they are, Buford, and mistakes are mistakes. Is there any chance that you could've made a mistake here?"

"It's possible, sir, but I doubt that all three of their RVs would be registered in the same weird town if I had."

After a pause, Clem said, "In the same what? Would you repeat that?"

"All three of the widows' RVs are licensed in Graham County, Arizona, so I made the usual inquiries. They're registered to a single post office address in a small town called Eden, Arizona, about fifty miles northeast of Tucson."

"Excuse me. Did you say Eden?"

"Yeah. Pretty weird, huh?"

"Maybe, maybe not. It could be one of those blue-hair retirement communities. Arizona's full of 'em."

"I don't care what kind of community it is; I'm catching a plane out of Lincoln tomorrow morning. I'll go door to door if I have to, but I'll have complete files on the widows by Friday afternoon or my name isn't Buford P. Pickett."

"Friday? That's too goddamned late. Cancel your flights."

"But . . ."

"I'll send the G200 down to get you. John Smith will call with the details."

"You're . . . You're flying me to Tucson in the bank jet?"

"If I get a good report, I might even fly you back. Is that all you've got?"

"Yessir. Thank you, sir."

"You do interesting work, Buford; wacky, but interesting. Have some more good news by seven tomorrow night."

"Your time or my time? I'll be two hours behind you."

"Split the difference. Make it eight p.m. my time, and don't be late."

"I won't disappoint you, sir."

A few minutes later, my Fiancé in Perpetuity called my son-in-law. "The NBP jet lands at Beatrice muni at five forty-five a.m. tomorrow, John. Make sure Buford gets to the plane on time, and then I want you to baby-sit him on a day trip to Tucson. You should be home by midnight."

"Consider it done, sir. May I ask what the mission is?"

"I'd rather not say, but I suppose I'm gonna have to deal with your goddamned scruples sooner or later. Have you heard of the three widows who are staying at the Come Again?"

"Everybody has. They're friends of Mr. Moore's."

"Buford came up with an interesting theory about their identities, but he has to go to Arizona to finish his investigation. Do you have a moral conflict with that?"

"Yessir, I do."

"I figured as much, but we have a deal, John: I called off the research into Vernon's background; you returned to work. I'm keeping my end; I expect you to keep yours."

"This mission is not within the spirit of our agreement, sir; not by a country mile."

"Spirit my ass, John. This is a goddamned business deal. Buford is going to Arizona with you or without you. Here's a quiz: will you be able to help Saint Vernon more by staying behind and looking for a job, or by going along as a valued employee of the Tucker Trust?"

John replied, "I'll keep my word, sir."

Chapter 23

THE PLANET MINUTIA

MR. MOORE AND THE WIDOWS were nowhere to be found when I got home that evening, so I turned down his bed and put a note on the dresser about the sunrise service and the big dinner at the River House. Then I took the back stairs down to the kitchen and got a chicken pot pie out to thaw.

My special cell phone rang the second I opened the freezer door. At least it was Loretta instead of Hail Mary, but she was bouncing off the walls like a maternal Super Ball. We had to sift through every single second of the widows' visit, from Laverne hiding under her bed, to the discussion of her gift, to "Auntie" Marion's warning and their whispery farewells.

I had two duties as Loretta's best friend, which you men might want to record for future reference. First off, I had to listen, which means paying attention and not interrupting. Second, I was obliged to pick one of two roles: either to play the sympathizer, which is always appreciated; or to be the dispassionate analyst, which is riskier. In the end, I chose option three: diversion. "Where was Mr. Moore while all the folderol was going on?"

"He was visiting petitioners, the rat. Casey Jaworski called around noon. Vern stopped at her place for tea."

"He did? How did that work out?"

"Well, they're not buying flood insurance, that's for sure. Rick went out for lottery tickets after Vern left."

"Lottery tickets? My dear Lord. That can't be good."

"Billie Cater called in, too."

"Oh, dear. What did she say?"

"Vern spent most of the time asking about crop yields and land values."

"Crop yields? Land values? Why would he care about that?"

"I have no idea, Wilma. Call Billie yourself; call Casey, too."

"Thanks, but I'm not calling anybody. Then they'll have my secret number and it'll be like opening the door to one of those bridal gown sales. Every woman in the county will come rushing through. That reminds me: Clem wants to have a dinner party for Mr. Moore and the widows tomorrow night. You and Calvin are invited. Laverne, too."

"A dinner party? At the River House? I'll need to check with Cal. He's not real comfortable around Vern yet, and the widows' stock didn't exactly skyrocket today either."

"Maybe so, but do you think for a minute that he'll turn Clement down?"

"Okay, but don't expect to see Laverne. For the time being, I'd like to keep her as far away from the widows as possible. I don't want her reading any minds either. Who knows what she might see?"

That's when I got the first real inkling of what Loretta faced for the next umpty-ump years. A woman's peace of mind depends upon the privacy of her thoughts. I couldn't imagine what it would be like to raise a child who could read them at any time.

I shuddered and closed the phone, then I looked down at my pot pie and was reminded that a watched pot won't boil and a watched pot pie won't thaw. Since I had only my own mouth to feed and there was nothing else I needed to fix for dinner, I decided to check my e-mail for the first time in two days.

Good Lord in heaven! I had an awful lot of e-mail, and there wasn't a complaint against the widows in the bunch. Mr. Moore, on the other hand, had raised a few hackles here and there. I found a return e-mail from Clara at the very bottom of the screen, and it turned out to be the bombshell of the afternoon, twice over. Besides agreeing to meet with Hail Mary, she asked if she could hitch a ride to Rev. Hooper's sunrise service with Mr. Moore and me.

As far as I know, recluses don't receive guests, and they don't go to church either. That's why they're called recluses.

DOTTIE HRNICEK GOT a call from Pokie Melhuse in the wee hours of the morning. As it turns out, Pokie had been burning the midnight oil at the county library with Tulip Orbison, the town librarian. Tulip, by the way, was born during World War II, but not in Ebb and not on this Earth. She was born on the Planet Minutia. The smaller an item is, the easier she can deal with it, especially fine print. She put on glasses in the crib, bifocals in the fifties, and trifocals the day after they were invented. She wears drab, ankle-length dresses with neck-high bodices to the office, and her hair is usually in a bun and has a pencil or a pen sticking out of it.

Despite her sartorial idiosyncrasies, Tulip was married once, for five months. Her husband was one of the first American soldiers killed in Vietnam. After the war ended, she went over to the county courthouse and changed her name back to Orbison. To this day, she claims to be a second cousin to the late, great Roy, and she has memorized every one of his songs to prove it. If you're ever at the grocery store and your hear somebody humming "Only the Lonely" a few aisles over, it's likely Tulip.

Dottie was sound asleep when Pokie's call came in, so Shelby picked up the phone. About two seconds later, she shook her partner and shouted, "Wake up, Dot!"

"Who the hell is it? The president? Have we been overrun by Communists?"

"Get a grip, girl. It's Deputy Melhuse. She's callin' from the library."

Dottie grabbed the phone. "It's the middle of the damned night, Pokie! What in God's name are you doing over there?"

"Drinking Baileys and talking on the hooter with a librarian in London, England. She's been real helpful."

"England? You've been on the phone to England? How much is that going to cost?"

"Take a pill, Dot. It was Tulip's phone. We found some info on Lohengrin's Children."

"You did? No shit? What?"

"I'll put the details in a report, but I thought you'd want the highlights tonight."

"I'm sitting up in bed, Pokie. I'm cool, calm, and connected. Gimme what you've got."

"Okay, here goes. Every reference we could find was between 1530 and 1649."

Dottie put the phone on her thigh for a second so she could stick her pinkie in her ear and squiggle it around, then she picked up the phone again. "Would you repeat that?"

"Between 1530 and 1649."

"You can't dig up anything more recent, say in 1993?"

"Nope. We've been working backwards. Tulip says we're

starting to push the frontiers of documented history. We're un-likely to find much of anything prior to 1500."

"That's a pity, Pokie! I was expecting you to trace Lohengrin's Children back to the damned Crusades! What did you say you've been drinkin'?"

"Baileys Irish Cream, by coincidence."

"By coincidence? What the hell does that mean?"

"You're not going to believe it, Dot. You are not going to believe it. Mr. Moore is not like us. He is really, really, really not like us."

In the background, Dottie could hear Tulip singing "Blue An-gel," another Roy Orbison tune.

Chapter 24

....

PROTESTANT DRAMA

THERE WAS A TIME in Hayes County when we had separate churches for the Baptists, the Episcopalians, the Methodists, and the Presbyterians, but they closed one by one in the fifties and sixties. The Lutherans still have a house unto themselves, but the rest of us Protestants share a nondenominational church and the reverend rotates every three years or so. During the drought, our congregation was led by an amiable Methodist minister from Minnesota named Sven Hooper. He was a blue-eyed, balding man with thick-rimmed glasses and a poor complexion who had found his calling in seminary school. Next to the Lord, he loved fried chicken, biscuits, and mashed potatoes with gravy, which he enjoyed at the house of a different divorcée almost every Sunday.

The church sits on a promontory overlooking Highway 4 and is otherwise bordered by corn and alfalfa fields, except during the drought, when it was surrounded by hardscrabble. It has white clapboard siding, a green composition roof that was recently patched, and a steeple with a bell that never rings. The rope just fell out of the belfry one day and nobody bothered to get a new one. Just about everything else is worn off or worn down, too. The pews were stained a dark color once, but they have bright shiny spots on them now where the worshippers put their buns. The carpets are frayed at the edges, the walls could use a fresh coat of paint, and the hymnals have seen better days, but none of that matters to my way of thinking because it all works well enough to praise the Lord. As I recall, He isn't much for conspicuous consumption anyway.

The sun had begun to peek over the horizon when Mr. Moore pulled his blue Mustang into the parking lot with Clara and yours truly on board. It had been a long time since I had seen that many automobiles and pickup trucks at church, not to mention boxcar-sized motor homes, and it turned out to be a fair indication of the number of parishioners who had come to the service. After the usher, a curly-haired bean farmer named Willard Bouwen, had recovered from the shock of seeing Clara Tucker and Mr. Moore at the door, he escorted us to a pew three rows from the rear. From our vantage point, I could see the Widow Marion sitting next to Calvin, Loretta, and Laverne, the Widow Birdie beside Marta and Connie Kimball, and the Widow Eloise between Marie Delacroix and Pearline O'Connor. Hail Mary and Dottie were in the front row hobnobbing with the county supervisor, and red umbrellas were as numerous as pocketbooks. I guess Bebe's plan had worked after all, after a fashion.

We hadn't been seated for ten seconds before the folks in the pew in front of ours began to turn in our direction, then whisper in the ear of a person close to them. The whispering began to spread forward from pew to pew, like a wave. Lulu Tiller, the town veterinarian and a former Queen Bee, was sitting six or seven rows up on our side of the center aisle. When she heard the news, she stood up and turned to face us. As warmly as you can imagine, she said, "Welcome back, Clara, and you too, Mr. Moore." Then she began to applaud, and another Circle girl got up, and her husband did, too. The next thing you knew, the entire congregation had come to their feet and they were clapping their hands for my two unusual lodgers: the one who couldn't leave, and the one who couldn't stay. It brought a tear to my eye, I have to say.

By the time Jenny McCallum played "Rock of Ages," the pews were packed cheek-to-jowl, little children were sitting on their mothers' laps, and young men were slouching against the wall the way they always do. As the last bar echoed across the multitude, Pastor Hooper appeared before the altar in his finest purple raiment. He held his arms up to the sky and said, "Ho, everyone that thirsteth, come ye to the waters. Let us sing to the Lord."

The first hymn was "A Brighter Dawn Is Breaking," which gave me the impression that Pastor Hooper was aware of the time of day. After we had finished singing, he walked up and down the aisle welcoming parishioners by name, including Clara, which gave me the impression that he was up to date on the Tucker situation, too. Then he returned to the pulpit and addressed the congregation.

"This is day one hundred and twenty-one of the worst drought in three generations," he declared as he opened his Bible. "We will not keep our light under a bushel; we have gathered together to pray for rain. Let's begin with a scripture from the Epistle of James, chapter five, verse seven: 'Be patient therefore, brethren, unto the coming of the Lord. Behold, the husbandmen waiteth for the fruit of the earth, and hath long patience for it, until he receive early and latter rain.' "

As the pastor closed his Bible, the strangest thing happened: Pearline O'Connor stood up, all by herself, with no warning whatsoever. Like a child in fifth grade, she raised her hand timidly and said, "Can I testify, father?"

"You'd like to testify?" the pastor asked from the pulpit. "It's been years since anyone testified in my church. Of course you may."

"The Scripture says we should be patient for the coming of the Lord. Isn't that what you just said?"

"Yes, child, I did."

"But what if a man says we don't have to wait? What if a man says he can make it rain? Isn't that a blasphemy?"

Everyone in the congregation leaned forward at once, as if the floor had been titled toward the altar, except for Mr. Moore. He sat back with a finger to his lips, as if he was contemplating the question himself.

"Do you believe that only God can make it rain, child?" the pastor asked.

"Yes, I do."

"Have you read your Numbers? Do you recall it?"

"Uh, not all of it."

He paged to the front of his Bible. "I'm speaking of chapter twenty, when the children of Israel were lost in the desert. A few of them went to Moses on a particularly bad day and said, 'Why have ye brought the congregation of the Lord into this wilderness, that we and our cattle should die?' Does that sound familiar?"

Somewhere in the pews, a man remarked, "It sounds real familiar, Reverend."

"It does, doesn't it? But Moses was a conscientious leader, so he called up God. Allow me to read from verses seven and eight: 'And the Lord spake unto Moses, saying, Take the rod, and gather thou the assembly together, thou, and Aaron thy brother, and speak ye unto the rock, before their eyes; and it shall give forth his water, and thou shalt bring forth to them water out of the rock; so thou shalt give the congregation and their beasts drink.'"

Pastor Hooper looked up and winked at Pearline. "Here's the clincher: 'And Moses lifted up his hand, and with his rod he smote the rock twice; and the water came out abundantly. And the congregation drank, and their beasts also.'

"So, who made the water pour from rock, child? Was it God, or was it Moses acting on His behalf?" When Pearl didn't reply, he continued, "The Almighty says to judge not. But, if you absolutely must, then at least give the man a fair chance to smite the rock, with God's blessing, of course. Shall we all pray for rain?"

Before the pastor could put in a word to the Lord on our behalf, Dinky Cater jumped up from his pew, holding a beet-red BlackBerry high in his left hand. "Praise God," he shouted. "It's raining in Minot! The weather service has raised the odds of rain to fifty percent for southeast Nebraska, come Saturday!"

For the second time that morning, the congregation stood and applauded. Mothers cried, men shook hands, little children jumped up and down, and everybody within arm's reach touched Mr. Moore on his sleeve or his back. That was the happiest, most grateful bunch of people I have ever seen in the House of the Lord.

The rest of the service was upbeat but otherwise uneventful, which was a blessing in itself. After the benediction, Mr. Moore hustled Clara and me out a side door, probably to avoid any more spontaneous touching. As we pulled out of the parking lot, I could see the farmers beginning to mill around by the front entrance, backslapping, high-fiving, and congratulating each other all over again because of the imminent arrival of rain.

My sweet, compassionate side couldn't have been happier for them and their families, but my dour, cynical side was reminded of the high school football games I attended as a Pep Squad parent. After each game was over, a bunch of shirtless males from the winning school would inevitably jump out of the stands and run around the field yelling, "We won! We won!" — while generally behaving as if they had just stopped the Huns at the city gate with their personal derring-do. Myself, I never understood a whit of it, especially the "we" part. It was not like they were on the field when the game was being played, and it was not like we, the humble citizens of Hayes County, were calling in the rain.

That was up to God, or Mr. Moore acting on His behalf, and the game wasn't even over yet. The odds of winning were still only fifty-fifty.

Chapter 25

It's the Thought That Counts

LATER THAT MORNING, Hail Mary Wade and Dot Hrnicek welcomed Mr. Moore into the county attorney's office at the courthouse. Once he and Dot had taken hard-backed chairs and Mary had made herself comfortable, she puckered up and said, "It's a pleasure to see you again, Vernon. I was afraid that you were avoiding me, and after all we've been through together."

"Forgive me. I would have been by sooner, but it's been an extraordinarily busy week."

"So I've heard. We saw you at church this morning with Clara Tucker, but you spirited her away before we could catch up and say hello."

"It was her first contact with the public in years. I didn't want to risk overexposure."

"Just her, or maybe yourself, too."

Mr. Moore smiled. "A little of both, perhaps."

"Well, that was probably wise on both counts. Clara didn't seem upset by the attention, though. Did she say anything about the service afterwards?"

"No."

Dot remarked, "So her vocabulary is still limited to 'yes' and 'no.'"

"Yes."

"That's a pity. We're all hoping that poor woman will release herself from solitary confinement some day."

"I hope so, too, Sheriff, but she's kept to herself for a very long time. We should expect that her return to public life will be gradual at best."

"You're right, of course," Hail Mary added. "She's a county treasure; we all need to be patient with her. Have you had the occasion this week to meet Pearline O'Connor, Clem's practical nurse?"

"Several times, at the River House."

"What did you think of her little stunt at church this morning? Did it make you uncomfortable in any way?"

"Not a bit. Why?"

"Because everyone in the congregation knew precisely who she was talking about."

"Perhaps, but I thought the reverend handled it remarkably well. Didn't you?"

Mary half-smiled. "If I was a suspicious person, I might suspect that he had been prepared for the eventuality. Am I mistaken, or wasn't one of your widow friends sitting next to Pearline?"

"Eloise Richardson. She's also been to the River House."

"I thought so. It seems to me that you and your associates have been wearing a path to Lord Clem's door. I suppose you've heard the rumor."

"The rumor?"

"That Clem has offered you a king's ransom for his life."

Mr. Moore sighed. "Ah, *that* rumor. Why do you ask?"

"Because we, meaning Dottie and I, don't want you to tarnish your legendary reputation by running afoul of the law. In this state, a single count of fraud, extortion, or deceptive trade practices can be punishable by up to twenty years in jail, plus fines."

"Deceptive trade practices? That's a new one. What's a deceptive trade practice?"

"A false representation. For instance, extorting seventy-five million dollars from a terminally ill man in return for an empty promise to save his life."

"Wow! That's a serious charge. Do either of you honestly believe that I could do such a thing?"

"No," Dottie replied. "For a fact, we don't, but we've been wrong before. Be advised, Vernon: we will have to put you in jail if you deceive Clem Tucker into paying you that kind of money. The law doesn't give us a choice."

Mr. Moore thought her words over for a minute, then he said, "I appreciate the advice, Sheriff. Whatever I do or don't do while I'm in Ebb, I promise that I won't extort seventy-five million dollars from Clem Tucker."

"So the rumor is wrong. You deny everything."

"I'm unaware of the full extent of the rumor, Mary. How can I know whether I denied 'everything'?"

"Okay. The same rumor says you're going to ask for Clem's life instead of rain, not both. Do you deny that, too?"

"Forgive me, but didn't you discuss the same issue with Marion yesterday?"

"Yes."

"And what did she say?"

"She evaded the question, just like you are. She said we all should have faith—in you."

"I take it that was the wrong answer."

"I'm the county attorney, Vernon, and the Queen Bee of the

Quilting Circle. I can't just sit on my hands if there's a chance, any chance at all, that you're about to sell us down the river for Clem Tucker's money."

"You can't? Why not? What's your alternative?"

Hail Mary was never at her best when the tables were turned against her. She replied, "Excuse me?"

"I repeat: what else can you do? Should you warn Clem of my intentions? If you do, I believe you'll find that he's already very well informed, but he may not be enthused to learn that rumors of his private business dealings have reached your office."

"So the rumors are true. You and Clem do have a deal."

"We have a contingent business agreement. Like all such agreements, the terms and conditions are confidential."

"Privacy won't get you a pass, Vernon. I don't need a complaint to get a conviction. If you extort money from Clem Tucker for a prayer, I will throw you in jail."

Mr. Moore smiled calmly and replied, "The last time I checked, Counselor, the rain was on its way. Are we done?"

Hail Mary cleared her throat. "I have one other item on my agenda, if you don't mind. What can you tell us about Lohengrin's Children, or is that confidential, too?"

"It's a travel club, as you know. I'm a member in good standing."

"I gather it's not-for-profit."

"It's a club, Mary."

"So I understand, but we were unable to find any incorporation or tax records for this 'club' as you call it, either in this state or any other."

"You investigated the tax status of a travel club? How thorough! Do you check up on reading groups and bridge clubs, too? Is it a matter of routine?"

"You're dodging the question, Vernon. We were unable to

locate any sort of filing for Lohengrin's Children anywhere, not even a mailing address. Why is that?"

"It's conjecture, but my suspicion is that you forgot to check England."

"England?"

"Our headquarters are in Winchester, southwest of London. I believe you'll find whatever you need over there."

"I'll be damned!" Dottie remarked. "Thanks for the tip. We'll get on it."

Mr. Moore gathered himself and stood up. "I'd love to stay and chat but extortion has a schedule, or is it deceptive trade practice? I'm due at the River House shortly."

My friend the county attorney looked up from her big mahogany desk and said, "Why do I get the impression that you're not taking this predicament seriously, Vernon?"

"I have no idea, Counselor. Like you, I take all of my predicaments very seriously. Have a lovely day. You too, Sheriff."

After he had gone, Hail Mary asked, "Do you think he got the message, Dot?"

"Oh, there's no doubt about that. Did you get his message?"

"What do you mean?"

"Were you reading his body language when you threatened him with jail? He didn't flinch; he didn't look away; he didn't twitch or tap his foot or start to perspire. A normal man gets more panicky than that when he is asked to dance."

"A normal man can't ask for directions, Dottie."

"That's what I mean, Mary. Vernon Moore is not your normal man. Hell, he may not even be a man, and he is not the least bit worried about being thrown in my jail."

"Then he underestimates me . . ."

"Or you underestimate him." Dottie looked up at the ceiling and asked, "I wonder: which is more likely?"

PEARLINE MET MR. MOORE at the door that morning, then the two of them disappeared into the bowels of the household. She reappeared in the kitchen by herself afterwards, crying a torrent of tears.

Marie grabbed a paper towel off the rack and handed it to her. "Are you okay, Pearl? Is there something I can do?"

Clem's practical nurse sat down at the table and wiped her eyes. "I'm perfectly fine. I had a talk with Mr. Moore, that's all."

"I noticed. What did the man say?"

She blew her nose. "He got me a job, and after all the trouble I was."

"He what?"

"Mr. Tucker won't be needin' me after Saturday, so Mr. Moore got me a job; a good-payin' job, too, and it's in Edgerton, just down the road from home."

"Did you tell him you needed a job, Pearl? You didn't tell me."

"I told Mr. Tucker; he must've mentioned it to Mr. Moore. Now, if you don't mind, I have to do my laundry. I need to get ready to go."

"Where is Mr. Moore now?"

"With Mr. Tucker, in his office."

"They're in the office? Oh no! You can't do your laundry now! You have to listen in."

"No, I don't, Marie. I'm not spying on anybody anymore. Anyway, Mr. Moore said it would be okay if you listened in this time."

At first, Marie reacted like any professional chef would. "But I have to cook a formal dinner for ten tonight!" Then she stopped dead in her tracks and said, "Mr. Moore knows?"

"He knows everything, and I mean everything."

I got a call about two seconds later. Two seconds after that, you-know-who was on the hook for dessert, then Marie said, "Thanks for helping me out on such short notice, Wilma. You're the exception that proves the rule."

"What rule?" I asked innocently.

"I don't mean to be disrespectful, but I'm not used to the boss helping out. That's all."

"But I'm not your boss, Marie. I'm your friend, and a fellow Circle girl. We always help each other out. That's the rule."

"Maybe so, but I appreciate it anyway."

I probably should have been thinking about dessert, but "the exception that proves the rule" kept gnawing at my innards long after I had hung up the phone. It's another one of those old saws that makes no sense. To my simple mind, an exception is a clear indication that the rule doesn't work. For instance, there are three teaspoons in a tablespoon. Nobody ever says that the exception is two teaspoons, which proves that it's really three!

As long as I'm at it, I have a bone to pick with the first yokel who said, "It's the thought that counts." My theory is that it was thought up by some empty-headed husband who forgot his anniversary, and then a thousand others bought into it. The next thing you knew, forgetful men everywhere were saying, "It's the thought that counts."

In the country, a nice thought and four dollars will get you a latte at Starbucks. Effort is appreciated, too, but when a person is in trouble, they need results. I can't imagine one farmer calling up another and saying, "Hey, Bert. I heard you needed to borrow my tractor to get your corn in before the hailstorm, but I was playing pinochle over at the Corn Palace and plain forgot. It's the thought that counts, though."

See what I mean?

Chapter 26

DIVINE INTERVENTION

MY FIANCÉ'S OFFICE was an impeccably decorated shrine to the ancient and masculine art of killing things. A gun rack hung on each side wall: one for high zoot shotguns and the other for various and sundry hunting rifles, most with straps and scopes. Clem also kept a gun safe in the far corner that looked like a small refrigerator. I never saw what he kept in there, but I doubt that it was cabbage and cheese. The Japanese sword set sat in its own rack on a long, waist-high table in front of the window behind his desk, and his collection of Pawnee and Lakota Sioux artifacts was in a glass case on the bookshelf. A Remington bronze of a cowboy on horseback had been placed on the table next to a leather reading chair, and a red, white, and black Navajo rug covered most of the floor in front of his desk.

It was a man's room if I ever saw one; a well-heeled, well-armed man's room.

When Marie peered through the crack between the door and the frame, all she could see was a narrow slice of Clem sitting comfortably behind his desk. An invisible Mr. Moore was saying, "The widows and I are all looking forward to it, but I was wondering if you could ask Marie to set one more place at the table."

"Who for? Not that imp Hail Mary Wade. She's been angling for an invitation to the River House for years."

"Actually, I was thinking of your sister, Clara."

"Clara? You're shitting me! She'd never come out here. I must've invited her a hundred times."

"I thought you might have heard, Clem. I escorted her to the sunrise service at church this morning. She handled it well . . ."

"You've been seeing my sister?"

"You knew I had, Clem. We've been friends since my first visit to Ebb."

"You told me you had seen her once. Since you two are pals, is it possible that you might have dropped a hint or two about our deal?"

"No. I thought I'd leave that to you."

"To me? Why?"

"You go under the knife in two days, Clem. Don't you have some contingencies to cover with the people close to you? For instance, who will assume control of the Tucker Trust in the unlikely event that you die?"

"Calvin will continue as custodian of the trust. It's all arranged."

"But who will become chairman, or should I say chairwoman?"

Clem mulled that over then said, "You know what, Vernon? You're absolutely right. I had a fixed impression of what this dinner was supposed to be, but I should've been broader in my thinking. Clara should be here. Tell her I'm rolling out the red carpet."

"It'll be my pleasure."

"Excellent! Now, do we have business to conduct, or do you need to knock a few more nuts off the family tree first?"

"Let's move on."

Marie made a mental note to appear surprised when Mr. Moore mentioned that Clara was coming to dinner. In the meantime, my fiancé reclined in his chair and said, "As I recall, you had convinced me yesterday that God couldn't intervene in the affairs of men, but then you mentioned some sort of loophole. Is that right?"

"It is."

"Then I take it that we're about to explore the loophole."

"We are."

"That's what I wanted to hear. Do you want something to drink?"

"I would, if you don't mind. A cup of tea would be lovely."

Without getting up from his chair, Clem yelled, "Pearline! Marie! Would one of you come in here and see me, please?"

Marie counted to five and entered Clem's office. After a brief discussion, which included the "surprise" addition of Clara to the evening's guest list, she agreed to bring Clem a double espresso and Mr. Moore a cup of tea. No one was on station while Marie was in the kitchen, but it appears that little of the conversation was lost.

After she had delivered the men their caffeine, Clem said, "Yeah. I played baseball when I was a kid. Little League. Why?"

"Was your coach an ex–baseball player?"

"I'd hate to have a coach who wasn't. He played college ball at Concordia, up in Seward."

"Was he a good coach?"

"He knew the game and he didn't molest anybody. Against modern standards, I'd say he was stellar."

"So it would seem. Did your team ever get behind?"

"In a game? Sure. Once or twice anyway."

"Did the coach put himself in to pitch?"

"I just love the way you think, Vernon. He was thirty-something years old. Why would an idea like that even enter a man's mind?"

"Why, indeed? The reason it wouldn't, of course, is that the result would be predetermined. That's why it's against the rules. Correct?"

"Yeah, but isn't the same true of God? Isn't that why he can't intervene, because the result would be preordained?"

"Not exactly."

Clem took a sip of his espresso. "This is crap! There's not enough sugar! Everybody in my household is a goddamned nutritionist anymore. Now, explain to me why God can destroy uncertainty when that's supposed to be the one thing He wants more than anything else."

"Let's try an example. Suppose God decided to intervene in one of your Little League games. What would have happened?"

"Depending on the side He picked, my team would've won or lost by a zillion to zero."

"Meaning God would have destroyed the uncertainty of the game."

"That's what I already said."

"But you were only partially right. As it turns out, your uncertainty would have been destroyed, but God's wouldn't have been materially affected."

"How the hell can you say that, Vernon? He fixed the goddamned ballgame. Are you saying that He doesn't care?"

"Not at all, but He's God. He exists on an entirely different plane than we do. What applies to us doesn't necessarily apply to Him, and vice versa."

"I take it we're finally down to the loophole you mentioned yesterday."

"We are, but it takes a little math to understand. Would you agree that an omnipotent God would live forever?"

"Hell yes. Otherwise, he'd be less than omnipotent."

"Right. What's infinity minus one."

"I got As in math, Vernon. It's still infinity."

"Correct. In fact, what's infinity minus any finite number?"

"Same answer; still infinity."

"That's the loophole, Clem. As long as God lives forever, He can intervene as often as He wants without harming His own uncertainty. It's still infinitely large."

"Okay. So God can dabble on Earth to His heart's content. Good for Him, but what about us Little Leaguers? He'd sure as hell destroy our uncertainty. And for the record, I don't want to stand out there at first base for a million years while the other team scores a zillion runs. It would kill my knees."

"But what if you lived forever, too?"

"Then I'd need new knees, and the game would still be ruined." Clem picked up his espresso cup and walked to the door. Marie Delacroix is not a fleet-footed girl, but she managed to scoot into the great room before he shouted, "Marie!"

She stuck her face around the corner a five-count later. "Yes, Mr. Tucker."

"Would you make me another espresso, please? And double the sugar; I don't care what Louise says. Espresso is crap without a quarter inch of raw sugar in the bottom."

"Yes, sir."

"How's dinner comin'? Are you making me a green bean casserole?"

"Yessir."

"Come on, Marie. You can't fool an old fooler. You have to be making a dish I didn't ask for; a fancy dish. What is it?"

"I wouldn't call it fancy. I'm fixing fresh asparagus with Béarnaise sauce."

"Asparagus? Yum! What's for dessert?"

"Blueberry pies. Wilma's making them."

"Wilma?"

"She wanted to, Mr. Tucker. What could I say?"

"Nothing. If Wilma wants to bake, let her bake. I have to powder my nose. I'd appreciate it if you could fetch me a proper espresso while I'm gone. Okay?"

"Yes, sir, Mr. Tucker."

MARIE FOUND MY LODGER looking over the Japanese sword set when she returned. "Mr. Tucker won't be a minute. Can I top off your tea or bring you a piece of pound cake?"

"No thank you," he said, as he ran his palm across the top of the long sword. "This is the katana. The short sword is called the shoto. They're beautiful pieces, aren't they?"

"Yes, sir."

"Have you ever been to Japan, Marie?"

"I'm afraid not, Mr. Moore."

"Go. Don't wait too long; just go. You'll find many excellent cuisines."

"So I've read, but there isn't much call for seafood at the River House."

"Try the yakitori and the shabu-shabu." Mr. Moore turned to face Marie, and continued, "Do you know what else makes the Japanese so exceptional?"

"Their cars?"

"I was thinking that they're an honorable race. That's not to say they're perfect but, like the English, their culture was founded upon the tenets of honor and, like England's, it has endured a thousand years."

"I thought our culture came from England, too, Mr. Moore."

"It did, but it's not clear that the honor gene made it across the Atlantic intact. Do you suppose that a society based on greed and self-gratification will last even half as long?"

Clem reappeared just then with a big smile on his face. "Boy oh boy. I'm getting healthier by the damned minute! Thanks for the fresh espresso, Marie."

"Will you be needing anything else, Mr. Tucker?"

"I'll call if I do." While Marie left the office, Clem said, "Were you admiring my sword set, Vernon?"

"Yes. I was."

"Eighteenth century, hand-forged and folded steel. Razor sharp; could cut through an engine block like whipped butter. I'd never give it a try, though. Too damned expensive. I left it to John Smith. He's still in to all that martial arts crap, but maybe you'd rather have it."

"It's a nice thought, but leave it to John. I have a set of my own."

"You do? Are you a collector?"

"Let's just say that I'm an admirer of bushido. Where were we before you excused yourself?"

The two men sat down again. Clem answered, "You were about to explain why God wouldn't mess with my Little League game."

"Actually, I was about to explore the opposite case. What if He wanted to affect the outcome?"

"I'm confused, Vernon. Why would a God bother to intervene in a goddamned Little League game in the first place?"

"To make a point, to preserve a principle, to reward a good act. To answer a prayer."

"Very clever, but I don't give a shit; He can't do it. He'd ruin the game for the rest of us. We already agreed."

"We did at that, but what if there's a work-around? Did your coach ever call in a relief pitcher?"

"Yeah, sure."

"Why?"

"Because the starting pitcher was getting crucified. Why else?"

"Was the relief pitcher an adult?"

"Hell no. He was another kid, just like . . ."

"So the pitcher was relieved, but by another child, so the uncertainty of the game was preserved, wasn't it?"

"What are you saying, Vernon? Are you saying that God can intervene as long as He delegates it to a Little Leaguer—like you, for instance?"

"I would never make such a claim for myself, Clem. I'm only pointing out that a benevolent God could intervene if He chose to delegate—as long as He also met another requirement."

"Which is what?"

"We could never know that He was behind the intervention, could we? Otherwise, we would become dependent and expectant. Worse, the greatest mystery of life would be revealed."

"So God has to remain anonymous."

"As we discussed yesterday, yes."

Clem inhaled deeply, then exhaled slowly. "I'm a simple country boy, Vernon. Is this a good time to summarize?"

"Sure. You or me?"

"I'll take the wheel, if you don't mind. You're saying that God can influence an outcome on Earth without destroying His uncertainty because of a loophole. Right?"

"I believe so, yes."

"Okay. But you're also saying that He has to work through intermediaries if He wants to preserve our uncertainty."

"That would appear to be the case. Otherwise, the consequences would be obvious."

"Are you one of God's relief pitchers, Vernon? Think before

you reply. A shitload of money could be riding on what you say in the next five seconds."

"Nice try, but you can't trap me that easily."

"Trap you? What the hell does that mean?"

"If I was one of God's intermediaries, how could I possibly admit it and preserve His anonymity? The answer, of course, is that only a charlatan, to use your own terms, could ever claim to be an emissary from God. A true emissary would be forced to deny it."

"So you deny it, even though it could cost you seventy-five million dollars."

"The money is insignificant against the consequences. Either I'm not one of God's relief pitchers, or I am and I can't admit it. Either way, I'm not."

"What about Christ? Didn't he claim to be the son of God?"

"I wasn't there at the time, but I believe he said that we are all children of God, and the rules were different then anyway. The human race was barely out of the Bronze Age. The sun revolved around the Earth and the elements were earth, wind, fire, and water. Tell me: how would the Sermon on the Mount have gone over if it had been based upon chaos theory?"

Clem shrugged. "From where I sit, all of this divine intervention shit is still pretty hard to swallow, and it's two thousand years later. I need a while to mull it over."

Mr. Moore stood up from his chair and stretched. "No problem. I'll see you tonight."

"Can you answer one straightforward question before you go? I don't want any long-winded explanations either. Be Clara for a minute; just answer yes or no."

"I'll do my best."

"Does God ever answer your prayers?"

"Yes."

"He does? How often? Once a year; once in a blue moon?"

"Every day."

"Every day? Jesus, Vernon! What do you pray for?"

"Just that, Clem. Every night before I turn out the light, I ask for one more day. So far, God has been incredibly generous to me."

"No shit! If Buford Pickett is even half right, you've seen a helluva lot more days than the rest of us will ever see, that's for sure."

"Maybe, maybe not. Have you considered the odds?"

"The odds? What odds?"

"The odds that Buford is right. When the day is done, doesn't your decision depend more on that than on any other factor?"

"I suppose it does, now that you mention it. What does your decision depend upon?"

"Another number, Clem, with a dollar sign in front of it. Get some rest. I'll see you this evening."

Chapter 27

. . . .

RELATIVE RULES

M R. MOORE STOPPED BY the Angles House that afternoon to pick up Laverne for another field trip. I don't know if he was expecting to be ambushed by the lady of the house, but ambushed he was. Loretta opened the door and bypassed the usual father-of-my-child, saver-of-my-life banter. "Lovey is in the den watching *Shrek*," she said. "Can we sit in the front room for a minute?"

Mr. Moore replied, "Sure. What's on your mind?"

"Birdie and Marion came by for a visit yesterday afternoon."

"Marion said that you were a bit upset. Birdie thought so, too. Why?"

"Oh, I don't know. Maybe it was because my daughter was scared to death before they came, but she had a doting 'auntie' by the time they left. Or maybe it was 'Auntie' Marion's use of colorful, thought-provoking terms like earthquake and nuclear accident."

"Laverne has an extraordinary gift, Lo. It may permit her to foresee certain catastrophic events, should they ever transpire, but it will also make her a handful to raise. Access to an 'aunt' with a similar gift will be to your advantage. Spend some time with Marion at the River House tonight. She's not as dangerous as you think."

"Dangerous? Why is she dangerous?"

Mr. Moore sat forward. "I was speaking ironically, Lo. Marion wouldn't harm a fly, literally. What's really bothering you?"

"What do you mean?"

"How could I be more plain? Something else is bothering you. What is it?"

After a pause, Loretta said, "I don't want my daughter to spend her life in a bus, Vernon, even if she gets to sit up front. I want her to do whatever she wants, as long as it includes the production of grandchildren to comfort my old age."

"You've drawn an incorrect inference, Loretta. Marion lives a nomadic life because she accepted an invitation to join Lohengrin's Children. I thought you would have heard of it by now."

"I did, from Hail Mary. Aren't you a member, too?"

"Yes."

"Then where's your bus? Didn't you get one for yourself?"

"I prefer to travel by car, but it's irrelevant. Laverne will never become a member of Lohengrin's Children."

"Excuse me, Mr. Vernon L. Moore. Are you saying that my daughter couldn't get into a travel club? Why the hell not?"

"You'd never want her to take the entrance exam, Lo; nor would I."

"The entrance exam! What kind of entrance exam?"

"It's the worst, most dangerous kind of happenstance. It would almost certainly kill her."

"It would what?"

"The odds are a million to one, Lo. Hence the term 'happenstance.'"

"But it didn't kill you, did it?"

Mr. Moore sat back and responded, "Use your own best judgment."

Loretta crossed her arms. "Four years ago, you told me funny stories and made love to me. Two years ago you raised me from the dead, twice, and don't bother denying it either. I'm not in the mood. Now, all of a sudden, my biennial knight in shining armor has reappeared, and I'm scared shitless. Why? What did I do wrong? Are you pissed off because I gave your daughter a father? Was that my mistake?"

"No. You did precisely what you should have done."

"Then what's going on, Vern? Why am I so upset?"

"Ask yourself, Lo. There's no danger to Laverne. Something else is on your mind and you still haven't told me what it is."

Loretta paused to choose her words carefully, then said, "I've been trying to unravel your deal with Clem ever since you got here. Only one explanation makes sense."

"Which is . . . ?"

"You're going to give Clem's money to the farmers, aren't you?"

Mr. Moore replied sharply, "Where did you come up with an idea like that?"

"In the first place, you would never keep the money for yourself, so the question is who you would give it to. It was a bit of a leap, but I ruled out Congress and the oil cartel. The farmers need it more than anybody, and you've been talking to them about crop yields and land values since Tuesday. Is that another odd coincidence, or am I right?"

"I can't say one way or the other."

"You can't? Why not?"

"Because you'll tell Wilma, and she'll tell Clem. It could kill the deal."

"How come?"

"Because Clem Tucker is not a charitable man."

"Then why didn't you sell him some, darlin'?"

"A salesman sells what the prospect will buy, Lo. Clem is in the market for faith because he fears death, but he won't buy charity. He never has, and he has no need to know what I intend to do with his money. That's my business and mine alone."

Loretta had two choices: she could beat a dead horse, or she could change the subject. She said, "Then will you answer another question—honestly?"

"Honestly, after so many lies?"

"I'm serious. When will you be back to see your daughter?"

"I don't know."

"She's your daughter, dammit! She deserves a better answer than that."

"I agree, but it's not my decision."

"It's not your decision? How can that be?"

"The Quilting Circle has rules, doesn't it? Unfortunately, so do we."

"By 'we,' I take it you mean Lohengrin's Children?"

"Yes, and I broke one of the rules."

Lo was taken aback, but not for the reason you might think. "Only one? Was it Laverne or me?"

Mr. Moore sighed. "You're right. I broke two, and they were very, very big rules."

"So you were a naughty boy. What can they do, take away your frequent flyer miles?"

At just that moment, a three-year-old jet streaked into the room and landed in Mr. Moore's lap. "Poppy, Poppy! The movie's over! Fiona turned green, again!" Laverne planted a kiss on his cheek, then she swiveled around to face her mother. "You're sad, Mommy. How come?"

"Poppy and I were talking about old times, Lovey. Grown-ups

can miss old times just like we miss our old friends, and that can make us sad."

Laverne leaped out of Mr. Moore's lap and into her mother's. "I told you before. Poppy's coming back."

"He is? How do you know?"

"Auntie Marion said so. She said you could take it to the bank."

"She said what?"

"She said you could take it to the bank, Mommy."

Chapter 28

. . . .

CLARA'S DANCE CARD

FOR A CHANGE, I didn't have my head in the refrigerator when Hail Mary walked into my kitchen. It was stuck in my oven, which is electric, thank you very much. On any given day, the owner of a bed and breakfast has to stick her head into a variety of kitchen appliances, but never a gas oven, a garbage disposal, or a blender. That's a safety tip.

"Hello, Wilma," she said. "I see that you're baking—for dinner at the River House?"

"Blueberry pies, Counselor; Clement's favorite. I'm pinch-hitting for Marie."

"Etiquette was never my best subject, but isn't a formal dinner supposed to have two desserts?"

You'd never think that girl was country-born herself, would you? "That's why there are two pies," I replied. "How was your visit with Mr. Moore? Did you and Dottie change his mind?"

"I hope so. At a minimum, we gave him something to think about."

"I was just curious, because Marie gave me a call not fifteen minutes ago. Mr. Moore and my Fiancé in Perpetuity had another discussion about divine intervention this morning. Apparently, it was impossible yesterday but perfectly possible today, which means he's still doing what he always does."

"Which is what, if I may ask?"

"Confusing people," I replied. While Mary was thinking that over, I added, "We're due upstairs to see Clara in a minute, but I may need to pull out and leave part way."

"Why?"

"I have to check on my two desserts again in about twenty minutes."

"Don't worry yourself, Wilma. If necessary, I can muddle through on my own. After all, it's only the future of the county at stake. I wouldn't want you all to be without your precious pies tonight."

BEFORE CLARA WOULD set her big toe inside my door, the third floor of the Come Again had to be decorated to her exact specifications. I take that back; "decorate" is an exaggeration. Actually, she converted the place into a home gymnasium, starting with fifteen hundred square feet of polished, Brazilian wood flooring. These days, it's checkered with just about every exercise gizmo you could imagine, plus a few odd-looking contraptions that may have been invented during the Spanish Inquisition. The rest of Clara's floor is arranged into a bedroom, a huge bathroom with a Jacuzzi tub smack in the center, an office, and a large, tile-floored kitchen which should have made her the steel industry's Woman of the Year. It has a huge, stainless-steel refrigerator-freezer, a Viking range, a steel Miele dishwasher, and a double, stainless-steel sink—for a woman who makes herself one meal a day, usually a salad with tofu or cashews in it. Otherwise, she eats my cinnamon oatmeal for breakfast and lives off yogurt smoothies.

On the edge of the kitchen, right next to the gym, there is an everyday, garden-variety wood picnic table where Clara likes to take her meals. Don't ask me why; every other piece of furniture she owns is top of the line. Did I mention the flat-screened televisions? Clara has no less than six of them sprinkled here and there, which gives the place the ambience of a sports bar or an airport waiting area.

A Fred Astaire movie was playing on every TV screen in sight when Hail Mary Wade and yours truly arrived for our afternoon appointment. Clara was watching from the picnic table, sipping a smoothie of one variety or another, and dressed in her usual uniform: a red tee shirt under a black leotard, white kneepads over shiny hose, plus running shoes. Her gray hair was in a ponytail, and she was sporting a red sweatband that was a mite pinkish and sweaty.

Any woman who was not raised in a barn would have offered us something to drink, but Clara's hospitality was hindered by her vocabulary. Instead, she muted the TVs with a clicker—all at once, I might add—and motioned us to join her at the picnic table.

Did I ever tell you that Hail Mary Wade can get a little gushy? Well, she can, especially around folks with money. I'm not familiar with the circumstances of her upbringing, but a lot of people who were born poor seem to have the same affliction. She began by saying, "Thanks so much for agreeing to visit with us this afternoon, Clara." Then she waited, as if she expected a two paragraph response.

Clara smiled. It was a tolerant smile in my opinion; the kind a wife gives a retired husband after he has passed gas at the kitchen table.

Mary figured out that a smile was all she was going to get, so she moved on. "I was so glad to see you at church this morning. Did you enjoy it?"

That was the sort of yes-no question that could have put Clara into the conversation, but she chose to nod, just a smidgeon. In my experience, that meant that she found the service tolerable, which Hail Mary seemed to divine.

"You have a lovely home," Mary said. "It's so athletic, so leading edge. Wilma tells me that you decorated it yourself. Is that so?"

Clara loosened up. "Yes."

"You must exercise a lot. You're in excellent shape."

Instead of answering, Clara smiled and took a sip of her drink.

"Did Wilma mention why I asked to see you today?"

"No."

"I just requested a meeting, Mary," I interjected.

"Do you hear that Mr. Moore is in town?"

Clara nodded. I guess she needed to give her voice a rest.

"He's been up to see her several times," I said on her behalf. "Isn't that so?"

"Yes."

"Are you aware that he's been visiting your brother every morning?" Mary asked.

Clara nodded again.

"Did Mr. Moore tell you what he and Clem are talking about?"

"Yes."

By then, Mary's eyes were the size of boiled eggs. I had no idea that such a small person could have such large eyeballs. "He did? You're completely up-to-date?"

"Yes."

My lawyer friend was unable to keep a lid on her emotions. "Really? Did you know that your brother has offered to pay Vernon the sum of seventy-five million dollars—for a prayer! Are you aware of that little detail, too?"

"Yes." It was a flat, emotionless answer. There was no stress or excitement in it whatsoever.

"So you're not worried about Clem."

"No."

"What about the drought? How worried are you about that?"

I couldn't tell whether Mary had forgotten my lodger's two-word limit or whether she was trying to trap her into a sentence-long response. For her part, Clara just looked at me again, like it was my job to get it all sorted out. I said, "We were hoping you could help us persuade Mr. Moore to ask for rain *and* Clem's life. Are we on a fool's errand?"

"Yes," she replied instantly.

Hail Mary put her hands on top of her head, like she was a prisoner of war. "We can't take 'yes' for an answer, Wilma. Clara has to help us. We have to find a way."

"It sounds to me like we're tardy to the party, Mary. I think her dance card is already full. Is that so, Clara?"

She said "yes," and then she picked up the clicker and turned up the volume on the TVs. Fred and Ginger were twirling across a stage to a brassy, big band number, but I don't believe that Hail Mary was captured by the moment like I was.

"What can we do?" she pleaded. "What can we do?"

"We can say thank you and leave."

"But we can't . . ."

"Yes we can, Mary. We've done our song and dance; now we're done. I have no intention of wearing out my welcome here." I said to Clara, "Thank you so much for allowing us to intrude on your busy day. We both appreciate it, very much."

She nodded, and then she walked over to a step machine and mounted up. I stood, too, leaving Mary by herself at the picnic table. After a second, she looked up at me and asked, "What's going on, Wilma?"

I had a little giggle to myself. "Are you kidding? Vernon Moore is what's going on. I was a fool to think for a minute that we could get in his way. So were you."

"Then I am not done being a fool. When you hear what Pokie has to say, you won't be done either."

Chapter 29

....

S-E-X

A GUARDIAN PASTRY ANGEL must have been perched on my shoulder that afternoon. I had forgotten my blueberry pies, but they were baked to a golden brown when I got back to my kitchen. I received a call on my police phone from Loretta while I was putting them on the rack to cool.

Have you ever tried to answer a cell phone with oven mittens on? Here's a piece of advice: don't.

"It's official," Lo moaned after I got the gloves off. "Lovey's gifted. Vern said so."

"I thought it was official yesterday," I replied. "Or were you hoping that the widows were blowing smoke up your nether reaches?"

"I don't know what I was hoping, Wilma. All I know is that I have an abnormal child."

"Welcome to parenthood, Lo. There's no such thing as a normal child. They all have their abnormalities; every one of them. It's what makes the little sweeties so lovable."

"But Lovey can read minds!"

"Okay, so that's an abnormal abnormality, but we both saw it coming. Besides, I thought you were worried that she would have to spend the rest of her life in a bus."

"I was, but Vern says there's no chance. He might lie to me about something else, but he would never lie about his daughter."

"Well, that's a relief. Now we can quit worrying about Laverne and get back to worrying about the drought. And Clem. And Buford and Beryl and Hail Mary. Did I leave anyone out?"

"Don't you change the subject on me, Wilma Porter. I'm still concerned about Lovey. She can read minds. What am I going to do?"

"Here's a strategy: when you're around Laverne, think nice thoughts."

"That's what the widows said, but what about s-e-x? How can I think about that if my daughter is listening in?"

"You'll probably have to give it up," I advised dolefully. "Come to think of it, she can probably read her father's mind, too. I'd say you're both done."

"I'm serious, Wilma! What am I supposed to do?"

"If you want, you and Calvin can come over here every once in a while to do the dirty deed."

"It'll be too late. We'll have already thought about it."

"Then you ought to talk to Marion tonight. Maybe she has some good advice."

"No way. I don't trust her; I don't care what Vern says."

"That's not you speaking, Lo; that's a mother's concern for her child. It's healthy, like broccoli. But don't overcook it; then it's not. Who else are you going to pester? Mr. Moore?"

"Vern, about s-e-x? How awkward would that be?"

"In that case, it seems to me that you have three choices: you can pervert the mind of my innocent little goddaughter, which isn't my first choice; or you can give up having sex with your husband, which likely isn't his first choice; or you can talk to a widow tonight and see if there's a way out of this mess."

"Okay. Fine! I'll talk to Marion."

"That's a good idea. Hail Mary and I just went upstairs to see Clara."

"Oh crap! I'd forgotten. How did that go? Was she talkative?"

"No more than usual, but Mr. Moore must've found some way to get through. He's bringing her to the River House tonight."

"Are you serious? That's two road trips in one day—for a recluse! Come to think of it, I guess I'm not all that surprised. That man is way, way ahead of us, Wilma."

It's not like I didn't agree, but the way Lo said it sparked my curiosity. "What do you mean?" I asked.

"You can't tell anybody. Not Clem, not Hail Mary; not anybody."

"I understand the rules, Lo; I invented the darned things. Now cough it up! Spill the beans. What did he do that's so darned earth shattering?"

"It's not what he did; it's what he said. He's going to give the money to the farmers."

"He is? Lordy, lordy! Of course, he is. I should have thought of it myself. It makes perfect sense, knowing Mr. Moore anyway. But Clem is Clem, whether he's on Death's Doorstep or not. What if he won't pay the money in the first place?"

"Then Vern will make it rain, or maybe he'll turn Clem into a pillar of salt. There's no telling what he'll do."

"Not so, Lo. We know two things for sure: come Friday night, Mr. Moore will be off to the hither and yon, and we'll still be here, holding the bag."

Now, why in heaven did I have to say that? The first image that crept into my mind wasn't a handbag, or a trash bag, or even a grocery bag, it was a body bag.

Chapter 30

. . . .

THE IRISH CONNECTION

IT WAS CLOSE to five o'clock when I left home for the Abattoir. My dead old oak had begun to cast the nub of a shadow across the parking lot, but the tarmac was still soft like cookie dough and the breeze reminded me of my ex: slight, shifty, and never there when I needed it most. In case you haven't guessed, my ex-husband was a devotee of the notion that "it's the thought that counts" — possibly because he rarely had one.

I was running a few minutes late, so I was the last girl to arrive at the meeting. Hail Mary checked her watch and said, "Thanks for coming, Wilma. Let the minutes show that the full board is present and accounted for, finally. Pokie Melhuse is also in attendance as my guest. She has some important information to impart to us all."

Pokie's head was resting on her forearms on the table, like she was catching a nap, but she looked up and nodded when Hail Mary mentioned her name. The poor girl's eyes were bloodshot, her lipstick was smudged, and her hair was in a state. If I hadn't known better, I would have thought that she had been in a bar fight. As it was, she had only been up all night.

"I'd like to dispense with the small talk . . ."

Loretta interrupted, "You always dispense with the small talk, Mary. Why can't we have a little small talk for a change?"

"Did you have something small to bring before the board, Loretta? I'd be happy to put it on the agenda."

"That's very sweet of you, Mary. My TV's been off all day. Has the forecast changed?"

Dot answered, "I checked with the National Weather Service just before we drove over. A high pressure area is building up west of the Rockies. There's a possibility that it'll push the rainstorm off to the east before it gets to us, so the odds of rain are still at fifty-fifty."

I remarked, "Well, being stuck on fifty percent is a lot better than being stuck on zero, which was where we were for months. I haven't seen a Buzzword for two days running. Does that mean that our members have stopped disappearing in the middle of the night?"

"My deputies are on the lookout. We'd know if they had."

"Well, then; that's good news, too. Maybe we should quit while we're ahead."

"I don't think we should adjourn just yet," Dottie suggested. "Don't you want to hear what Pokie has to say? It'll curdle your cottage cheese; I can promise you that."

I admit it; I have a weakness for cottage cheese. I like the medium curd with cling peaches straight from the can, but that's another item I can never serve my guests. Canned fruit doesn't cut it in the hospitality business nowadays. It has to be fresh, even in the wintertime.

Loretta responded, "By all means, Dot. Let's not quit while we're ahead. What has Pokie found out?"

"Are you ready?" Mary asked.

"Yes, ma'am." Pokie stifled a yawn and opened up a small

notepad that had been hidden under her forearms. "As you all know, Mr. Moore and the widows belong to a travel club called Lohengrin's Children, so Sheriff Hrnicek asked me to look into it. I didn't have any luck with the law-enforcement data bases we're allowed to access at the office, so I went over to the library to see if Tulip Orbison could help. We were hard at it till five a.m. this morning."

"I take it you found something," Loretta observed.

"It wasn't easy; that's for sure. We found thousands of Internet entries for some opera, but we couldn't find a single reference to any kind of group or club called Lohengrin's Children. But Dottie said the club is headquartered in Winchester, England, so Tulip called Edith Pickerel, a librarian at Oxford College that she met at a conference one time. Edith gave us the URLs for some private catalogs they have and we both started poking around. We were getting nowhere at all until we started diggin' into the letters of an English baron named William Cecil, who lived from 1521 to 1598."

"Who lived when?" Loretta asked.

"In the sixteenth century," Mary answered. "You might want to hold your disbelief until the end. There's more to come, isn't there, Pokie?"

"Yes, ma'am. Mr. Cecil was secretary of state during the reign of Queen Elizabeth the First, and later the lord high treasurer. He also wrote a lot of letters, which makes him an important historical source."

"You're going to tell us that this Cecil character knew Vern, aren't you?"

"It wouldn't have surprised me, Lo, but no. The baron had a close advisor named John Warren. He was a favorite in the court of Henry the Eighth, but he got thrown in jail in 1542 for opposing the Witchcraft Act. That same year, Henry razed a chantry at Winchester Cathedral called the Chapel of Lohengrin's Children."

"In the same Winchester?" Lily asked. "What's a chantry?"

"Edith said it's a place where people go to chant."

"Okay," Loretta commented. "Chanting, chantry; I can see how that works. But how is the razing of a chantry connected to John Warren?"

Pokie referred to her notes again. "For one reason or another, Mr. Warren was eventually released from jail. Edith figures the queen gave him a pardon after Henry passed. Anyway, Mr. Warren became a confidante to the baron, who later referred him to an Irish judge named Nicholas White. Apparently, Mr. Warren was good with numbers . . ."

"He was good with numbers?"

"Uh huh, but he got into some kind of trouble with Queen Elizabeth, so the baron wanted to ship him over to Ireland until things cooled off."

"When was that?"

"In 1568 or 1569. Mr. Cecil didn't say why."

"Okay, but I still don't see the connection."

"In two of his letters to the judge, the baron described Mr. Warren as a disciple of 'Lohengrin's Children.' "

I was starting to get the heebie-jeebies, but Loretta kept her cool. "Really? What else did the letters say?"

"The baron described Mr. Warren as a smart man and a loyal adviser, but a bit contrary in his thinking."

"Contrary?"

"Those were his words, Lo, and it struck me as a coincidence, too."

"Did any of the judge's letters survive?"

"Not a one, but we do know that he fell out of favor with the queen a few years later. Edith figured it was Mr. Warren's fault.

Anyway, Judge White was arrested and eventually died in the Tower of London."

"So that was the end of John Warren."

"Not quite," Hail Mary countered.

Pokie continued, "Edith and I started rooting around in Irish history after that, and we found one last connection to Lohengrin's Children. A man named 'John Warren, Lohengrin's Childe'—which was spelled with an 'e' on the end—was listed among the battlefield casualties at a place called Drogheda Castle."

"It appears that Mr. Warren made a habit of being on the wrong side," Loretta observed.

"No kidding. When did Drogheda Castle fall?"

"In 1649, Mary."

"Would you repeat that for everyone?"

"In 1649. Even if John Warren was a child in the court of Henry the Eighth, he would've been one hundred and twenty years old when he died, on the field of battle."

"No shit!" Lily remarked. "That makes perfect sense! Wait till I tell you what Buford found out about the widows."

That piqued my curiosity, but the ever-officious Mary beat me to the punch. "You're next on the docket, Lily, but let's close this item first. Is that all, Pokie?"

"Yes, Ms. Wade."

"On behalf of the Quilting Circle, I'd like to thank you for doing a terrific job. Please pass our appreciation on to Tulip, as well."

"You might want to buy her a bottle of Baileys, ma'am. She keeps one under the counter for after hours, but we finished it off this morning."

"I'll send it with the gratitude of the Circle."

"That'll be nice, thank you. If you don't mind me asking, what are you gonna do about Mr. Moore?"

"We haven't decided yet. Why?"

"Can I offer my own opinion before I go?"

Dottie looked at Hail Mary, who said, "Of course. We're all aware of your past relationship with Mr. Moore."

"I don't claim any relationship with Mr. Moore, but I have seen what that man can do. Whatever he is, he's not one of us. I wouldn't want to land on his dark side, that's for sure."

"What are you trying to tell us, Pokie?"

"I'm saying that he has a way with the weather, and with life and death. That's a proven fact. If I was close to Mr. Moore, I'd be privileged to hold his hat, but then I'd stand back."

Mary smiled. "Speaking for the board, I can say that we're all privileged to be acquainted with Mr. Moore and very appreciative of his past efforts."

"You could've fooled me, ma'am. Where I come from, which is right here, we don't normally launch investigations into folks we're privileged to know."

"Perhaps, Deputy, but the circumstances in this case are highly irregular. You may have noticed a few irregularities yourself last night, but thank you for your advice. We'll take it under careful consideration."

The rest of us sat in silence while Pokie closed her notebook and left the room, then Hail Mary opened the floor. "Questions? Discussion?"

"Why don't we hear what Buford found out about the widows first?" I proposed.

Loretta, Bebe, and Dot practically fell over each other seconding my motion, so Mary said, "Are you ready, Lily?"

"Am I ever! Hang on to your pixie dust, girls! You're about to be transported from Olde England to Never Never Land, where dead people never die."

It wasn't easy, but I did my best to sit still and keep my mouth shut while Lily related what Buford had learned about the widows. When she was done, Loretta whispered in my ear, "Vern was right. My daughter is *not* taking the entrance exam for Lohengrin's Children."

Hail Mary inhaled deeply and said, "Math was never my best subject, Lily. How old is the Widow Birdie now?"

"It's hard to say, but she ran a secondhand store more than a hundred years ago . . ."

"That is one well-preserved fire victim," Bebe observed on behalf of a board that remained generally awestruck and pixie-dusted. "I'd like to hire her mortician."

"You might want to retain Marion's mortician, too," Lily advised. "She was sixty-something when the *Titanic* went down. That makes her what, a hundred and sixty-odd now? In comparison, Eloise is a mere child of eighty-five or ninety."

"Like Mr. Moore," I added, as if it made him less of an age-related oddity.

Hail Mary frowned. "Is there anything else, Lily?" she asked.

"Yep. All three of the widows' RVs are registered in a town called Eden."

"Eden? Did you say Eden?"

"I'm not making this up, Mary. All three of 'em are registered in Eden, Arizona. Buford took the company jet down to Tucson this morning. John Smith went with him."

"They did?" I said. "What do they expect to find?"

"Maybe they'll find a black swan," Lo remarked.

"A what?" Dottie inquired.

"Pokie mentioned the legend of Lohengrin. Did any of you bother to look it up?"

"I went to the opera," Mary kindly reminded us all.

"Then perhaps you'd like to tell us about it."

"I would, but it was in German."

My best friend rolled her eyes and said, "Then why don't I give it a try? You can fill in the gaps. The legend of Lohengrin dates to German Arthurian literature in the twelfth century. He was the son of Percival, a knight of the Round Table, and in possession of certain special powers, but his twin brother inherited the family's wealth so Lohengrin became a Grail Knight. Later on, he was dispatched to a place called Brabant, where the local duke had died without a male heir. Luckily, our man was single at the time and in search of a duchy he could call his very own. He arrived to save the day in a boat pulled by a black swan; sort of like widows arriving in motor homes with dolphins and seagulls on them, but I digress."

Everybody looked at each other while Loretta pressed on. "Lohengrin agreed to marry the deceased duke's daughter, Elsa, but on the condition that she never ask him to disclose his true identity. Elsa may have been a duchess, but underneath all the jewelry and designer clothes she was just another bony, weak-kneed woman. Eventually, she was overcome by her feminine curiosity, so she asked her husband who he really was. He answered truthfully, but then he stepped back into his swan boat and disappeared forever."

"Forever?" I remarked. "But Mr. Moore has been back to Ebb twice."

Mary scowled. "It's just a legend, for God's sakes! Vernon didn't arrive in a boat. He doesn't stick around. He didn't marry anybody."

"But he has powers, and he gave Loretta a child. We don't know who he is either, not really. What if Buford finds out? What if he can never return?"

"I'm done," Bebe announced. "Five-hundred-year-old travel clubs, people with secret identities and special powers, dead widows who live to be a hundred and whatever. I'm all in; my 'no shit' reservoir is empty. I want to go home and do something that puts me in touch with the real world, like read *Cosmopolitan* or watch a reality show on TV."

"It's too incredible, isn't it?" Hail Mary lamented. "Every report seems to defy logic even more than the last, but the future of our county is at stake. We need to step back and focus on what we know for sure."

"Okay," Loretta said. "What do we know for sure?"

"If you boil it all down, only two things matter: Vernon Moore is in Ebb, and he's going to ask for Clem Tucker's life tomorrow."

"How can you be sure of that? The rain's already coming. What if Vern asked last week? What if Clem refuses to give him the money? What if he has a different plan up his sleeve altogether?"

The room fell silent, then Hail Mary said, "Okay, Lo. What's your plan?"

"It hasn't changed, Mary. My plan is to leave the salvation of the county to the expert. My plan is to put my faith in Vernon L. Moore."

"Loretta's right, Counselor," Dottie interposed. "We're way, way out of our league here. We need to shut up and let the man do his work."

"How can you say that, Dot? The county . . ."

Lily interrupted midsentence. "Have you been listening to anybody in this room today? Things are going on here; weird, spooky things that we have no business putting our noses in. We need to have some faith in the man, or the widows, or whatever the heck they really are."

"But, but . . ."

Dottie shook her head. "Goddammit, Mary! Read the tea leaves and put a sock in it! We're all in accord here. I move that we adjourn. Who seconds?"

My hand shot up like a Patriot missile. Loretta's, Lily's, and Bebe's did, too.

Lo looked around slowly, then said, "I'm no authority on Robert's Rules of Order, but I believe it's time to call for a vote, isn't it?"

In the end, it was five votes for faith and one for whatever takes its place in the hearts of those who've lost it. By then, I felt sorrier for Hail Mary Wade than for Rufus and Winnie Bowe. They might have lost their farm, but I bet they kept their faith. At least, I hope they did.

Chapter 34

....

REVELATION, PART II

EXCLUDING THANKSGIVING, my Fiancé in Perpetuity hosted about one big dinner per year at the River House. As often as not, it was to reveal some sort of stratagem. Three years ago, it was the Big Buyback, when Clem sold the Tucker Trust's farm holdings to tenant farmers as long as they got their mortgages at the county bank, which Clem owned lock, stock, and barrel. A year later, the big soirée was to announce that he had sold Hayes County Bank to the National Bank of the Plains, also known as NBP, which is the biggest financial institution in Nebraska and the Dakotas. He must have forgotten to tell us that he would use the proceeds to take over NBP and throw out the CEO later the same week.

Maybe it was the drought, or maybe it was the revelations of the day, but the idea that Clement might be announcing something momentous didn't even enter my mind until I was choosing my attire for the occasion. All of a sudden, I had no idea what to pick, as if the prospect of a blockbuster announcement had changed the dress code for the evening. In the end, I decided to wear my little black dress. It wasn't all that little, but it was the safest item in my wardrobe, and I was thinking about safety at the time.

Road Rage offered me a ride to the River House with the widows, but I turned him down in favor of Mr. Moore. That bought me a return visit to the tiny rear seat in his Mustang, with a blueberry pie in my lap to boot, but it gained me a spot where I could keep an eye on my other pie, in Clara's lap. Maybe it was an irrational thought, but I was expecting her to start barking like an old-school auctioneer at any minute. As it turns out, Mr. Moore and I talked about the farmers and their various predicaments all the way down, and Clara didn't utter a word, not even "yes" or "no."

Pearline met us at the door—I swear she nearly bowed when she saw Mr. Moore—then she assumed custody of the pies and ushered us into the great room, where we found Clem tending bar for the widows. Rather than pajamas, he was dressed in a black blazer, a black knit shirt, and black slacks. His head had been polished to a high sheen, and he was wearing a big, toothy grin. Clem always had good teeth; "all the better to bite you with," he would say.

The Millets arrived shortly after we did and the party began in earnest. Consuela and Pearline passed through the gathering with trays of hors d'oeuvres and flutes of champagne, Clem was on his best behavior, and the widows were as sweet as cotton candy, but the conversations reminded me of past reunions with distant relatives. Everybody was outgoing but reserved at the same time, and no one mentioned anything pithy like Clem's illness, the weather, or anybody's age. Meanwhile, Clara sat on a barstool with a glass of champagne, occasionally responding to a question with a yes, a no, or a nod, but mostly watching the proceedings in the same way she watches movies: with amused detachment.

Just before dinner, Loretta and I managed to cut Marion off from the herd and corral her on the edge of the library. The widow said, "Wilma, dear, your fiancé is such an engaging man, and he has such an air of confidence about him. One would never imagine that he was ill."

"You should've been here a week ago," I replied. "Clem hurt so bad that he couldn't raise his voice, but Mr. Moore came along and he got better overnight."

"So you believe that Vernon is responsible for the improvement?"

"Take a look, Marion. He's taking the same pills that made him sicker than a dog last week, but now he's his ornery old self. Only one thing has changed. That would be the arrival of your Mr. Moore, and he has a track record."

We both looked at Loretta, who struck a pose and said, "Ta da-a-a!"

Marion shifted her weight from one foot to the other and asked, "Is something on your mind, Loretta? I get the sense that there is."

"You would, wouldn't you? My mind has been chock full of somethings ever since you and Birdie left my home. Are you absolutely certain that Laverne can read minds?"

"Oh yes, dear. Aren't you?"

"I'm doing my best to get used to the idea, but won't it give her an unfair advantage at school? Won't she able to read the teacher's mind and get all As?"

"Yes and no. If Laverne is taking a test, for example, she will have the ability to tune in to her teacher's mind, but it won't be much of an advantage unless the teacher happens to be thinking about the answers at the time. If she's thinking about something else . . ."

"Like s-e-x? What if her schoolteacher is thinking about that?"

Marion smiled. "I take it that the question is more personal, but you needn't worry. What Laverne sees in your mind will be under your control."

Loretta exhaled and replied, "Thank God." Then she asked, "But why?"

"Think of your brain as a library. Unless Laverne is truly extraordinary, she won't be able to browse through your bookshelves. She'll only be able to look over your shoulder at whatever you happen to be reading at the moment."

"Okay, but suppose I happen to be reading a book about s-e-x. What then?"

"You would be wise to avoid it while she's in your presence, dear. If she decides to tune in . . ."

"So distance helps?"

"It does, but distraction is best, especially sensory interference like TV or music. But neither will help you with the problem that's really on your mind. There's no defense for that."

That confused the heck out of me. "What does that mean?" I asked.

Marion answered, "We should rejoin the group, don't you think? I believe we're about to be summoned to dinner."

Lo began to follow Marion across the carpet, but I grabbed her by the elbow and held her back. When Marion was further down range, I asked, "What was she talking about, Lo?"

"It's nothing, Wilma."

"Don't you fib to me. I may not have the gift, but I can read you like a book. Something is eating at you. I can't worry about it properly unless you tell me what it is."

"Ask me again on Saturday."

"Saturday? Why is that . . . ?" Then it hit me. "Mr. Moore will be gone, won't he?"

"Yes."

I nearly dropped my half-full flute. "Oh my God, Lo! You still love him, don't you?"

She touched me on the cheek, and then she walked over to Calvin and took his arm, bless her soul. After a moment of reflection, I said a little prayer for my best friend, and then I pulled up my hostess socks and went to check on the dining room. A magnificent bouquet had been placed in the center of the table, full of lavender-colored foxglove, sunflowers, purple dahlias, yellow wildflowers, and angel hair—but the table had been set for ten. That struck me as odd, so I counted the guests on my fingers. Clem, Clara, Mr. Moore, Calvin, and Loretta made up one hand, which left the three widows and me. I was a diner short and pretty darned sure that Road Rage wouldn't be eating with the adults, so I stuck my head in the kitchen.

Marie was zipping from one pot to another like a water bug, while Pearline and Consuela were putting croutons and Parmesan on the Caesar salads in assembly-line fashion. No one noticed poor little me until I said, "Hi, everybody! How's dinner coming along?"

Marie stopped moving long enough to put her hands on her hips. "One of these days, I'm going to figure out how to prepare a formal dinner two days in advance and have it taste like it was made at the last minute. Until then, I'll be in a froth till the last minute. By the way, the pies look wonderful; thank you."

"You're more than welcome. When do we eat?"

"Consuela will be placing the salads in a few minutes. Pearline will call you shortly after."

"I noticed that the table is set for ten. Will you be joining us for dinner?"

"Take a look at this kitchen, Wilma! How could I possibly do that? I'd be running back and forth all the time."

"But I counted ten places. There are only nine guests."

"Speak to your Fiancé in Perpetuity. I was just following orders."

"Clem didn't tell you who it was?"

"He said to set the table for ten, Wilma. What else was I supposed to do?"

I hate it when people follow orders—except for mine. Don't you?

Chapter 32

....

THE MYSTERY GUEST

CLEM AND I WERE SEATED at the ends of the table, which meant I couldn't enjoy the glare from his shiny new head because Connie's bouquet was in the way. Calvin, Birdie, an empty space, and Loretta were to Clem's right, meaning that Lo was sitting to my left. Mr. Moore was to my immediate right, then Clara, Marion, and Eloise. I wouldn't go to all this trouble, but you need a mind's eye view of the seating chart in order to get an idea of who was talking to whom.

We started off with the Caesar salad, which is Clem's favorite, probably because it requires the minimum number of vegetables (one) to be called a salad. The main course was USDA prime porterhouse steak—Clem won't eat choice and he can tell the difference in a second—plus asparagus with Béarnaise sauce, fries, and the inevitable green bean casserole.

According to Lo, Clem skipped the asparagus but put Béarnaise sauce on his fries, which reminded me of a birthday dinner I shared with my father long ago. He drank bourbon on the rocks and ashed a cigarette in his salad before inhaling a sixteen-ounce prime rib, plus all of his fries and half of mine. The night before he died, he told my mom, "I can't go the doctor; I'm too sick." I kid you not. He was a man's man.

My paternal reminiscences aside, the moratorium on conversational pith remained in place until Pearline and Consuela served dessert, when none other than our very own Pastor Sven Hooper materialized out of thin air.

Clem jumped up from the table and said, "Welcome, Reverend!" Considering my fiancé's views on religion, that was a tad more enthusiasm than a certain person would have expected. "Have you met everyone?" he asked.

"Except for Mr. Moore, who I know by reputation." He and my lodger shook hands, and then he continued, "I'm sorry for being late. My adult Bible class held a debate on evolution this evening. A few of the men very nearly came to blows."

"So Christianity hasn't changed in my absence. I can't say I'm surprised. Can I offer you dinner, Reverend?"

"Thank you, Mr. Tucker, but we had mac and cheese at church."

"Then how about a slice of Wilma's homemade blueberry pie?"

"Pie? Dear me! I should decline in the name of moderation, but it looks so delicious!"

"A la mode or straight up?" Pearline asked flatly, like a bored waitress.

"A la mode, please. I don't suppose you have any chocolate sauce."

Pearl glanced at me and I nodded. "If that's what you want," she said.

"Bless you, my child. And bless you for having the courage to testify at service this morning. I hope my regular parishioners were taking notes."

Pearline muttered something under her breath and disappeared, only to reappear two minutes later with a soup bowl heaped full of blueberry pie, ice cream, and chocolate sauce.

"My heavens!" he exclaimed. "The Lord is bountiful tonight. Would you care to join me in prayer?"

From the other side of the bouquet, I heard Clem say, "You go ahead on your own, Reverend. The rest of us will talk amongst ourselves. I'll save the news until you're done."

There it was; another stratagem was in the offing. Loretta had the same dumbfounded look on her face I had, but her husband didn't. Calvin was in on it, and we weren't.

AFTER THE DISHES had been taken away and coffee had been served, Clem tapped his spoon on the side of his water glass. The time I was dreading—the moment of the big announcement—had arrived. He stood up and said, "Thirty-six hours from this very minute, I'll be undergoing an operation that will determine whether I live or die. The odds are not in my favor, but there is an advantage to the prospect of unsudden death. It is the ability to prepare for the eventuality. With that in mind, I beg your indulgence while I make a few announcements.

"First off, I'd like to thank Vernon, Eloise, and their friends for visiting us this week. It has been the best medicine an unwell man could get."

Marion and Birdie nodded while Eloise replied, "You're more than welcome. It was our pleasure." Loretta took my hand and squeezed it.

"Next, I'd like to thank Calvin Millet, who has been the finest friend an arrogant old codger could have for the last four years. I may not have another opportunity, so I'd like to present you with a small gift as an expression of my gratitude."

Clem pulled an envelope out of his jacket pocket and handed it to Calvin, who accepted it with a simple, "Thank you." I wasn't expecting that. Judging from the look on Loretta's face, she wasn't either. We were dumbfounded again.

Clem turned his attention to his sister. "We haven't had much of a chance to visit because of my health, Clara, but you should know that Calvin has agreed to stay on as the custodian of the Tucker Trust for as long as you wish. He's also agreed to help you put together a new board. I apologize for giving you such short notice, but you two will need to get started on that next week."

There it was; that was the big surprise. "But why, honeypot?" I protested. "You're going to be just fine."

"I hope you're right, Wilma, and more than you know. As of midnight tomorrow, I will resign my positions as chairman of the Tucker Trust and the National Bank of the Plains. If I survive, I intend to spend my autumn years golfing, hunting, and doting over my new wife."

The room froze at the utterance of "new wife." Loretta squeezed my hand so hard that my fingers turned white.

Clem walked around the table to my end. "Forgive me for not getting down on one knee, but neither one can take the weight alone. Before I go under the knife, I'd like to propose marriage one last time."

Dumbfounded does not begin to describe my reaction. I attempted to unlock my jaw, but I couldn't find the key. All that came out was a solitary, "Uh . . ."

"Don't get your tail in a knot about the prenup. I've amended the bylaws of the trust and changed my will. It doesn't matter whether you say yes or no, you'll be taken care of for the rest of your life."

"But, but, but this is so sudden . . ."

"A friend of ours says that uncertainty is the spice of life, Wilma. What could be more uncertain than an impromptu wedding on the eve of major surgery? Pastor Hooper is ready to say the words. Calvin has the bands and will be my best man. Tell me if I'm wrong, but you may be able to recruit a maid of honor at the table here. Let's do it right now."

The first thought that entered my mind was my previous experience with the institution of matrimony. The second was, "I can't get married; I have guests!" The third, which actually came out of my mouth, was, "What about a marriage license?"

"Good try, but Calvin took care of it on Tuesday."

I was the victim of a conspiracy! Holding back the tears, I announced, "This is too much of a surprise, honeypot. I need a minute to myself."

Loretta knew what I meant by "myself" and beat me to the powder room. You might assume that we didn't have much space to maneuver, but it was Clem's powder room, in the River House. It had a shower stall, two sinks, a toilet, and a bidet—yes, a bidet, in Nebraska—and there was enough space left over for a bar-sized pool table.

"Holy shit, Wilma!" my best friend shrieked. "Did you know this was coming?"

"Of course I did; that's why I dressed in black—for my own wedding! I bet the widows saw it, though. At least one of them might have had the good grace to warn me before I chose my attire for the evening."

"Well, they didn't, and you can't hide in here till Sunday, either. What are you going to do?"

"Go get Mr. Moore."

"That's it? That's your answer? You're so overwhelmed by Clem's proposal that you're forming a committee."

"After I pee. Get Mr. Moore."

Loretta is such a trooper. That woman would take on a pack of wolves with a nail file and a hairbrush if I asked her to. She knocked on the door a few minutes later, just as I was washing my hands. After she and Mr. Moore filed in, I closed the door and locked it.

"How is Clem?" I inquired. "Is he okay?"

"He's at the bar," Loretta answered, "playing gin rummy with Calvin."

"So he's not too disappointed?"

"I wouldn't say that, darlin', but you can probably rule out suicidal."

"What about Clara and the widows?"

"Relax, Wilma. They're shooting the breeze with Pastor Hooper on the back porch. You wanted me to bring Vern; he's here. Let's get on with it."

He could have said something nice to break the ice, but he didn't. I was left to ask, "What should I do, Mr. Moore?"

This is the point in the movie where the music crescendoes and the wise man is supposed to say, "Follow your heart, Wilma." But he didn't. Instead, he said matter-of-factly, "It's tomorrow morning. You're married to Clem. How do you feel?"

"Scared, trapped, afraid I made a mistake."

"Okay; let's try your other option. It's tomorrow morning, but you didn't marry Clem. Now how do you feel?"

Loretta sighed and put her arm around my shoulder. I replied, "I'm in a bit of a box, aren't I?"

He smiled and kissed me on the cheek. "I'm meeting with Clara in the morning anyway. I'll take care of her oatmeal."

Chapter 33

I AM FARFETCHED

DESPITE THE SPONTANEITY, I have to say that it was a lovely little wedding. Calvin and Consuela rearranged the furniture on the porch so we had room to gather together, Loretta filched a few flowers from the table and made me a cute bouquet, and Pastor Hooper kept the words short and sweet. I halfway hoped that somebody would object at the last second, but no one who could read my mind was inclined to intervene. After we said our "I do's" and smooched, the party applauded as if they meant it and Marie threw Uncle Ben's converted rice on everybody.

Clem stood by my side while we weathered the inevitable congratulations, but then he whispered in my ear, "Can you steer our guests to the bar? I need to have a quick mano-a-mano with Vernon."

That was it; that was the entire ceremony. My first sexual experience was a marathon in comparison. "Right this minute, honeypot?" I asked, hoping to savor my bliss a little longer. "You can't put it off?"

"I wish, but I can't put anything off; not anymore."

"How long will you be?"

"Fifteen minutes, twenty max; I promise. Organize a square dance; play Scrabble with the widows. I'll be back before you can spell dosie-do."

"I'll be organizing a firing squad if you're not back in half an hour. I know where you keep your guns."

"You're a hoot, Wilma. Thanks for makin' an honest man of me."

"Don't thank me, you scallywag. You haven't made it through the night yet."

Clem whispered into Mr. Moore's ear, then the two of them disappeared into his office down the hall. I noticed Marie heading that way just a minute later.

After they were settled in, my new husband said, "Before we get going, I have to thank you again for coming down tonight. It means the world to Wilma and me, and I appreciate you bringing Clara along, too. Tell me if I'm wrong, but she seems to be enjoying the evening."

"I believe she is, including the spontaneous wedding."

"How about you? Were you surprised?"

"Pardon me for saying so, but no, I wasn't."

"Is that so? What was the tell?"

"Heirs. You had one estranged daughter at the beginning of the week. Tonight, you acquired two stepdaughters, two grandsons, and two granddaughters. It was quite a coup."

"In case you didn't notice, one of my new grandsons just happens to have the sharpest head for numbers I've ever seen. But don't make the mistake of believing that heirs were the only reason I got hitched. In fact, that's why I wanted to chat tonight. My thoughts should be with my new bride, but this deal of ours is weighing heavily on my mind."

"Uh oh! 'Weighing heavily' isn't the sort of phrase an old

salesman likes to hear. Should I be steeling myself for disappointment?"

"That depends on you, Vernon. I've tried my damnedest to buy your story, I really have, but I'm not comfortable with it. To be brutally honest, I think it's a pile of theoretical horseshit."

"That's a pity. Where did I fail?"

"Everywhere. I can't bring myself to buy a word of it."

"I'm sorry, Clem; I did my best. Is that all you wanted to tell me?"

Mr. Moore began to stand but Clem said, "Hold on there, cowpoke. I don't want to go under the knife thinking that I might've thrown the baby out with the bathwater."

"I can see why. The image is terrifying. What can I do to help?"

"For openers, you can help me sort through all this uncertainty shit. It's like nothing I ever heard before. It's just too farfetched."

"Too farfetched or too illogical?"

"What do you mean? Aren't they the same thing?"

"Not at all. If all the mass in the universe was condensed into a single ball, how big would it be?"

Clem frowned then answered, "I don't have any idea, Vernon. I don't have any idea why it's relevant either."

"Humor me; take a shot at it anyway."

"We're talking the entire universe, right?"

"End to end."

"Okay. It has to be a trick question, and I read someplace that atoms are mostly space, so I'd guess that it could all be squeezed into a ball the size of a single star, like our sun."

"The universe is comprised of hundreds of billions of galaxies, Clem, each with billions of stars. How could so many be squeezed into a single star?"

"You asked me to take a shot at it; that's my shot. Are you

gonna tell me the answer, or are we gonna bat the little white ball back and forth across the net until sunup?"

"Your second guess was closer. According to the latest research, all the mass in the known universe was compacted into a space the size of a golf ball just before the Big Bang. One trillionth of a second later, it was spread across the visible universe. A trillionth of a second! To me, that's the very definition of farfetched, but it's also consistent with the latest data analyzed by the world's best cosmologists. In layman's terms, it's logical."

"So God made heaven and Earth out of a golf ball. He's omnipotent; He's supposed to be able to do that kind of shit. What's your point?"

"That the universe is so large, so fantastic, and so old that anything we say about it, even something as simple as its origin, will ultimately be farfetched."

"We're not talking about the origin of the goddamned universe, Vernon. We're talking about little old me."

"Fair enough. Name something that isn't farfetched; anything at all."

Clem picked up a paper clip. "How about this?"

"Good choice. What could me more common than a paper clip?"

"Exactly. I rest my case."

"How many are made each year?"

"Jesus, Vernon! I have no idea."

"Hundreds of millions? Billions? Tens of billions."

"Let's not go overboard. A few billion, max."

"Fair enough. What were the odds that that one paper clip would end up on your desk?"

After a pause, Clem said, "Okay. How about Wilma? That woman is the salt of the earth. She's as unfarfetched as anybody I've ever met."

"Really? What were the odds that Wilma's parents would meet and marry, much less conceive a child with her exact genetic composition, and what were the odds that their parents would meet, marry and produce them? If you think about it, you quickly come to the conclusion that the odds against any one individual's existence are beyond astronomical. Ultimately, only one mathematical condition permits it. Do you know what it is?"

"No, but I'm willing to bet that I can rule out destiny."

"The correct answer is a chaos theory, Clem. It says that everything becomes impossibly unlikely over time, but some things must ultimately exist, even a wonderfully farfetched concoction like a Wilma Porter."

My new husband wasn't impressed. "Net it out for me, Vernon. What the hell are you trying to say here?"

"That you can't dismiss any idea simply because it's farfetched, because *everything* is farfetched through the lens of time. However, you may dismiss any idea if it's illogical. That, in fact, is the very essence of intellect."

"I still don't get it."

"Everything that you and I have discussed about 'reasoned faith' may seem farfetched, but it is a logical extension of a single, simple assumption: that the universe is a massive uncertainty engine created by a self-serving but benevolent God. What more logical, less farfetched alternative do you have? The Bible?"

"No way, cowboy. I'm not fallin' into that trap. If I even hint that it's less farfetched, I'll get an earful of arks and parting seas. Thanks, but I don't even want to go there."

"Why not? It doesn't matter whether those stories are fact or parable; what are they really about?"

"It's the Bible, Vernon. It's about God."

"Think about it Clem. Is the Bible really about God, or is it a collection of stories about men like Noah, Moses, and Jesus? And how are they portrayed: as men, or as men with special powers who intervened in the affairs of man on behalf of God?"

"So they were Biblical relief pitchers? Is that what you're saying?"

"Exactly! The Bible can't be more or less farfetched than an uncertainty-based theory of divine intervention because it's the same story, only told from an ancient perspective."

Clem had to think about that for a second, then he said, "Okay, then I have another problem. If God delegates intervention to men, doesn't that put a cap on the size of miracles? Doesn't that mean that little ones are in but big ones are out?"

"Big miracles? Like what?"

"Like calling in a rainstorm, for instance."

"There are many kinds of relief pitchers in baseball, Clem: left-handers and right-handers, long relievers, short relievers, set-up men, closers. In the vast expanse between God and man, who is to say that some of His aces can't part a sea, or heal the sick, or send for rain?"

"So you can bring the rain. Is that what I'm supposed to believe?"

"You're supposed to believe what your heart will allow you to believe. From a purely theoretical standpoint, though, the real problem isn't scale; it's scarcity. In order to maintain uncertainty, the quantity of miracles would have to be extremely low, wouldn't it? Otherwise, the cumulative weight of so many 'impossible' outcomes would inevitably lead to the conclusion that a supernatural force was intervening in the affairs of men."

"What in God's name are you selling now, Vernon? Are you trying to tell me that I'm getting a cheap deal because miracles are scarce?"

"We're only discussing the theory of divine intervention,

Clem, but the theory says that intervention must be invisible, delegated, and scarce. It's not my job to tell you whether I'm offering you a good deal or not. You'll have to come to your own conclusion on that one."

"Thanks, but I may have figured that out by myself. Right now, my conclusion is that seventy-five million dollars is one hell of a lot of money to pay for a goddamned theory."

"But why? It's virtually identical to yours."

"Identical to mine? What the hell does that mean?"

"On Monday, you told me that men make miracles and God has abandoned us. Think about it. What has changed since then?"

My new groom couldn't come up with an answer, so Mr. Moore did it for him. "One thing has changed, Clem, and only one: the men are still making the miracles, but God is back at the helm. Do you remember the Deist's Paradox?"

"I'm sorry; I was going to write it down but I forgot."

"Not to worry; it goes:

A benevolent God would intervene in the affairs of men from time to time;
But God has not intervened in the last two thousand years;
Therefore, He has abandoned us.

"Now, however, we understand that a truly benevolent God would not intervene in the affairs of men, at least not directly. But, by a quirk of math and your own accounts, it appears that He continues to intervene indirectly nonetheless. Therefore the paradox is solved, and not only once, but twice! Isn't that good news?"

My husband groused. "I suppose."

"Then I'm mystified, Clem. Why aren't you thrilled? More to the point, why aren't you willing to pay me more today than you were at the beginning of the week?"

My new spouse said, "I can't put it in words, Vernon, but my gut is telling me that I'm missing something, and it's damned important."

"Now, that's a fair objection. For the kind of money you're paying, you shouldn't miss a thing, important or otherwise. What can I do to help you find it?"

"Nothing for the moment. I need to return to my bride or I'll be sleeping on the porch tonight. We're on again at ten a.m., right?"

"Yes, but tomorrow's meeting will have to be our last. I leave immediately afterwards."

"Well, then, it'll have to be a damned good meeting, won't it? Otherwise, you could be leaving empty-handed."

"If I do, Clem, who stands to lose the most: you or me?"

"You're a smart man, Vernon. I'll see if I can figure that out between now and tomorrow morning."

Chapter 34

....

A PIG IN A POKE

A ROUND ONE A.M., after the curtain had come down on my unrehearsed wedding and the last of the supporting cast and conspirators had left, the groom and I retreated to the master suite with a chilled bottle of French bubbly. A gentle breeze was blowing in from the river so it was cool enough to cuddle in bed, and I was almost in the mood.

Clem put his arm around me and said, "We need to think about a honeymoon, Wilma. Where'd you like to go? Pick anywhere in the world."

"I haven't given it a minute of thought, honeypot."

"Europe? Australia? The South Pacific?"

"I'll go anywhere, so long as it's not Las Vegas or a country where a girl can get diseases. Why don't you pick the place and surprise me?"

"You want another surprise? You didn't take much of a shine to my dinner surprise, not at first anyway."

"I didn't see it coming, that's all. If I hadn't been so busy with Mr. Moore and the widows, I might've thought of it myself." A Circle girl is always a Circle girl, even on her nuptial night. I snuggled up to Clem and added, "You had your twenty minutes with Mr. Moore and then some. Are you two still talking about the same old business deal?"

"You mean the deal he never should've told you about in the first place?"

"Uh huh."

"We're down to the short hairs, but something is gnawing at my gut. I can't seem to put my finger on it."

"You can't?"

"My gut is never wrong, Wilma. If I don't pay attention, I could end up paying a king's ransom for a pig in a poke."

I was never a professional salesperson, but "pig in a poke" didn't sound like a buying signal to me. For the first time in my life, I broke a promise to my best friend. "I wouldn't want one of those either, honeypot, but did Mr. Moore tell you what the king's ransom is for?"

"Why would he tell me that? Is it material to the deal?"

I allowed one last wave of cold, wet regret to wash over my body before saying, "Lo says he's going to give the money to the farmers . . ."

Clem's face turned red-orange in a flash and a purple vein jumped out of his forehead. "He's going to give my money to the goddamned farmers! That's the . . ." Then his anger subsided as quickly as it had surfaced and he did something that scared me to death: he thanked me. "You've helped me more than you could imagine, Wilma. That's the last piece of the puzzle. Now I know how to play out the hand."

"You do?"

"Clear a spot on the dining-hall wall, Wilma. I've got Saint Vernon dead to rights."

For all his confidence, Clem's stomach was a bit unsettled after we turned out the lights, so I stroked the back of his neck for a while and he nodded off like an old hound dog. Naturally, I couldn't get to sleep myself. I was worried about my sick husband. I was worried that I had said the wrong thing. I was worried about Loretta and my goddaughter. I was worried about my guests, especially Mr. Moore.

I hadn't packed an overnight bag.

I was still wide awake when Clem went to the bathroom in the middle of the night. For those of you who have yet to reach your silver years, three a.m. trips to the toilet are not uncommon amongst the older set. But Clem stayed too long, even for a man, so I decided to take a peek. He was sitting on the toilet with his head in his hands.

"I feel like shit," he moaned.

"What did you expect?" I replied valiantly, just like a bona fide wife. "You ate a pound of porterhouse steak and you put Béarnaise sauce on your fries—Loretta saw you—and then you had a big bowl of blueberry pie a la mode and half a magnum of champagne."

He groaned again and waved me off, so I left him alone, but you know what I was thinking: that he had deluded himself into believing that he could defeat Mr. Moore, and that his healthy days were over.

I was thinking that I had married a dead man.

CLEM RETURNED FROM his sojourn in the bathroom and was sawing wood again in no time, but I had no such luck. After tossing and turning for two more hours, I dragged myself out of bed and headed for the kitchen. I needed to cleanse my soul, but it was all of five twenty-five by the time I had the coffee pot on, and that was too early to call to anybody except the poor sod who had night duty at the 9-1-1 switchboard in the firehouse. Being the courteous person I am, I waited until the sweet scent of freshly brewed coffee filled the room, then I dialed Loretta.

She whispered, "Wilma? Is that you?"

"I'm sorry for calling so early . . ."

"What time is it, darlin'? My alarm clock says five thirty-one. That can't be right, can it?"

"I couldn't wait, Lo. Clem is going to turn down the deal."

"He's what? Give me a minute to put on a robe and go downstairs."

I took a sip of hot coffee and looked out the window. There was a faint, pinkish-yellow glow on the eastern horizon, which I interpreted to be a sign that the sun was coming up and the world hadn't ended after all. Either that, or Missouri was on fire.

"Wilma? Are you still there?"

"Where else could I go at this hour?"

"You're right; it was a silly question. Can we start over? What's going on, girl? It's your wedding night. You're supposed to sleep till noon."

"Clem got sick to his stomach, Lo, and I know why. He's going to turn down the deal with Mr. Moore."

"He is? I don't believe it! What did he say?"

"He said he won't pay a king's ransom for a pig in a poke. Those were his exact words."

"I've been living in farm country for more years than I can count, Wilma, and I still have no idea what a pig in a poke is. It doesn't sound like something I'd pay seventy-five million dollars for, though." Loretta paused, then carried on. "Wait a minute. We're talking about your scurrilous, sick bastard of a husband here. Are they meeting again this morning?"

"As far as I know."

"Then the deal might not be dead, Wilma. He might be thinking that he can force Vern to lower the price."

"Maybe so, but he said he had Mr. Moore dead to rights, and it's my fault."

"Your fault? How come?"

I swallowed a mouthful of dark, bitter-tasting betrayal and replied, "I told him what Mr. Moore was going to do with the money."

"Oh no! Tell me you didn't."

"I did, and I am so sorry, but I just couldn't help myself. I was desperate; I thought it might change his mind." I couldn't see the disappointment on my best friend's face, so I had to await my rebuke. Even though it was only a few ticks of the clock, it reminded me of sitting alone in my childhood room with the door shut, waiting for my father to come home.

Happily, Lo is not my father, rest his soul. "That's okay, dar-lin'," she said. "I might have done the same thing if I had been in your shoes, but now I need to get my fanny in motion. Somebody has to get over to your place and tell Vern that the cat's out of the bag."

"Will you call me afterwards?"

"I will, darlin'. In the meantime, you need to think about something else."

"What?"

"If Clem and Vern can't make a deal, what happens to the odds of rain?"

"Oh my God, Lo! I was so worried about my husband that I didn't even think about the drought. Hang on for a minute. I'll turn on the Weather Channel."

It was almost time for "local weather on the eights," but a commercial for Las Vegas was just finishing up. As a big, black limousine pulled away from the airport, the slogan "What hap-pens here, stays here" flashed across the screen in neon colors. It was my just deserts; I deserved it.

"Wilma? Are you still there?"

"Hold on, Lo. The weather's coming on any second." The bright lights of Las Vegas faded away and a smiley, bearded salesman in a flannel shirt and an apron popped up on the screen. "I was wrong," I reported. "It's a commercial for stain remover."

"There's no rush. We've got half the morning."

After he was done removing grape juice, mustard, grass stains, and engine oil from a white shirt, a lithe, skimpily dressed blonde appeared on the TV, bouncing along the floor on a silver-colored ball the size of a hassock. I wondered if Clara had one. As far as I knew, she had every exercise gadget ever invented.

"Wilma?"

"It's another darned commercial. If this is the Weather Channel, don't they have to put the weather on sooner or later? Oops! Wait a second, Lo. There it is. Hang on. The temperature's going up to ninety-nine this afternoon, and the humidity will be up, too."

"Only ninety-nine? What about tomorrow?"

I watched in anticipation, but then I closed my eyes and sighed. "The front is still headed in our direction, but it's moving eastward, too. Omaha may get rain, but not much. The chance of measurable precipitation in the tri-state area has dropped to twenty-five per cent."

"That can't be right. If the odds of rain are going down, the odds of a deal have to be going up."

"No they don't, Lo. It's the official weather report. We're all going to lose out. Everybody's going to go bust."

I admit it. Somewhere between the drought, the deal, Clem's cancer, and my sudden marriage, I had misplaced my faith, but Lo would have none of it. "Wilma Porter Tucker," she said, "you go straight to the nearest sink and wash your mouth out with soap. Vernon Moore did not come back to bear witness to our defeat. He came to save us."

"Then why don't I fell like I'm being saved?"

"That's a darned good question. You just married the richest man in southeast Nebraska, and there was no prenup. Since I'm your best friend, and because my curiosity was eating me up, I asked Cal how much money you're worth last night."

"You did? What did he say?"

"He said it was confidential."

"He wouldn't tell you? Why not?"

"Because I'd tell you. Where did he get an idea like that?"

Chapter 35

....

AT THE CORNER OF THIRD AND PEA

SEAGULL AND DRAGONFLY, the motor coaches owned by Eloise Richardson and Bertha Fabian, were already gone by the time that Loretta and Laverne got to the Come Again. Laverne wanted to peek inside the Dolphin, but her mother was less than enthused about the prospect of an unchaperoned encounter with Road Rage. After a short but emotional dispute, Lo managed to steer my sweet little goddaughter across the parking lot and into my house, where they found Mr. Moore and the Widow Marion fixing Clara's breakfast in the kitchen.

"Poppy!" Laverne shouted.

"Sweetheart! What a nice surprise!"

Mr. Moore smiled and gave his little girl a giant-sized hug while Loretta said to Marion, "Have Birdie and Eloise already left?"

"Sadly, yes, but they wanted me to pass on their best wishes, especially Birdie. She's quite fond of Laverne, you know. Can I offer you a glass of orange juice or a cup of tea?"

"Thanks, but I was hoping to speak with Vern. Alone. Oops! I guess you knew that."

Mr. Moore replied, "Can it wait a few minutes, Lo? I promised Wilma I'd take Clara's breakfast up this morning."

Loretta checked her watch. "That depends. Will you have time to walk Lovey and me to preschool?"

"Lions, tigers, and bears couldn't keep me away."

"Then go ahead. I wouldn't want Clara to miss out on breakfast. Would you like to go, Lovey?"

"Can I, Mommy?"

"Uh huh. Maybe Poppy will give you a ride on his shoulders. Can you do that, Vern?"

"I am my daughter's steed," he replied, "except when I'm carrying a tray of cinnamon oatmeal, orange juice, and banana nut bread up two flights of stairs."

After Mr. Moore and my goddaughter had left for the loft, the Widow Marion inquired, "Did you enjoy the dinner party last night, dear?"

"Yes, and the grand finale was, well . . . so unexpected. Out of curiosity, did you or your partners see it coming? Wilma wanted to know."

"Even if we had, we could never have said anything. It would've spoiled the surprise. Not the sort of thing a guest should do, wouldn't you say?"

"I suppose. I take it you're leaving this morning."

"Yes, very shortly."

"Where are you headed?"

"I haven't quite decided. West, most likely. Do you have any recommendations?"

After a pause, Lo answered, "If you haven't been already, you might think about visiting the Little Bighorn National Monument in Montana. It's the spookiest place I've ever seen."

"The spookiest? Why, pray tell?"

"More than two hundred cavalrymen died on the battlefield at Little Bighorn, plus an ungodly number of Sioux. I stopped by with a friend on what we thought was a perfect summer day, but the weather turned cloudy, windy, and cold as we pulled up to the monument, as if the combatants were still haunting the plain and fighting mad to boot. When we returned to the main road afterwards, the sun was shining and it was a warm, clear day again. I'm not a superstitious person by nature, but that was not the sort of thing I could explain with microclimates."

"How fascinating! I'll make a point of stopping by."

"But you won't stay long, will you?" Loretta surmised.

"What do you mean?"

"Your role is different, isn't it? You don't stay for six days at a time like Vern does."

Marion nodded. "Very good, dear. That's quite correct."

"But you can't tell me any more, can you?"

"I'd love to, but you'll have to find that out for yourself, I'm afraid."

"Where should I start? Winchester?"

Marion did a double take, then said, "I'd forgotten; Vernon mentioned it to your county attorney, didn't he? It's a lovely town to be sure, one of my favorites. You'd never guess it was once the capitol of England, except for the great cathedral, of course."

"So you've been there."

"Oh yes, many times. I was born in England, you know."

"I thought you might have been." Without missing a beat, Lo added, "Just out of curiosity, did you come to the U.S. on a ship?"

"By ship? Do you have a particular ship in mind, dear? I have a sense that you do."

"The *Titanic*."

"Well, well, well. Someone's been doing their homework, haven't they? It is true: an Englishwoman by my name did perish on the *Titanic*; a milliner traveling third-class. Many of the lifeboats were already at sea when the third-class passengers made it top-side, or so I've been told. It must have been heartbreaking."

"You didn't answer my question, Marion."

"I'm sorry, dear, but I mustn't. It would be against the rules."

"Against whose rules? Lohengrin's Children?"

"Of course. Isn't that what we've been discussing all along?"

The conversation was cut short by the return of Mr. Moore and Laverne, who was riding high on her Poppy's shoulders. He kneeled to the ground so she could dismount, then she stuck out her lower lip and said, "Auntie Clara cried."

"She did? Is she okay? Should Mommy go upstairs?"

Mr. Moore replied, "It would be better if you left her alone. She'll be fine."

"Then why was she crying?"

"Because Poppy's going away," Laverne answered, pouting herself.

"She cried because you're leaving, Vern? What's going on be-tween you two?"

"We're friends, and we've just said good-bye. I need to return a call before we head off to preschool. Is that a problem?"

Loretta frowned. "Not if you make it snappy, darlin', but don't think you're off the hook yet. I have more questions about you and Clara."

While Mr. Moore was upstairs, Loretta and Laverne walked the Widow Marion out to her motor coach, where they said their fond farewells. There were no tears, whispered messages, or secret psychic handshakes as Loretta had feared. Marion was the proper English aunt, even a bit detached. I figure the wid-ows were used to leaving people. Either that, or their husbands taught them detachment, just like mine taught me.

• • •

AT LAVERNE'S INSISTENCE, Mr. Moore hoisted her up on his shoulders again for the short walk to preschool. As they left the shade of my porte-cochere and strolled down the driveway, Loretta remarked, "It feels odd, doesn't it? Only a few hours ago, Wilma's parking lot was cheek-to-jowl with giant RVs. Now it looks so empty. Will they ever be back?"

"Auntie Marion will," Laverne said from high on the saddle.

"When, Lovey?"

"I dunno. Giddyup, Poppy! Go faster!"

Mr. Moore picked up the pace, but Loretta grabbed his elbow. "Don't you even think about it, Vern. Lovey's school is only a few blocks away and I have questions."

Mr. Moore dutifully slowed down. Laverne said, "Phooey!"

"That's better. Now, what's the deal between you and Clara? Should I be jealous? And don't tell me she's too old. Some folks say you're old enough to be her father."

"Is that so? I take it that the *Lady Be Good* theory has resurfaced."

"It has, but don't tell me your real age, for God's sake. It would scare me to death. I just want the skinny on Clara."

"There's no mystery, Lo. If her brother dies, Clara will become the controlling shareholder in the Tucker Trust. She had to be prepared for the possibility, but Clem was too ill to take care of it himself so I stepped in on his behalf."

"Of course you did. Why'd I even ask? Are you stopping at the River House on your way out of town?"

"Yes. Why?"

"I have a little tidbit of information you'll need before you see Clem." Myself, I would have beaten around the bush, but Loretta just blurted it out. "He knows about your plan to give the money to the farmers."

Mr. Moore stopped in his tracks and turned to face Loretta.

"That was pure speculation, Lo," he said through gritted teeth. "I never said a word."

"Which means you didn't deny it either. I broke my promise and told Wilma, and she broke her promise and told Clem, just like you said she would. It was my fault, Vern. I should have listened, but I thought it would help Wilma understand what you've been up to all week."

"Did you tell anyone else?"

"No, of course not."

Laverne pulled on Mr. Moore's white mane and said, "Gid-dyup, Poppy! I have to go to preschool!"

As they resumed their journey, Mr. Moore asked, "How did Clem react? Did you get any feedback from Wilma?"

"She said that the deal is all but dead."

"Dead?"

"Her words, not mine, and I disagree anyway. Did you see the weather report this morning?"

"No. I haven't checked."

"The odds of rain are down to twenty-five percent, darlin'. If your deal with Clem is on the rocks, then why aren't they going up? Have you lost your touch?"

They turned the corner of Third and Pea just then and Laverne shouted, "Whoa, horsey! There's my preschool! You have to let me down, Poppy!"

Hayes County Elementary is a one-level cement and glass structure with a flat gravel roof and exterior hallways. The grade school was closed for the summer, but the kindergarten and pre-school remained open year round for the convenience of work-ing mothers. A thin, yellow haze hung over the grounds when the three arrived, but it was cool enough in the early morning for laughing little children to play on the swings, the slide, and the jungle gym.

Laverne pointed. "Those are my friends. Over there! I have to go."

Mr. Moore put his daughter on the sidewalk ever so carefully, as if she was a bowl of soup that had been filled to the brim. "Will you do your best in preschool? Will you do what your mommy and daddy say?"

"I'll be a good girl, Poppy, but you better come back. If you don't, I'll get sick and you'll have to come."

Loretta kissed her daughter on the top of her head. "Go and play with your friends, Lovey. I'll walk Poppy home."

I guess my unusual lodger had flunked detachment class.

"One last hug, sweetheart?"

Laverne held out her arms and Mr. Moore swept her up. He closed his eyes and squeezed and squeezed, until Lo touched his shoulder and said, "You have to let her go, Vern. You have to let her go."

"Good-bye, Poppy," Laverne whispered as he put her down, then a single tear trailed down her cheek. It was the first time she had cried—ever, since the day she was born. She felt the dampness with her index finger, then tasted it and looked up at her mother.

"It's just a tear. Now go. Go to your friends."

"Will Poppy be okay?"

"He's our knight in shining armor, Lovey. He's invincible."

Lo rarely underestimated Mr. Moore, but that was the exception. He put his hands on his knees and wept openly as his daughter ran away. Lo rubbed his neck for a few seconds, but then she took his hand and led him across the street. "Lovey can't see you like this, darlin'. She'll come back and you'll have to go through it all over again."

"I don't suppose you have a Kleenex on you."

"I'm sorry. That's Wilma's department. Be a man; use your sleeve."

They stopped at the corner so that Mr. Moore could wipe his eyes. According to Lo, it took both sleeves.

"Lovey has never cried," she said. "Did you know that?"

"No, but it was one tear."

"Well, it was a start. Thank you for that. A girl has to cry."

"Apparently, so do old men." Mr. Moore inhaled deeply, then said, "We have to say good-bye here, Lo."

She wasn't prepared for that. "Now? Why? I can walk you back to Wilma's. I can fix you a cup of tea."

"An old man's heart won't stand another break. Please, let me go."

"But I have more questions, Vern, a lot more."

"And I have my last appointment with Clem. I can't be late, Lo; I have to go."

"Then answer one more question. Just one more, for Lovey?"

No man can refuse a daughter, not even in the third person. "Okay," he replied, "but please make it quick."

Without a smidgen of hesitation, Loretta locked her eyes on Mr. Moore's and asked, "Did Marion and the other two widows suffer like you did?"

"Excuse me?"

"Everything started with the *Lady Be Good,* didn't it? You were lost in the desert for days, without a drop of water. Did the widows survive horrible, near-death experiences, too? And isn't that why you said that you'd never want Lovey to take the entrance exam?"

"That's more than one question, Lo, and I can't answer any of them."

"Then let me try this another way. What was the point? Why was so much misery necessary? Was it a metaphor for Christ's suffering on the cross?"

Mr. Moore looked toward the horizon, as if he was thinking, "Funny; it didn't feel like a metaphor at the time." Then he answered, "Are we speaking in theory?"

"Of course we are, darlin'. Isn't that how we always talk?"

Loretta swore that time froze for the next fifteen seconds. Nothing moved, not the trees, not the wind, not even the children at the playground. In the stillness, Mr. Moore said, "The theory is that a man or a woman who can endure impossible hardship must fully value the gift of life, and must thus be incorruptible."

"So it is like Christ on the cross."

"He was already incorruptible, Lo, and my time has passed. We have to say good-bye."

Loretta knew that her time had passed, too, so she took Mr. Moore in her arms, right there on the corner of Third and Pea, and whispered, "You better come back. If you don't, I'll hunt you down like the scoundrel you are. Remember, I have Marion's number."

He kissed her lightly on the cheek and said, "I love you." Time started up again, laughing children could be heard in the distance, and he turned and walked away.

Loretta waited until he was out of sight, and then she counted to twenty. When he didn't return, she crossed the street and took a seat on a green bench at the edge of the playground. Lulu Tiller, the town veterinarian, came by with a few of her dogs just before lunchtime. It was the one hundred and twenty-second consecutive day of the drought and steaming hot, but Lo was still there. I never asked her why, but I don't believe she was waiting for Laverne, or even for Mr. Moore. I believe she needed some time to herself before she could go back to her home with Calvin.

Chapter 36

....

A GIFT HORSE

JOHN SMITH WAS WAXING Clem's black-on-black Porsche 911 convertible in the shade of the garage when Mr. Moore arrived at the River House. To me, that car looked like a giant doodlebug on wheels, but Clem loved it with an unnatural ardor. Before he got in, he would run his finger up the fender from the headlight to the driver-side mirror, like he was caressing it, and then he would say, "Are you ready to rumble, baby doll?" One weekend last spring, my wagon was in the shop and John was off somewhere with the limo, so I asked Clem if I could take the Porsche into Ebb to see my friends. You'd think that I had asked the man to fry a Fabergé egg. In the end, he drove me to town himself, grumbling all the way.

John walked over to Mr. Moore's Mustang and opened the door. "Morning," he said. "Mona tells me you're shipping out today. Is that so?"

"As soon as my meeting with Clem is over."

"I'm sorry to hear it, Mr. Moore. The Old Man goes on the chopping block at oh seven hundred tomorrow. Is he gonna make it?"

"I hope so. I hope he comes through with a clean bill of health."

"Me, too. That man will never be decorated for compassion, that's for sure, but I've seen worse. I don't suppose anybody told you where I was yesterday, did they?"

"No. Is it information I ought to have?"

"I was in Eden, Arizona, with Buford Pickett. We were investigating the widows."

"Eden? I've never been. How was it?"

"It's a ghost town, but Buford half expected it. He told me on the flight down that the widows died years ago. One of 'em was on the *Titanic*. He says you died in World War II."

"Is that so? How do I look for a corpse? Better than average?"

"For all I care, you could've caught a Minié ball in the Civil War, Mr. Moore. I'm not the kind of man who looks a gift horse in the mouth. Every day, my wife and I thank our lucky stars that you came here to help us, and so do our sons. If you ever need backup, anywhere in the world, just pick up the phone. I'll be on the next plane."

John extended his hand. My unusual lodger shook it. "Thanks for the offer. I may take you up on it one day. How are the newlyweds this morning?"

"That's a good question. The Old Man has been in his office all morning with the door shut. Mom's in the kitchen with Marie . . ."

"Mom?"

"She may be the new duchess, but she's still my mother-in-law."

"So she is. Doesn't that mean that the duke is your father-in-law, too?"

"I hadn't given it thought," John answered, "but I guess it does. Maybe he'll take me to a ballgame after he's better."

The TV was on when Mr. Moore walked into the kitchen, but

it was just background noise. Betwixt and between the twenty-nine congratulatory calls I had received from various Circle girls that morning, I was trying to explain to Marie that I had no intention of taking over the household cooking chores as long as she allowed me to bake every once in a while.

My erstwhile lodger took one look at Marie and asked, "Should I come back later?"

She sniffed, "Don't worry about me, Mr. Moore. I've been dicing onions for salsa. Can I make you a plate of huevos rancheros for brunch?"

"Thank you, but I've already eaten. I just wanted to check in before I see Clem. Tell me if I'm wrong, but it appears that the mistress of the house didn't get much sleep last night."

That's what a woman likes to hear from a man. "I didn't get a wink," I confessed. "The lord of the manor may have planned every detail of last night's ambush in advance, but he didn't spend five minutes thinking about the consequences of his trip to the hospital, like who was going to manage the manor or pay the bills while we're away. As soon as Marie and I get that sorted, I have to figure out what the heck I'm going to do with Clara and the Come Again."

"A short-term solution may be easier than you think. She'd like to accompany you and Clem to Omaha."

"She would? That's so brave! But are you sure she's up to it, Mr. Moore?"

"She'll be in your care, Wilma. She'll be fine."

"Then I'll handle all the arrangements. Clement and I have to stop by this afternoon anyway. It's not like I packed a bag last night." I don't know how other minds work, but mine jumps from one topic to another like it's got a mind of its own. Not packing a bag reminded me of the wedding, the wedding reminded me of the party, and the party reminded me of the widows. "Are your friends still in town?" I added. "I enjoyed their company so."

"They left this morning, but they wanted me to pass on their profuse thanks and their very best wishes. You have my credit card imprint. Send me the bill."

"I could be living out of a shopping cart under the Nemaha Bridge and you couldn't pay me a dime, Mr. Moore, and I don't want to hear any arguments either. You need to save your breath for my husband. He's in the office waiting for you."

"Fair enough. How's he feeling this morning?"

"He lost a rematch with the Béarnaise sauce and the blueberry pie in the middle of the night, but he's better now. I wouldn't call him cheery, though." I gulped and added, "Did you have a chance to talk to Loretta this morning?"

"I did."

"Then you're aware of how well informed he is, fully aware?"

Mr. Moore sighed. He didn't have to do that; I already knew he was unhappy with Lo and me. "I spoke to Loretta. Would you care to walk me down to Clem's office?"

As if I would even consider refusing. On the way, I tried to lighten up the conversation. "Did you ever see Silas the Second?" I asked.

"I didn't, but it was only a small disappointment, Wilma."

"It was?"

"There are other gentle ghosts, and I have time. I'll meet one face-to-face someday."

A thousand questions flooded into my mind just then, starting with, "Exactly how much time do you have?" But then the oddest thing happened: I discovered that all I wanted was the questions. I didn't know why—and it's not like the circumstance favored introspection—but in that instant I knew that I had had enough of answers.

We walked the last few steps to my husband's office in silence, and then I knocked on the door. From the other side, Clem hollered out, "It's open!"

Mr. Moore turned the knob and let himself in. From the hallway, I could see the groom sitting sideways behind his desk, cradling a long-barreled hunting rifle with a green khaki strap on his lap. That's not the sort of picture a bride wants to see, especially on the day before the big operation, but he looked up and waved. "Come on in. Take a load off."

"Are you okay, honeypot? Can I bring you a cup of tea?"

"I'm fine. I might have an espresso later on, but I'm still a little queasy in the tummy right now. How about you, Vernon?"

"Nothing for me, thanks."

"Then can you leave us to our own devices, Wilma? I'll call if I change my mind."

"Just give a shout," I replied. "I'll be close by." I left the door open a crack and ran to the kitchen to retrieve Marie. It's not like I couldn't listen in myself, but that woman can hear a cat crossing a carpet during a Stones concert.

"Have you ever seen one of these?" Clem asked. "This little jewel is a .416-caliber Winchester Model 70 with a Zeiss scope. It's not the most expensive hunting rifle out there, but it's one of the best. I took down the bighorn and the elk in the dining hall with this gun, both at more than a hundred yards. Those were two of the finer shots of my life."

"I wonder if the bighorn and the elk shared your opinion."

"I don't believe they had opinions. That's why they're called animals. Pardon my manners, though. I had forgotten your distaste for the sport of hunting. Give me a minute while I put ol' 'Chester back on the rack."

Mr. Moore observed, "You seem to be in a reflective mood this morning."

"Should I be doing handsprings across the lawn? I'm about to be opened up like a goddamned watermelon. If you've already fixed me, I'd like to know right now. I'd be happy to skip the operation and work on my golf game instead."

"Do you really think that that would be wise, Clem?"

"No, I don't. Since you won't give me any kind of guarantee, I believe that would be the second stupidest thing I could do."

"The second stupidest?"

"Begs the question, doesn't it? If that's the second stupidest, then what's number one?"

"Putting Béarnaise sauce on your fries again?"

"Good answer! I'll never repeat that mistake; I promise you that. But the stupidest thing I could do is pay you seventy-five million dollars. Do you know why?"

Mr. Moore hesitated, then replied, "Presumably because I failed to persuade you that God is still with us."

"You should give yourself more credit than that, Vernon. I wouldn't say I'm convinced, but I'm not convinced that He isn't on board either. That has to be a feather in your cap. What's more, I've upgraded my assessment of your ability to save my life."

"You have? As I recall, you had me at one in three on Monday. What am I today?"

"Conservatively, two-to-one in my favor."

"Then I'm confused, Clem. If your faith has doubled, then why don't we have a deal?"

"That, Vernon, is the seventy-five-million-dollar question. The answer is that I know what you intended to do with my money."

"You do? How could you know that?"

"Because you told Loretta, and that was a bonehead mistake, by the way. Expecting that woman to keep a secret is like letting a fox into the henhouse and expecting it to have creamed corn for dinner. It's contrary to the nature of the beast."

"I didn't tell her, Clem. She guessed."

My husband sat forward. "Then look me in the eye and tell me you didn't plan to give my money to the farmers. Go ahead."

"What if I did? Why would you care? You don't need the money to support your elaborate lifestyle, and you'd still be leaving millions to your heirs."

"Are you shittin' me, Vernon? Do you honestly believe that giving my money to those poor sodbusters would make a speck of difference? The family farm is finished in this part of the country; it's a relic of the past. The future is fuel-grade ethanol, but the only way we'll be able to compete against foreign producers is with economies of scale. A mom-and-pop farm is the opposite of economies of scale; it's the economics of futility. It's too much overhead, too little buying power, and a threadbare balance sheet wrapped into a puny, pea-pickin' package."

"Why? What happens if the farms are no longer drowning in debt? What happens to their buying power? What happens to their staying power?"

"Are you really that naïve, or are you just plain innumerate? There is no goddamned way that you can emancipate the farmers in this county with a measly seventy-five million dollars. Ten years from now, maybe twenty, they'll all be back at the same trough and Hayes County will be out of the ethanol race. In the future, eastern Nebraska will be tilled by large, efficient corporations who can leverage scale from seed to silo to biofuel plant. It's the only way we can be relevant in the second half of the century."

Mr. Moore didn't respond immediately, but then he said, "I'm starting to get the idea that you're not going to change your mind."

"It's not a change of mind, Vernon; it's a reversal of strategy, and a pisspoor reversal at that. Why the hell do you suppose I divested the trust of its tenant farmland three years ago, and why do you suppose I took over the National Bank of the Plains? I did it for one reason, and one reason only: to position the Tucker Trust, meaning my heirs, to benefit from a statewide shift to corporate ethanol production. Why in God's name would I consider spending even a dollar of my own money to defeat my own plan? It makes no sense to me at all. In fact, like I said, it would be the stupidest thing I could do."

"But you're not writing off the family farm, Clem. You're writing off a way of life, and it's not just their way of life; it's yours. Hayes County is the womb that spawned seven generations of Tuckers. If you don't save it, then who will?"

"Excuse me for stating the obvious, but isn't that your department? Weren't you sent here to save us for the third goddamned time? Haven't you already asked for rain?"

That must have set Mr. Moore back on his heels. "What do you mean?"

"If I've got a handle on this divine intervention shit, then there are only two possibilities: either you're not in God's Bullpen and it doesn't make a damned bit of difference what you do; or you are and you just might have an impact. I was on the fence until last night—when Wilma told me what you were going to do with my money. That convinced me that you're one of God's right arms after all, and nothing I've heard this morning has given me cause to change my mind. You see where I'm headin', don't you?"

"I believe so, yes."

"If you're really a man of God, then my money is immaterial; it's a nonissue. You've already asked for rain and you've already asked for my life. That's why the weather forecast changed, isn't it? And it's why I feel so much better, too."

"I can't take any credit for either, Clem."

"I've been payin' attention, Vernon; I got that part. What I don't understand is why you didn't ask me to write you a check on day one. You were in the hunt until I found out what you were goin' to do with the money."

"I needed time to put God back into your life," Mr. Moore answered. "I thought you'd be more amenable to a contribution if your faith in God was restored."

"A contribution? Jesus, Vernon! Did it ever enter your mind that seventy-five million dollars was a bit pricey for a goddamned contribution?"

"Not considering the source, and not considering the scale of the problem. It would save hundreds of farms."

"I'll tell you what will save hundreds of farms: some measurable goddamned precipitation. Is it gonna rain or not? The forecast was down this morning."

"I don't know."

"Then you don't know if I'm going to survive the operation either, do you?"

"I'm just like you, Clem. Sometimes I get what I ask for; sometimes I don't."

My new husband smiled. "You're an interesting man, Vernon, but we're no more alike than chalk and cheese, you and me. I'd be pleased to look as good as you when I'm pushing a hundred, though. If you could put in an extra word, I'd be very grateful."

"Really? How grateful would you be?"

The rest of the conversation was drowned out by two of Dot's cruisers, which pulled into the front courtyard one after the other with sirens on full howl. I ran to the foyer and threw open the door to see the sheriff and Pokie emerging from their respective vehicles, one to admire Clem's Porsche, the other to admire John Smith.

Dottie turned to me and said, "Congratulations, Wilma! The news is all over town. I'd give you a hug, but it'll have to wait. We've come for your famous lodger."

"Oh no! He's still in with Clem. You're not going to throw him in jail, are you?"

"Hell, no! He's got an appointment with the lieutenant governor at noon. We've got to get him to the county line by eleven o'clock."

"The lieutenant governor?"

"I'm just a poor civil servant, Wilma. I have no idea what that man is up to now. All I know is that I have to escort him to the county line."

From behind, I heard Mr. Moore say, "It's okay. Clem and I have completed our business. I'm ready to go."

I turned. "You have? You're all done?"

"Yes?"

"Did you make a deal?"

"You should discuss that with your husband."

"But Mr. Moore . . ."

"I have to go with Sheriff Hrnicek and Deputy Melhuse. Please keep an eye on Laverne and Loretta for me. If you ever need anything, don't hesitate to contact Marion."

What's a girl to do? As I began to well up, he took me in his arms and whispered, "I love you, Wilma. I'll miss you more than you could possibly know."

I tried to hold him, but he slipped from my grasp and was halfway across the courtyard before I could blubber out a fare-well. "Good-bye, Vernon," I cried.

He waved one last time before he got into his car, and then

Dottie led him away with Pokie bringing up the rear, sirens screaming and red-white-and-blue cherry poppers flash-dancing across the roof.

As they took off in a cloud of dust, I heard Marie shout above the din, "I'm so sorry, Wilma. The deal fell through. Clem didn't buy it."

Chapter 37

. . . .

SOMETHING OLD

I AM A COUNTRY GIRL. I don't typically have difficulty dealing with the harsher realities of life, but I was in the Marianas Trench of denial that day: I couldn't believe that I had married Clem Tucker on the spur of the moment after a four-year engagement; I refused to concede that Mr. Moore had left us again, possibly forever; I couldn't understand why my husband had turned down his help, no matter what the price was; and I couldn't face the possibility that I might be a widow in less than twenty-four hours. So I just stood there in the doorway staring at nothing in particular, while saline tears trailed down my cheeks and into the corners of my mouth.

Given enough time, I might have rooted to the spot, but Pearline called me to the kitchen phone. It was the Queen Bee, who may have been the last person on Earth that I wanted to talk to at that moment. "Wilma, you old fox!" she said. "I just heard from Lily that you and Clem tied the knot last night. Congratulations!"

"Thank you," I sniffed. "I'm thrilled."

"You might have warned us, girl. We would've had a proper bachelorette's party at the Abattoir: cheap wine, chocolate fon-due, Chippendale dancers, all the deadly sins."

"I had no idea that Clem was going to repropose, Mary. I wore black to my own wedding, for Christ's sake! Do you suppose that's bad luck?"

"A black dress? For the bride? How could that be bad luck? I heard that the widows left this morning. Did you have a chance to say bon voyage?"

"We said our bon whatevers last night after the ceremony. Why?"

"Flathead didn't show up at the firehouse this morning."

"He didn't?"

"Beryl's not home either. It wouldn't be such a mystery except that Virgie saw them walking up your driveway around six a.m. It seems that Beryl was carrying a stack of paperbacks and Flathead was pulling a suitcase."

"They were not!"

"It's an eyewitness report, Wilma. Dot sent a deputy over to Beryl's an hour ago. Their closets were half empty and the fridge was as clean as a whistle."

"Oh my! Do you know where they went?"

"No, but I thought you might. The widows were staying with you."

"Nobody said boo to me, Mary."

"Not even your famous lodger? Did he mention anything this morning?"

"Uh uh."

"Then Dot'll have to file a missing persons report. She just checked in, by the way. I take it that Vernon and Clem are done trying to outmaneuver each other."

"They're all done, Mary."

"I don't mean to be indelicate, but I need to know: did they reach an agreement or not?"

I sighed deeply. "You can relax. There was no deal."

After a second, she replied, "I'm sorry, Wilma, but I was afraid that's what you'd say."

"You were? How come?"

"The jet stream moved again. The storm front has turned due south and is picking up steam. It's expected to make Omaha by midnight."

"It is? What are the odds that we'll get rain in Hayes County?"

"Back to fifty percent and rising. Now they're saying we could get as much as half an inch by Saturday night."

"Oh my God!" I exclaimed. "It's happening. Mr. Moore is bringing the rain after all."

"Hold on a minute. My AA just stuck her head in my door." Mary came back on the line half a tick later. "Marta Kimball stopped breathing at Connie's flower shop not fifteen minutes ago. The EMT team got there in no time, but they couldn't revive her. Doc Wiley just pronounced her dead at the scene."

I am not a Catholic, but I genuflected anyway. "May she abide in heaven. That poor woman was never a particle of herself after Dean passed away." Then my mind bounced from poor Marta to my new husband, and in less time than it takes a hummingbird's heart to skip a beat. "I have to go, Mary. I have to check on Clem."

The door was shut when I got to his office, but I took a deep breath and just plunged on in. Calmly, he said, "I know we're man and wife now, but I'd appreciate it if you'd knock. I could've been in the middle of a long-distance conference call."

"I'm sorry, honeypot. I will from now on."

"Thank you. I saw the sheriff escorting Vernon off the lot. Is he under arrest?"

"Not so far as I know. Dot said he has an appointment with the lieutenant governor."

"The lieutenant governor! That liberal turncoat bastard! What in God's name is Vernon selling him?"

"How would I know? I thought he might have said a word to you."

"Well, he didn't, but I can guess. We just spent thirty minutes debating the fate of the family farm. That man is a goddamned relic; he was born in the wrong century. Wait a minute; I take that back. We don't really know what century he was born in, do we? Did he tell you that we concluded our business?"

"He said to check with you," I replied, as if I wasn't already in the know. "How did it end up?"

Clem sat back in his chair and opined, "You have to give the man credit. He was gracious in defeat."

"Gracious in defeat? I thought you were trying to make a deal."

"We went over this before, Wilma. Every business deal is a contest; there's winners and losers. I told you Vernon was going to lose last night. You shouldn't be surprised."

"But what about your cancer?"

"Please! I'm not that stupid. He fixed me up at the beginning of the week."

"He did? Are you sure?"

"As sure as I can be. Why do you think I'm feelin' so much better?"

"Then did you offer him any money, any at all?"

"Why in hell would I do that? He wasn't asking for money; he was asking me to throw half my legacy down a goddamned rathole. Given his purposes, a few million here or there wouldn't have amounted to a wood tick on a coon's butt anyway."

"But . . ."

"No buts, Wilma. If Saint Vernon is a straight-shooting man of God like everybody seems to believe around here, then he needs to quit putting his hand out and start calling in the rain. Last I heard, the forecast was down this morning."

"That's not right, honeypot. The odds jumped up again—right after Mr. Moore left with Dottie."

"They did?"

"The weatherman says we're looking at half an inch this weekend, maybe more."

"Well, I'll be damned, Wilma! I'll be damned! I'm going to make it."

"You are?"

"Hell, yes. If Vernon Moore can bring the rain, then he sure as hell can cure a chicken-shit case of cancer."

Isn't it strange how two separate grown-ups can get the same exact news and react in opposite ways? I see Democrats and Republicans do it all the time, but I had forgotten that husbands and wives do it, too. Clem was reassured by the imminent arrival of rain, but I was petrified by it. All I could remember was Mr. Moore saying, "A deal is a deal, Wilma. I'll ask for one and not the other."

Would a man of God lie about something so important?

EARLIER ON, I EXPLAINED to you that rich folks do not use telephones like normal folks. Well, they don't go to hospitals like normal folks either. That afternoon, Clem and I drove up to Ebb in the Porsche, with the top down and the air conditioner running full bore, while John Smith followed in the limousine, which was stuffed to the gunwales with suitcases, hang-up bags, and briefcases—all Clem's. It was all I could do to keep the man from bringing golf clubs and a sidearm.

When we got to the Come Again, Clem went upstairs to retrieve Clara while I went to my room to pack a bag. To my surprise, I found a suitcase on top of the bed that had already been filled with all the clothes I would need. Sitting right next to it was a large white box tied in blue ribbon. Inside, I found a greeting card with a photograph of a giant sea turtle named "Harriet" on the front. That's right, a sea turtle. The description overleaf said that Harriet had lived in an Australian zoo until the ripe old age of one hundred and seventy-five.

A note was written on the opposite page:

Dear Wilma:

Please accept this gift as a small token of our thanks. It's a day late, but the box is borrowed, the ribbon is blue, Harriet was magnificently old, and the hat is quite new.

I hope to visit again someday. In the interim, please don't hesitate to call.

Best wishes,
Marion Meanwell

Underneath the card was a brand new panama hat with a red Paisley band. Not only did it match my official Quilting Circle parasol, it fit my curly locks perfectly.

I made a few strategic additions to my suitcase and added a makeup kit, and then I donned my new panama and met Clem and Clara in the parlor just as John Smith was pulling up to the porte-cochere. He had picked up Louise Nelson, Hank Wiley's nurse, who was riding up to Omaha in the limo with Clara.

Here's a wardrobe safety tip: don't wear a panama hat in a Porsche convertible with the top down and a madman at the wheel, even if the madman insists that his perfectly engineered wind guard will prevent it from flying off. You are riding in a Porsche, and panamas are impervious to German-made wind guards. What isn't obvious about that? I hunkered down low, but I reached for the brim too late. The wind snatched it from my grasp as Clem accelerated onto I-80 at a dreadful rate of speed and John Smith, who was doing his darnedest to keep up, nearly flattened it as it flew by. I wanted to go back but my sentimental husband said, "We're not turning around, goddammit! I'll buy you another one." My "something new" was last seen heading south toward the border, and Panama.

We picked up the first signs of the cold front as we crossed the Platte River midway between Lincoln and Omaha. The clouds were on the edge of the horizon, but I could tell that they were tall and purple, which was a sure sign of rain as long as the jet stream didn't change its fickle mind again. Clem pulled off the highway at the next rest stop to powder his nose while John guarded the Porsche and watched the top put itself up. It was the first time I had had a moment to myself since Mr. Moore had left, so I gave Loretta a call on my police phone.

"Are you en route?" she asked.

"We're almost there. I just lost my brand-new hat."

"Your new what?"

I told Loretta about Marion's note and my recently departed wedding gift, but she was more interested in Harriet. "That turtle was thirty at the beginning of the Civil War," she said. "Do you suppose that Marion was trying to tell us something?"

"It's a possibility, but I've seen prettier critters in my day. If that's the price of longevity, then I'll have to think about it. Did you hear about Marta Kimball?"

"Yes, bless her soul. She would've been the first to admit that she was ready to go. Here's a question: do you send flowers to a bereaved florist?"

"That's a tough one, but I'll leave it to the Condolences Committee, if you don't mind. I suppose you heard about the deal. I would've called myself but it was all I could do to get Clem ready for the hospital."

"I got the word from Hail Mary. I'm so sorry, Wilma. Is there anything I can do?"

"You can pray," I replied. "That's all any of us can do anymore."

That's when it hit me; it must have been my forty-first revelation of the week. The only reason we pray to God for divine intervention is because the men who have the means to help us don't do it. If Clem had given Mr. Moore the money, then hundreds of Hayes County farmers would have made it through the year, no matter what God did with the weather.

A long time ago, Mr. Moore said there were four kinds of people: the weak, who need help from others to get by; the self-sufficient, who help themselves; the strong, who help the weak; and the pathetic, who take from everybody. On the rest of the trip up to Omaha, I tried to decide which definition fit Clement best. I didn't want to be unfair to a man who had cancer, but the only category I could eliminate was "the strong."

Mr. Moore had tried his best, but he had failed to rehabilitate my husband. The realization made me very sad.

Chapter 38

. . . .

My Kingdom for a Hershey's Bar

THE WAKE-UP CALL from the hotel desk arrived at the undignified hour of six a.m. I could have rolled over and slept till noon, but Clement was due at hospital admissions at seven sharp. He beat me to the bathroom, so I put on a white cotton robe and threw open the curtains to get a tenth-floor panoramic view of the Omaha weather. Dark, mean-looking clouds filled the sky, raindrops streaked down the window in long diagonal trails, and a gale-force wind was blowing sheets of rain across the parking lot.

My heart nearly stopped. It was exactly like the day that Mr. Moore had saved Loretta. I yelled out to Clem, "The heavens have spilled over, honeypot! It's a monsoon; a deluge!"

He didn't respond, so I rapped on the bathroom door and opened it a crack. "Are you okay?"

My husband was facing the mirror in his striped shorts and a farmer's tan, meaning his face and arms were brown as a berry but the rest of his skin was as pallid as mozzarella cheese. In the reflection, I could see two tiny pieces of tissue stuck to his chin by red dots of Tucker blood. "I cut myself shaving, goddammit! You'd think a man could shave his own face in the morning."

"Do you need a Band-Aid? I brought some."

"No, I don't. I need three scrambled eggs on toast, hash browns, half a dozen strips of bacon, and a pot of fresh coffee."

"You can suck on ice chips, honeypot, but that's the limit. Doctor's orders. I'll get a bucket from the machine as soon as I get dressed."

"I suppose a bucket of fried chicken is out of the question."

"It is unless you want to vomit all over the doctors and nurses who are trying to fix you up. I hear that's frowned upon in operating circles."

"How about a Hershey's bar?"

"How about I bring Nurse Nelson in here, with you in your shorts?"

That's how it went all morning. I tried my darnedest to get my husband ready to meet his surgeon, but all he wanted to do was eat. If it hadn't been for Louise, I doubt that I would have gotten him past the restaurant in the lobby. When John Smith pulled up in the limo, Clement said, "Take me to a pancake house. There's one on Dodge about thirty blocks west of here."

On behalf of his entourage, which included a dour-looking Clara wearing a black slicker and matching rain hat, Nurse Nelson replied, "You're not the boss this morning, Mr. Tucker; I am. If the doctor okays it, I'll see if the hospital kitchen can fix you an egg-white omelet tomorrow night."

"Goddammit, Louise! By tomorrow, I may be a friggin' omelet."

Nobody had the temerity to talk back, but you know what I was thinking. I was thinking, "If you are, it's your own darned fault."

IT'S NOT LIKE I have ever been associated with a hospital in a professional capacity, but I suspect that a psychologist was on the decorating committee. After Clem was led away to be prepped, Clara, Louise, John, and I were shown to a private room with light-blue carpet, comfy chairs with sea foam–colored cushions, and prints of pretty pink sailboats hung on the walls. Suitably soothed, I took a seat next to an end table, where I sifted through a pile of old magazines until I found a dog-eared copy of *People*. In Nebraska, every waiting room is required by law to offer at least one copy of *People* magazine to the public, the rattier the better. Lo must have a dozen old issues in her salon.

Clara was never much of a *People* person, so she turned on the television and began to surf through the channels. I suppose she was looking for an old movie, but she settled on an ancient *I Love Lucy* rerun on Channel 23, out of Lincoln. Louise and John watched with her for a spell, but then Louise drifted off to see about the recovery room and John went downstairs to the cafeteria to fetch coffee, so Clara and I had the room to ourselves when a news flash came on-screen. A young, confident-looking anchorman behind a studio desk said, "We apologize for interrupting our regularly scheduled programming, but we have breaking news from the capitol. We now take you directly to Courtney Stockton, our roving reporter, who is live on the steps of the state house. Courtney, you look drenched! How's the weather over there?"

The camera cut to a windswept, soppy-haired blonde in a tan raincoat. She reported into the microphone, "We're soaked to the bone, Frank. The downtown area has gotten three-quarters of an inch in the last four hours, and traffic is backed up on Holdrege out to the Ag Campus because of flooding in the streets. We've received reports of half an inch of rain or more in Hayes, Pawnee, and Nemaha counties, and there's minor flooding in Gage County, too."

"For the benefit of our viewers, could you please explain the lieutenant governor's disaster declaration? From where I sit, it's a tad on the tardy side."

"The same question was asked at the press conference minutes ago. According to a representative from the department of agriculture, corn, soy, and alfalfa harvests in eastern Nebraska are still expected to come in fifty to eighty percent below average, and that assumes normal levels of precipitation for the rest of the season."

"So the rain is too little, too late."

"That's the story, Frank. Forty-one counties in the eastern third of the state have been officially designated a federal disaster area, an emergency loan team from the USDA's Farm Service Agency is in the air, and the governors of Iowa, Missouri, and Kansas are expected to follow suit early next week."

"Well, late or not, that has to be good news for our beleaguered farming community. But speaking of governors, where's ours? We've been unable to reach him from the studio. Have you heard any word from the mansion?"

"According to a staff member who wishes to remain anonymous, the governor is on a fishing expedition off the island of Hokkaido and can't be reached for comment."

"He's incommunicado in Hokkaido?"

"What else can I say, Frank?"

"Not a thing, Courtney. Thanks for the report." The screen switched to the anchorman, who looked into the camera and said, "Well, there you have it, folks. The drought is officially over. The lieutenant governor has declared eastern Nebraska a disaster area anyway, emergency loan assistance is on the way from Washington, and the governor's gone fishing in Japan. We now return you to our regularly scheduled programming, but don't touch that dial! For the latest in news, weather, and sports, stay tuned to Channel 23!"

I had an urge to call Loretta, but I decided to wait until the lightning bolt hit or we got news about Clement, whichever came first. I was reading a year-old article about the Emmy Awards when a sweaty-looking character out of *ER* appeared at the waiting-room door in an aqua green outfit, matching booties, and a shower cap. "Are you Mrs. Tucker?" he inquired.

"I am. This is his sister, Clara."

"My name is Ben Regier. I'm the chief surgeon here at St. Joseph's."

Clara clicked off the TV. I stood up. "So soon? How is my husband?"

The doctor crossed the room and took my hand. "I'm so very sorry, Mrs. Tucker. He passed away on the operating table minutes ago."

My legs buckled. If I hadn't been standing in front of a chair, I would have landed on the floor. As it was, I sat down with a thud.

"I can't explain it, ma'am. Your husband's stomach, pancreas, and liver were riddled with malignancies. It was a miracle that he could stand up, much less eat. The pain must have been excruciating, but he was confident, even cheerful, during prep. Just before the anesthesiologist put him under, he said, 'A thousand dollars for a Hershey's bar!' "

"Those were his last words?"

"From a man facing death. I've never seen anything like it."

To the immortal ether, his sister muttered, "You were a fool, Clement. You were a damned fool." When I looked at her with my mouth agape, she added, "I'm sorry for your loss, Wilma. It's my loss, too, but it's not like he didn't make his own bed."

The surgeon offered, "Mr. Tucker's body has been wheeled into recovery, ma'am. Nurse Nelson is already there. Would you like me to escort you in so you can say good-bye?"

I nodded and stood up again, but on shaky legs. As the doctor took my arm, Clara said, "You go ahead, but leave your cell phone, please. I have to call Calvin."

"Calvin?" I whimpered.

"He's the executor of my brother's will. You go with the doctor. We'll take care of everything."

One minute, my husband was impossibly hale and hungry and my permanent boarder was a mute recluse with more quirks than an attic full of animal astrologists. The next minute, he was dead from cancer and she had assumed command of the complete catastrophe, plus the full breadth of the English language.

It was more than I could take. I blacked out.

Chapter 39

. . . .

IN MEMORIAM

M AYBE IT WAS THE GRIEF, or maybe it was the shock, or maybe it was the little pills that Louise gave me after I came to, but I don't have a good recollection of the rest of that day. Mona, Winona, and Loretta converged on me in the hospital room like I was the last artichoke in the rabbit compound and took turns handing me tissues until I was composed enough to say good-bye to my husband. Afterwards, John drove Mona and me home to the Come Again, where I proceeded to do my best impression of a bereaved recluse for the next three days: I stayed in bed and watched old movies on TV, I cried and ate pimiento-cheese sandwiches, and I refused to speak to anybody except Loretta, Mona, Winona, and Clara, plus Clem and Mr. Moore, although the latter two never had the courtesy to return my calls.

Clara, I learned during one of our several, rather morbid conversations, had a lifetime of funereal experience. As a child, she attended the burials of all four of her grandparents and an undetermined number of aunts, uncles, and other Tucker kin. Later, as an adult, she arranged the interment of her parents and both her husbands, even though the death of the second eventually pushed her into two decades of seclusion. But thanks to Mr.

Moore, she was back into fine managerial form for her younger brother's final voyage. It went off without a hitch.

The first memorial was held on Wednesday morning at St. John's Cathedral on the Creighton campus, only steps away from the hospital where my husband had died. It was a formal affair presided over by two Jesuit priests and attended by hundreds of businesspeople, politicians, and employees of the National Bank of the Plains. Fabrizio Santoni, the CEO, made a very nice speech about how Clem had saved the bank and thousands of jobs.

Pastor Hooper held a wake at the Protestant Church in Ebb that night. I worried that nobody would come, but the Circle girls and their families showed up in force, bless their hearts, and Calvin Millet, Buzz Busby, and Buford Pickett said more nice words about the business genius of my dearly departed.

On Thursday morning, after a short service for family and a few close friends, we accompanied Clement's casket from the church to Tucker Cemetery, which is on the banks of the Missouri only a few miles south of the River House. It was a cool and blustery day, more like the end of September than the beginning of August. The sun peeked in and out between the clouds, the green canopy over Clem's grave flapped and furled in the wind, and the grass felt slippery and damp beneath my feet.

I sat on a folding chair at graveside with Loretta and Calvin to my right and Clara and Mona to my left. The Reverend Hooper said a few final words, then a man from the mortuary began to turn a crank and Clem's body descended slowly to his final resting place. I tried my best to cry but my reservoir was dry, so I sat on my chair like a lump on a stump, staring at the disappearing coffin and wondering, like a small child, how many cranks it would take to hit bottom. When it finally did, Loretta ushered me over to the grave, where I reached into my pocketbook and fished out a Hershey's bar. As I tossed it onto his coffin, I said, "You'd be proud of me, honeypot. I saved us nine hundred and ninety-nine dollars."

Chapter 40

··

A PILL FOR BEREAVEMENT

MARIE FIXED A NICE SALMON and brie salad at the Come Again after the funeral, which I couldn't touch, and then we remained in the dining room afterwards for the reading of Clem's last will and testament. Besides Clara and yours truly, Calvin and Loretta were there, plus Mona, John Smith, and four lawyers from Omaha who had joined us during coffee. Once introductions had been made, the three younger attorneys took seats by the wall while a grumpy, salt-and-pepper-haired counselor with glasses and a beard took Clem's chair at the head of the table. He removed a thin, blue folder from his briefcase, inhaled deeply through his nose, and said, "Thank you for coming, folks. I'm very sorry for your loss, but my role today is to inform you that you all have benefited from Mr. Tucker's untimely end. Are there any questions before we begin?"

I had a zillion questions like, "Why in the heck do we need four lawyers to read one will?" But I held my tongue.

Everybody else did, too, so Grumpy opened the folder and continued, "Mr. Tucker's estate was organized into two parts: his stake in the family trust, and his personal investments. At the time of his death, he owned 36.2 percent of the Tucker Trust which, as of the close of business last night, was valued at approximately two hundred and eighty million dollars."

He allowed the figure to sink in, which took a while given all the zeros and commas, then he went on, "Mr. Tucker bequeathed half his holding, or 18.1 percent, to Clara Tucker Booth Yune, his sister. The balance is to be held in beneficial trust for Mark Allen Breck, the son of Mona Smith and . . ."

Mona grabbed John's arm and squealed, "For who?"

"Mark Breck. He's your son, isn't he?"

"Yes, but . . ."

"There are codicils, Mrs. Smith. Mark does not become eligible for the bequest until the fifth anniversary after he has officially assumed custody of the Tucker Trust, at which time he will inherit the full 18.1 percent. Until then, it will be held by the National Bank of the Plains. If, for any reason, your son does not assume custody of the Tucker Trust by the age of thirty, then the fund will be liquidated and donated to the National Rifle Association or its successors."

I can tell you now that there is a pill for bereavement. It is called a mean, manipulative, outrageously male will and testament. It made me so angry that I shouted, "A hundred and forty million for the NRA, and not one red cent for the farmers of Hayes County! That's crazy! Did you know about this, Clara?"

"Yesterday. I stopped by Bill's office after the memorial at St. John's."

"Why didn't you tell me?"

"I'm sorry. I didn't want to ruin the funeral."

"Well, it's good and ruined now. Tell me why. Why did he do it?"

Calvin answered, "Clem wasn't that fond of the NRA, Wilma, not really, but he was a big believer in the carrot and the stick.

Whatever we may think of his methods, his intention here was clear: to use a very large carrot and an equally large stick to ensure custodial succession of the Tucker Trust."

"So you knew about this?"

"Yes, but I was sworn to silence."

"What if Mark wants to be a cello player? Can't we contest the will!"

Grumpy said, "Even if you had cause, and you don't, I would advise strongly against it. You don't want to give the NRA the notion that they're an accident away from a hundred and forty million dollars. They're heavily armed."

So Grumpy had a sense of humor.

"Mona! What do you think?"

"It's too soon to say, Momma. I want to read the will myself, and we need to talk with Mark, too. He and Clem weren't close, but they discussed his future a number of times. For all I know, he expects to head the trust some day."

Calvin said, "Regardless, is there anything we can do about this today, Bill?"

"No. If you wish, my team and I will be happy to research the matter at a future date, but we need to complete the reading this morning. May I continue?"

Clara stared off into space and remarked, "And people wonder why I became a recluse. Go on, please."

"In addition to his interest in the family trust, Mr. Tucker had significant personal investments in stocks, bonds, derivatives, mutual funds, and real estate. The River House was bequeathed in its entirety, including the acreage, automobiles, equipment, and furnishings, to Wilma Porter Tucker with two exceptions. Mr. Tucker left his eighteenth-century Japanese sword set to Mr. John Smith and his firearm collection to Mr. Fabrizio Santoni. In addition, Mr. Tucker transferred a personal holding, his thirty percent interest in Millet's Department Store, to you last Thursday. Is that correct, Mr. Millet?"

"It is."

"Even though the certificates were postdated, there may be tax complications because the physical transfer occurred prior to his death. I'm not prepared to discuss it now, but we can cover it later on this week."

"No problem."

Grumpy turned the page. "The remainder of Mr. Tucker's testament is refreshingly straightforward. He left five million dollars to Mrs. Wilma Tucker, to be paid in cash . . ."

I had rolled the possibility around in the back of mind for days, but there it was in black and white: I was filthy rich. After working my tail to the bone for just this side of forty years, I got five million dollars for being married to a man for forty hours. That might be more than some lawyers make.

". . . two million dollars to Calvin Millet, two hundred and fifty thousand to Marie Delacroix, and one hundred thousand to Consuela Bocachica. Another five hundred thousand dollars has been placed in trust for Matthew Breck, who will be eligible to receive the bequest upon his release from Anamosa State Penitentiary in Iowa.

"In addition to his sword set, Mr. Tucker also bequeathed to John Smith a fifty-dollar shopping spree at the nearest Chuck E. Cheese's. I am required to add, 'The free pizza party with the four-hundred-pound rodent is in return for being a constant pain in the ass.' The balance of his estate, net of taxes, is to be transferred to the Tucker Trust. Are there any questions?"

"What about his daughter, Mary Beth?" I asked.

"She was not named in the will, Mrs. Tucker."

"She wasn't? He gave away all that money and he didn't leave her a dime?"

"I'm afraid not," Clara replied. "Perhaps we can discuss it later. Are we done, Bill?"

"We are."

"Then would you please dismiss the other attorneys with our thanks?"

"Yes, ma'am."

As the three silent lawyers stood to leave, Clara said, "Calvin, I would appreciate it if you could escort Bill's associates to the courthouse. Stop at Starbucks on the way if you wish and tell Olga to put it on my bill. John will tag along as well."

"May I ask why, Mrs. Yune?"

"I'd like to have a private conversation with the girls. We won't be long."

I had no idea what was going on. Judging from their looks of bafflement, Mona and Loretta didn't either. After a few pecks and squeezes, we women were left alone in the dining room with Bill the Grumpy Lawyer, who seemed perfectly comfortable with the arrangement.

Loretta said, "This is all very mysterious, Clara. What's on your mind?"

She replied, "Buford Pickett called a few hours ago, as a courtesy. On Monday, he intends to lay off nine bank employees and send fifteen foreclosure notices to local farmers. He would have done it a week ago, but he decided to wait until after the funeral. Wasn't that respectful?"

"Why? We just got an inch of rain. Didn't that help?"

"I had the same objection, Wilma. He told me it was too late."

"But what about the disaster declaration?"

"I brought that up, too. His position is that cheap, guaranteed loans will help the larger, better capitalized operations, but it will do little more than postpone the inevitable for the smaller, weaker farms in the region. If the weather is dry again next year, he says that hundreds more will fail in the tri-county area."

"Hundreds more? Did you say hundreds more? Ebb won't survive."

"That's right, Loretta. Life as we know it will end, which means that we have a decision to make. We can decide, like my brother did, that the quality of human life is little more than a consequence of the laws of economics, or we can decide that here, in Hayes County, the laws of economics can be rewritten." Clara turned to Grumpy. "We're among friends, Bill. How much richer am I today than I was a week ago?"

He inhaled through his nose, then exhaled, "A hundred and seventy million dollars."

"And how did you arrive at that figure?"

"The portion of the trust you inherited from Mr. Tucker is valued at a hundred and forty million. He left another eighty-two million from his personal portfolio to the trust, of which you now own 49.1 percent. Net of taxes, that rounds off to a hundred and seventy million."

"Do you suppose that some of that could be used to rewrite the laws of economics?"

"For that kind of money, you could rewrite the laws of physics."

"I believe we'll set our sights a little lower to start. Does anyone have any thoughts about how we might rewrite the laws of economics here in Hayes County?"

"I have an idea," Loretta answered. "If you gave some of your money to the farmers, they might be able to stay in business."

Clara smiled. "As you must have guessed by now, Vernon and I discussed the same matter at length last week. What you may not know is that I offered to give the money to the farmers myself. He was amenable, but only if he failed with Clem."

"Okay," Lo said. "Now I'm confused. If you had already agreed, then why was the deal with Clem so darned important?"

"Vernon wanted to restore my brother's faith in God before the operation, but he needed time to sell it. Clem could never resist a deal. It bought Vernon the time he needed."

"So he asked you to stay on the sidelines."

"Yes, but Clem was too smart for his own britches. Instead of listening, he tried to beat Vernon at his own game. I'd rather not make the same mistake." Clara turned to Grumpy again. "Bill, I'd like to endow a foundation for the benefit of family farmers in southeast Nebraska."

"How much would the endowment be, Mrs. Yune?"

"Half the day's gains to start. What's that? Eighty-five million?"

"Yes, ma'am. For my own edification, what would this foundation do exactly?"

"I haven't had time to figure out how the mechanics will work. In principle, though, we'll loan sums to distressed farmers at zero interest. Not large sums, but big enough to do some good: a hundred thousand to two hundred thousand per grant or thereabouts, and repayment will be strictly voluntary."

"Are you sure, Clara?" Lo asked. "The IRS will treat a loan like that as a gift; so will the state. There'll be serious tax consequences."

"Actually, Mrs. Yune, that may not be the case. The farmers who receive foundation grants will be able to write them off against any losses they incur in the same fiscal year. If their losses are substantial, then the tax consequences may be negligible."

"Start working on the details, Bill. I'll chair the board, but I'll need someone to manage the day-to-day. I've been a bit out of touch the last few years. Who do you recommend, girls?"

"How about Calvin?" I suggested.

"He's a sweet man, but I don't want to make money; I want to give it away. For that I'll need a woman. How about you, Loretta? You've got a head for business."

"Lily Pickett's is better. She a whiz with taxes, too."

"Then hire her as our treasurer. Please note that Loretta Parsons Millet will be our inaugural chief executive. She'll join me on the board, along with Wilma and Mona here. Leave one seat blank; we'll add a fifth member later. That's enough to get you started, isn't it?"

Grumpy made a note. "I'll need a name, Mrs. Yune."

"Didn't I mention that? We'll call it the Tucker Foundation."

"I'll also need an address."

"Oops! Old age is such a nuisance; I forgot that, too. I'd like to locate the foundation's headquarters here so I won't have to leave to attend to business. Is that okay with you, Wilma?"

I knew the answer, but I asked the question anyway. "Does that mean that I won't have a bed and breakfast any more?"

Clara smiled. "Tell me if I'm wrong, Bill, but I don't see how one place can be both at the same time, not unless there's a legal entity called a bed and breakfast foundation."

"You may be right, Mrs. Yune, but the matter should be researched."

"You all do a hell of a lot of research, don't you?"

"Yes, ma'am. One last thing: you'll need to open a bank account for the foundation. Otherwise, money will be flying all over the place and the taxes will get mixed up."

"Will a million do?"

"We can probably open a door or two with that."

"Good. Will you follow me upstairs when we're done, Loretta? I'll write a check and you can take it to the bank. Bill will go along and help you with the paperwork."

"Me? I can take it to the bank?"

Clara grinned broadly. "You're the new CEO, dear. Stop in and see Buford while you're there, if you don't mind. Tell him to expect a call from Omaha."

Well, there it was. All I had to do was hold a mirror up to my face to see that Mr. Moore had been to Ebb again. In six short days, I had gone from being perpetually affianced to instantly married to widowed and enriched by the sad but preventable death of my arrogant, foolhardy husband. The drought had been brought to an end; my cute little goddaughter had been declared gifted by two of the oldest and oddest women on planet Earth; the Circle had discovered a secret club that dated back to Henry the Eighth; Beryl and Flathead had disappeared; Marta Kimball had passed away; the lieutenant governor had declared half the state a disaster area; my grandson had become a zillionaire under construction; my mute, reclusive boarder had turned into a chatterbox and the most philanthropic woman in state history; and my bed and breakfast career was all but over.

You know what I was thinking. "But what about Mr. Moore?" I said plaintively. "What if he comes back?"

"You can keep the entire second floor for yourself, Wilma," Clara replied. "Can you spare one room?"

JUST BEFORE SUNDOWN, Bett Loomis, who is the town postwoman, appeared on my stoop with a big, brown express envelope in her hand. I was wearing a ratty pink housecoat, a hairnet, and running shoes when I opened the door, but it wasn't like I lived in Buckingham Palace, was it?

"You're working late," I said. "Is that for me or Clara?"

Bett has been trying to quit smoking for so long that she has become addicted to nicotine gum. "It's for you," she replied between chews, "and it's postmarked *England*." In case you were wondering, we don't see a steady stream of mail from Europe around here.

"England?"

"Take a look for yourself."

Pretty red and blue stamps with pearl-white profiles of a young Queen Elizabeth adorned the upper right-hand corner, but there was no return address. "I can't tell who it's from, Bett. Should I open it?"

"It ain't a bomb," she answered, like I was a sissy. "I'll open it if you want."

"No, no. That's okay. As long as you're sure it's safe." I tore open the edge of the envelope and found a smaller one inside made of textured off-white paper and addressed to me. It contained a card of the same stock with a pretty, hand-painted watercolor of a black swan swimming on a translucent blue-green lake. A shiver ran down my spine as I read:

Dear Mrs. Tucker:

On behalf of Vernon, Marion, and all of Lohengrin's Children, please accept my sincerest condolences for the untimely death of your beloved husband. Forgive us for being unable to attend his memorial, but other matters required our immediate attention. I hope you will understand.

With sorrow and regret,
John Warren
The Managing Director

I reread the card, which made me a little woozy in the head, so I sat down on the stoop to regain my sense of equilibrium, and then I read it again.

"Who's John Warren?" Bett asked, looking over my shoulder.

"He's an old friend of Mr. Moore's," I answered, "from the court of Queen Elizabeth — the *first*."

Bett is a philatelist, not a history buff. She slacked her gum and remarked, "That's nice. Can I have the stamps?"

Aftermath:

. . . .

KEEPING THE FAITH

R AINFALL LEVELS RETURNED to normal in Hayes County for the rest of the season, but it was too little, too late, just as Buford had predicted. Crops were nonexistent to flat awful, but no foreclosure notices were sent out and nobody was laid off. Clara put in a call to Fabrizio Santoni, the CEO of the National Bank of the Plains, to request that he give us a few extra months to get our county house in order. He is a nice man, but Clara's emergence as his largest individual shareholder may have contributed in his consent. There is also a rumor running around the Abattoir that Lily threatened her husband with a painful, public, and extremely expensive divorce, but she never said so much as boo to me or Loretta about it.

My bed and breakfast business is history now. I accepted a few return guests for the county fair, such as it was, but they were the last. The downstairs is being converted into offices now, and most of my appliances have been moved up to the second floor, where Buzz Busby is building me a new kitchen with a center island. The parking lot is also being enlarged, and Clara, who rarely leaves the third floor except to come downstairs for a meeting, is having the roof retiled. It didn't need it, but she said she would be the first to suffer from a leak.

In case you were wondering, Silas the Second appeared on the back stairs the night after Buzz's workmen started tearing down my kitchen, and he has been back twice since. I get the impression that he is not fond of the changes. I have regrets myself from time to time but, given the circumstances, there was no way on Earth I could refuse.

Thanks to Grumpy and his troop of legal beagles, the Tucker Foundation was up and running in only thirty days. Casey Jaworski, who is an expert at farming, dairy operations, and lean times, became the fifth member of the board. As you might expect, her selection pushed a certain person's nose out of joint yet again. Hail Mary believes that she should have gotten the nod, but Clara forbade it. I guess she failed to make an impression when she had the chance.

By Columbus Day, the foundation had loaned $4.7 million to thirty-one farmers in Hayes, Gage, and Pawnee counties. We're still getting upwards of fifty applications per week, but we all agreed that we couldn't deplete the fund too quickly, so we limit ourselves to one grant per day. Even that has attracted the attention of the press, which has kept poor Lo running all over the place. Somehow, she has still found time to raise my goddaughter, although it has to be a bit of a chore. Last week, Laverne came home from preschool and announced, "I hate meatloaf!" Marie, who cooks for Calvin and Loretta nowadays, had taken the ground round out of the freezer to thaw, but she hadn't even cracked an egg.

It would have been a tragedy to board up the River House, so Mona, Mark, and John moved there in my stead. The very next day, Consuela and her husband disposed of all the toothy dead heads on the dining hall wall. Mark is working for Calvin and the Tucker Trust after school, and John has been retained by the foundation to find Mary Beth Tucker, Clem's estranged daughter, plus Herb and Barb Knepper. He caught up with Rufus and Winnie Bowe in Geraldine, Montana, two weeks ago and they are on their way home, but nobody is on the lookout for Beryl and Flathead Williams. I hope she has found her ocean by now.

The news of John Warren's sympathy card pushed Lily Park Pickett to the verge of apoplexy, of all people. The next thing I knew, she had formed an official Circle committee to investigate Lohengrin's Children. Pokie, Tulip, Louise, and a dozen other girls have thrown in with her, plus Edith Pickerel, the librarian from England. Lately, they have organized themselves in subcommittees: one is researching the widows; another is looking into the mystery of the *Lady Be Good*; and a third has just been created to investigate a legendary oasis called Zerzura on the Egyptian border near Libya. Coincidentally, it was thought to be inhabited by descendants of the Crusaders, and it was located within a few hundred miles of where the *Lady Be Good* went down.

Lily invites me to all their meetings, but I have yet to go. I make up some kind of excuse as a rule, but the real reason is that I don't want to know any more. In particular, I don't want any more facts. I have nothing against knowledge; it's just that I want to keep my faith in Mr. Moore intact. A person can't have faith in a fact; it's a fact. Faith is a belief; it requires a measure of doubt. For that matter, so does hope, and I hope with all my heart that he can find his way back to Ebb one day. Until then I will keep his room ready, and I will await his return, along with Loretta, Laverne, and a thousand others.

Wouldn't you know it? Mr. Moore was right all along.

Uncertainty is the spice of life.